The White War

PATRICK RAYMOND

The White War

A NOVEL

CASSELL

LONDON

CASSELL LTD.
35 Red Lion Square, London WC1R 4SG
and at Sydney, Auckland, Toronto, Johannesburg,
an affiliate of
Macmillan Publishing Co., Inc.,
New York.

First published 1978

ISBN 0 304 30188 4

Typeset by Inforum Ltd, Portsmouth
Printed in Great Britain by
Richard Clay (The Chaucer Press) Ltd.
Bungay, Suffolk.

Though in the trade of war I have slain men,
Yet do I hold it very stuff o' the conscience
To do no contrived murder

OTHELLO, Act I, scene 2

For Diana

'. . . the vision stays, and keeps me in its warmth, and wherever I go I cannot lose it.'

R.C. HUTCHINSON, *Testament*

INTRODUCTION

By the Former Officer Commanding,
Royal Air Force Uxbridge, Middlesex

The story of Prince Karolajczyk and the White Squadron appears in no history of the Second World War, and indeed it would have remained untold had it not been for an elderly visitor to Uxbridge who, in January 1974, first drew my attention to the antics of this strange company. On a second visit, when he felt assured of a welcome, he gave me an account of an operation which must surely have been the most astonishing of the war, and which was performed by an aircraft of the White Squadron in the last hours of the conflict. I had almost used the word 'disgraceful' to describe it, but that would miss the point: better to call the Prince's action both heroic and culpable, and to relate it without embellishment, as the author of these pages has aimed to do.

When my visitor made his first tentative entry into my office I knew him at once for a military man. Despite his advanced age (he was then seventy-six), he was precise in his movements and he spoke from the repose of a perfect discipline. He told me his name was David Armstrong and that he was a group captain who had been nearly thirty years in retirement. At first I had supposed he was simply revisiting the old RAF Depot where he would have undergone his basic training more than half a century earlier. Many such courtly old gentlemen would come back to look at the square and the barrack blocks and to recall with affection how they spent their days in these rough places. Or perhaps he was chasing the legend of Lawrence of Arabia at the unit where that strange airman first served. But after a while I realized that my visitor had something to tell me — some shadow lay upon his conscience — and that he had returned to 'the Depot' to make his peace with the service at its oldest and most fundamental station.

1

I could not help liking this quiet, dignified old man who was still troubled by the part he had played (unavoidably, it seemed) in the guilty endeavours of other people. In particular he was concerned at having told less than the truth to his Air Officer Commanding of the time, and he wondered if some way could be found to repair this omission. Well, by then Air Marshal Sir Edward French had been twenty years dead, and the Group of which he had the wartime leadership had been dead for much longer: nothing remained of the once gallant formation but for a seldom disturbed bundle of records in the Air Historical Branch. I none the less agreed to place on file any statement he might care to make, and subsequently I was to receive from him a carefully written account of his involvement with the White Squadron in the last year of the war. To this document he had annexed the statement made by Captain Wolkow on 29th April 1945 (which appears as Chapter 12 of this book) and a photostat of the letter from Prince Karolajczyk which is printed in the last chapter; the original of this letter he wished, naturally enough, to retain. For want of a better resting place, I put these papers into the Station Commander's safe at Uxbridge; I saw no need to give further circulation to material that might damage the reputation of a distinguished commander who had been so long in retirement; and there they lay until recently. As far as I was concerned, Armstrong had fulfilled his obligation to the service by reporting the whole truth to a responsible officer of the present day and could relax his mind on this account.

So matters would have rested but for a revival of journalistic interest in the White Squadron in 1976. At that time it seemed as if a definitive account of their activities (so far as they could be determined) would at least put the record straight and correct the many fallacious stories then in circulation. Group Captain Armstrong had died in November 1975 — with calmness and dignity, so I was told by the staff at Princess Mary's RAF Hospital, Halton — and had left no descendants or close relatives who might wish his part in this story suppressed. A group of retired officers and other interested organizations therefore invited Mr Raymond (a writer not unfamiliar with the service) to reassemble the evidence and to present his findings as a continuous narrative. In this task Mr Raymond has been assisted by many former members of the RAF station at Moreton Valence, not-

2

ably by Mr Albert Thorpe BEM, by the Reverend L.P. Shenstone, until recently Rector of St Michael's, Holme-in-Barton, Yorkshire, and by Sir Vincent Keeble, the classical historian.

Finally let me assure those readers who may have known David Armstrong during his service (1916-45), or in his long retirement, that this story shows little to his discredit; indeed, he is revealed as a man of honesty and courage whose only fault was his failure to arrest Prince Karolajczyk in the last week of April 1945.

P. E. BLAKE
Group Captain
RAF Retired

July 1978

3

Darkness. A darkness so complete it was relieved only by the tongues of flame from the inboard engines and the luminous tracery of the instruments. Despite the thrust of the engines the aircraft hung in the enfolding dark as if motionless; even the pitch and yaw that had beset the laden machine on the outward journey had now softened into a gentle undulation which the still upper air did nothing to accent. The aircraft was trapped in the earth's shadow in some cessation from war and its consequences. The crew fought to keep awake. The fear that had lain like frost in the body's core had lifted when the bombs fell out of the racks and the aircraft cleared from the target area. Far astern, but still visible from the rear guns, a scatter of fires showed where the Ruhr was burning.

Group Captain David Armstrong kept the control of the machine in his own hands and did not engage the automatic pilot. It was a small act of conscience that no one noted but which would allow him better to avoid a collision if one was threatened. His course lay north-west across the Schelde and the intervening sea to Yorkshire — a royal road, followed that night by six hundred heavy bombers; and the darkness rolled with them, giving its cover, concealing the great retreating army from enemy view. Armstrong knew that the war to which he had given his whole mind in the last five years was nearly won. The German air weapon had distinctly weakened. In the west Patton's armour had crossed the Marne. In the east Rokossovsky's army had closed upon the Vistula and Warsaw was within range of his guns. Another winter would see the end of the conflict in Europe. It was July 1944.

Fifty minutes more and the dawn light drew the wing surfaces in ghostly outline and gleamed in the propeller arcs. Armstrong could see a thickening of the darkness under the port bow. He spoke to the navigator, saying, 'Landfall — Humber. Beginning my descent.' He pushed the nose down and adjusted the aircraft trim to take the weight off the steering column; he eased the throttles backward to check the air speed. He flew as always with quiet attention to the rules of airmanship which had helped him to survive the last turbulent winter. He saw no need to play into the hands of a malevolent chance. There was a dull, wicked light upon the Humber as he completed his descent to the altitude at which he would steer an independent course to his airfield. The white dawn disclosed the homing aircraft: above and below him, to left and to right, the Halifaxes were revealed as they crossed the estuary and broke towards their parent airfields. Of course, they had been there all the time, his companions in the dark, but he had not seen them until now.

He spoke to the tower at Moreton Valence. 'L for Love. Joining the circuit.'

He could see the familiar configuration of the runways below the port wing as he went into a left-handed orbit of the airfield. He heard the voices of the other captains, each known to him, as they broke their silence and spoke to the tower, confirming their return, but he did not count their number. Later there would be time for that. Later he would turn his mind to the missing. Not now. He kept his aircraft in an exact orbit of the airfield waiting for his instruction to land.

Armstrong cleared quickly through interrogation and went to his office. One aircraft had failed to return; it might have landed away; they would tell him when there was news. As Station Commander he could not sleep no matter that his mind was limp with tiredness. It was now eight-thirty. The Station Warrant Officer and an untidy line of airmen defaulters were obstructing the passage outside his office door, but he had no time to deal with them now.

'Later, Mr Thorpe,' he said. 'I have a duty first. Say, ten-thirty. If that airman is still intoxicated, his case had better wait until tomorrow.'

He closed his office door, placed his helmet and gloves in the locker and changed his flying boots for walking shoes. He sat for a moment behind his desk trying to expel the sensations of flight from his limbs. Once, twice, his mind was clouded by sleep, but each time he shook himself awake, conscious of weakness. He took up the telephone and called the Adjutant in the neighbouring office.

Flight Lieutenant Jarvis replied in the harsh voice of the former NCO that commissioning had done nothing to soften. 'Sir!'

'Call my car, if you please. Ask the Clerk of Works to meet me at the Polish site. I will be out for half an hour.'

'As you wish, sir.'

Jarvis always said that — the words of an old regular airman who would take no responsibility for the caprice of authority. Armstrong heard him open the window and bellow across the tarmac to the MT yard. 'Station Commander's car. At once! What are you waiting for?' He could have used the telephone, of course.

Armstrong allowed himself five minutes of rest as he was driven round the perimeter towards the site where the contractor had thrown up a new concentration of Nissen huts. Here there was accommodation for a second squadron with messes and hangarage to scale. The airfield at Moreton Valence had been cut out of the wheatfields three years earlier and contained not one permanent building; it was a wartime expedient, without past or future. Armstrong would have preferred to command one of the old stations of spacious brick where the Royal Air Force was in touch with its own history and not this place of abject utility; but the discipline that had governed his life since he first put on uniform twenty-eight years before obliged him to accept the duty given without complaint. True enough, many regular officers younger than him were now wearing marshals' plumes and were famous names besides — true, too, he had been passed over by some temporary officers who were just gifted civilians brought in by the war — but Armstrong was honest enough to admit the limitations of his mind which had closed the higher ranks to him and to concentrate on doing his best in his present appointment. It was without much distinction or glory, just a part of the Main Force of Bomber Command, but at least he had sight of the war. Beyond the investing wire Armstrong could see where the haymakers were taking in the harvest.

The Clerk of Works met him at the new site where the huts,

painted green, were aligned with a straight-edge and covered perhaps ten acres. Glaziers were still at work on the windows, and in the domestic lines parties of airmen were unloading beds and lockers from motor transport. The Clerk of Works, a shapeless civilian from the building trade, conducted Armstrong through the site with that contempt for the military mind which obliged him to explain every feature with slow and heavy emphasis. The buildings still smelled of wet concrete, but they were at least complete and Armstrong was satisfied.

'Admirable,' he said. 'The Polish squadron will be well quartered. You have done well.'

The Clerk of Works simply grunted, for he was not amenable to compliments from this source.

They emerged into the sunlight at the end of the barrack lines and at a moment when a Halifax passed overhead and obliterated their voices. Armstrong looked up in sudden hope; but it was not the missing aircraft, only a Halifax on local detail.

The car had shadowed them during their walk through the huts and now drew abreast of Armstrong, stopping so that the rear door was exactly in front of him. An experienced driver; probably a regular. The Station Commander was about to enter the vehicle when a figure at a distance caught his eye and held it. An officer, tall, elegant, of calm authority — an officer walking towards him as if to speak but with no increase of pace. Armstrong could not read the badges of rank from where he stood: the languid approach suggested a rank superior to his own, and Armstrong was puzzled because he had heard of no exalted visitor to the unit that morning. The figure gained in detail as he covered the last yards and then Armstrong saw him to be wearing Polish ensignia, the braid of a *pod porucznik*, the lowest commissioned rank and many times his junior.

He was vexed, but it was his rule never to show impatience if he could avoid it. The Polish officer compounded his offence by failing to salute.

'Pilot Officer Count Feliks Nikolski,' he said, as if he were presenting a nosegay. 'I am called Niki. Liaison officer to the Polish squadron. I come ahead.'

He was certainly a surprising figure to spring out of the Yorkshire loam. The face had an aristocratic cut, but it had been made elsewhere than here; the eyes were dark, remote and

7

touched with deep fatalism. Armstrong waited to hear more.

Nikolski said, 'You are the principal officer at this — er — establishment?'

'I am the Commanding Officer of Moreton Valence.'

'Of course. My greeting. Together we shall expunge the enemy. The squadron flies in this afternoon.'

'I was aware of it,' Armstrong said. 'Nikolski, if you wish for an interview with me, I suggest you come to my office at — shall we say — two-thirty this afternoon? In the meantime I have to hear charges.'

The Pole stood looking at Armstrong with courteous detachment. Perhaps he had not heard. 'Tell me, Commanding Officer — you will have authority over the Polish squadron when it is resident here?'

'A strange question. The matter is plain enough. The squadron will be under the operational control of the Air Officer Commanding at Group Headquarters, but the commander will report to me in station matters. They will handle their own discipline.'

'That is — the invariable arrangement?'

'What did you suppose? The officers will have been briefed in this respect.'

'But there are shades of authority, degrees of obedience.'

'None that I know of. The squadron will be no different from any other Polish unit serving with the British forces. They will accept normal command. And now, if you will excuse me . . . '

Nikolski was still following some thought of his own. Armstrong guessed him to be a civilian in borrowed outfit with little knowledge of the military obligations, chosen for his title and fluency in the host language. He wore his uniform like a lounge suit.

The liaison officer said then, slowly, 'The squadron has a thirst for war. They have borne great frustrations.'

'I dare say they have, Count Nikolski. I am aware of Polish suffering. But while they are at Moreton Valence they will behave with restraint, or I shall be obliged to make a report to the Polish Air Force. I will put up with no indiscipline. For the moment, you should inspect the accommodation and plan your allocations. You can report to my office later.'

Nikolski bowed. 'As you direct.'

'One thing more. In our service it is customary to address the Commanding Officer as "sir" and to offer him your salute.'

'As you wish.'

'It is not my private wish, Nikolski; it is the unbreakable habit of military men.'

Armstrong drove back to his headquarters wondering of what operational quality the Polish squadron would prove. He was not encouraged by his meeting with Nikolski. When a thousand bombers crowded into the air poor discipline could lead to the loss of innocent aircraft in collision. He did not want RAF lives sacrificed to the madness of the Poles. He knew them to have suffered abominable cruelties at the hands of the Germans, but he knew too that war had to be fought with a rational mind, from the repose of discipline, if the worst excesses of violence were to be avoided. This was his central belief at a time when faith had no point. This was his religion in time of war. He sent the car back to the MT yard and returned to his office.

He telephoned the Group operations room hoping they would have news of the missing aircraft, but they could tell him nothing. He paused for a moment, his hands covering his eyes. There were no words in his head, only regret and tiredness. Then he instructed the Adjutant to arraign the defaulters.

Flight Lieutenant Jarvis, the Adjutant, stood beside the Commanding Officer's desk as the accused airmen were one by one marched in under escort. It was an old ritual, played with a certain style and lying at the heart of service life: the wrong-doer was brought before authority, the charge was examined, the punishment awarded. Usually the accused acknowledged his error and seldom was there rancour. With something like affection Jarvis watched the file of petty offenders, the drunks, the malcontents, as their cases were quickly disposed of.

Jarvis had entered the RAF as an apprentice clerk shortly after its formation and was firmly of the ground. His figure had been assembled with a clumsy hand and his uniform hung about him in wilful disobedience. He lacked the grace of flight. He belonged to a class that administered the service with rough method but which, denied access to the air, had to accept an inferior moral stature, and a raucous manner made up for this deficiency.

A charge of malingering was followed by one of insubordination, and both men received seven days' confinement to camp. Jarvis had to admire the quiet dispatch with which Armstrong issued his judgements; he made a centre of restraint in a world of diverse weakness. The Adjutant saw a spare man, not tall, a face finely worked and one which a celibate discipline had wiped clean of blemish. The eyes were grey, not without charity, alert even in his tiredness; the small mouth was designed mainly for silence. Jarvis knew him to be unmarried, but he knew little else about him. He had a mother living somewhere in London. He played a good but not exceptional game of squash. He drank very little.

The last defaulter presented by Mr Thorpe, the Station Warrant Officer, was an airman well known to Jarvis because he had appeared before the Commanding Officer many times: Haines, the kitchen-hand.

'You are Aircraftman Haines, Arthur Percival, cook second class?' the Commanding Officer asked.

'Sir.'

'You are charged as follows . . . '

Armstrong paused when he looked at the charge sheet, for the list of offences continued to the foot of the page. He might even have smiled.

'Haines, you are charged with drunkenness, with creating a disturbance in the airmen's latrine, with using obscene and abusive language, with assaulting the orderly corporal in the discharge of his duty, with doing wilful damage to public property (to wit, the guardroom) to the amount of three pounds and six shillings by breaking two windows and by urinating on a pile of folded bedding. You understand the charges?'

Haines understood them, and so did everyone present: they were part of the underlying disorder, the abyss of human depravity that came to light at the Commanding Officer's orderly-room. The evidence of witnesses was taken that proved the charges beyond any doubt.

'Well, have you something to say?' Armstrong asked.

The accused had nothing to say; he had been driven by an impulse words could not describe; he was just a bad lot. Jarvis saw a short man, splay-footed, pig-eyed, his complexion marked by every kind of delinquency.

'I'll see the record of conduct,' Armstrong said. The Adjutant passed him the bulging envelope, from which he took the catalogue of offences and laid it on the table before him. 'I see. A shocking record. You waste my time and that of the disciplinary staff. We have better things to do than chase after defaulting airmen.' He spoke not with anger but with paternal severity. 'Will you accept my punishment? You may elect trial by court martial if you prefer.'

Haines elected the Commanding Officer's penalty: they always did.

'Very well. You will go into detention for fourteen days. You will pay three pounds and six shillings to make good the damage to public property. March out, Mr Thorpe, if you please.'

The accused and escort disappeared into the passage with all the clatter of a properly organized society.

Armstrong sighed as he took off his cap and laid it on the table. 'The task of making an airman out of Haines is, I think, impossible. He has an antipathy to discipline.'

'There's one on every station,' Jarvis said.

The Station Warrant Officer came back a few minutes later having delivered Haines into the custody of the orderly sergeant. Like Armstrong and Jarvis, he belonged to the regular air force — a tall, angular, taciturn man, hardened by years of foreign service. His uniform was grey with age and the stitching showed white where the sun had burnt it. Usually an SWO guarded his unpopularity with fierce devotion, but the dislike in which Mr Thorpe was held at Moreton Valence was not total, and he was known sometimes to treat offenders with less than contempt. His eyes showed a patience that the rasp of his anger did not exactly match.

'Sit down, Mr Thorpe,' Armstrong said. 'You too, Jarvis. I wanted to speak to you.'

They took chairs on either side of the Commanding Officer's desk. Jarvis could see that Armstrong was tired, so tired his mind would not move easily, but his movements were as brisk as ever.

The Adjutant said, 'I will arrange for Haines to be committed as soon as possible, sir. Until then, I'm sure the SWO can find him suitable employment.'

Mr Thorpe nodded without smiling: it was his job to purge the

11

guilty, to wipe out the stains of excess. 'He can assist the sanitary party in the collection of night soil,' he said.

'Naturally,' said the Commanding Officer while his mind was elsewhere. Haines was an untouchable, rightly dismissed to the most menial of human duties. 'It was not Haines I wished to discuss. He is a symptom of a condition I want to avoid, but he is not important in himself.'

An airman brought coffee in thick china cups.

Armstrong said, 'I have fears for station discipline. Well, fear is too strong a word, but I am certainly concerned. As you know, the Polish squadron is flying in this afternoon bringing their own ground personnel, and our strength will be nearly doubled. The Poles are not noted for their temperate habits. They are — shall I say — driven by their suffering to much eccentric behaviour. I have already met their liaison officer, Count Nikolski, and I cannot say that I was impressed. I do not want to see our standards of conduct, already weakened by the presence of so many temporary airmen, decline any further. Of course, we are regulars ourselves . . . ' He paused, looking at the Adjutant and SWO, the professional fulcrum of Moreton Valence. 'I will look to you to maintain the type of conduct we believe in.'

'There's always the sanitary party,' Jarvis said, and laughed. Thorpe said nothing, but his silence implied agreement.

'In Iraq, on the Canal, we managed somehow,' Armstrong went on. 'We held ourselves together despite foreign influence and we must do the same now. I know you will help me.'

He stopped. He seemed to be keeping his eyes open with an effort.

'You should go to bed, sir,' Mr Thorpe said. As senior airman, he spoke from a summit of authority similar to that of the Station Commander. Jarvis would not have allowed himself this liberty.

'I will, Mr Thorpe, very shortly.'

The telephone was ringing on Armstrong's desk. He took it up and listened. Jarvis could hear a voice speaking at the other end, but he couldn't distinguish the message.

'I understand. Thank you,' Armstrong said.

He went to the window which opened on to the airfield. Now the sunlight shone in the grass and Armstrong shaded his eyes as he looked to the far end of the main runway. He said, his voice

not wholly his own, 'The missing aircraft is returning. It has suffered damage. Yes, I can see it in the approach.'

One aircraft more or less mattered little to Jarvis and he didn't
bother to look. He gathered together the charge sheets and prepared to leave the office with the SWO.

'May I call your car, sir?' he asked from the door. 'You will
wish to go to your quarters.'

'In a minute,' the Commanding Officer said.

He had not moved from the window, where he stood erect as if
he were receiving an august personage. He passed his fingertips
along the undersides of his eyes.

Jarvis shrugged, making nothing of this; then he went out
holding the bundle of papers to his chest.

TWO

Wing Commander Hayden Chance, commanding the Halifax squadron at Moreton Valence, heard the squeal of the tyres as the overdue aircraft touched down on the runway. He was a tall, bulky Canadian whose quiet voice and languorous manner did not conceal his forcefulness. His frame was so large he had difficulty in the narrow spaces of the Halifax. He looked up from the litter of squadron business covering his desk, raised two fingers in the direction of the sound, murmured an acknowledgement to the gods of war, and tried to continue working. But he could not suppress a smile at this escape from perpetual darkness, for the aircraft must have been at the limit of its endurance when it reached home.

Chance watched while a clerk amended the board on which the squadron order of battle was presented: against R for Robert he deleted 'Aircraft missing' and wrote instead 'Aircraft returned'.

So, they were all back; the squadron was complete at this early muster. He knew the wayward aircraft to be captained by an American alcoholic named Peter Marek whose continued existence was important to the station at this moment. Marek had pressed his chances beyond the proper limit many times, and he had survived by a combination of drunkard's luck and inspired airmanship. The Squadron Commander left his desk, took a bottle of whisky from his locker and went out into the sunshine where, at a distance, he could see R for Robert moving off the perimeter road. He jumped on the running board of a passing bowser and rode in the direction of the dispersal.

Hayden Chance was a non-regular officer, a part of the great inflow of civilians who had increased the RAF to many times its regular size. A war in Europe had not been his concern; he came from the opposite side of the earth and his proper business was in the timber trade of British Columbia, where he was a wealthy segment of a vigorous industry. His nearest connection with Britain was three generations back. He had come from a sense of tribal obligation mixed with an instinct for war which had ensured his command of an RAF squadron after only four years. He was an amateur drawing upon a professional heredity. He had no belief in the political motives of the warring nations; he saw the war as a natural disturbance like the lightning fires of the eastern forests. He believed the war had its origin in the darkened mind of an Austrian corporal and that it had been carried east and west by an insane impulse until checked by powers of greater strength. He did not see these powers as particularly beneficent but as opposing forces arising naturally. When the war was over, as soon it would be, he would go home and forget it.

As the bowser neared the dispersal he saw the damage done to the Halifax — damage done by night but now revealed: the port wing tip torn off down to the aileron, the outer engine stopped and in strange alignment, the navigator's compartment gaping open as if entry had been forced violently from the outside. Plainly a shell had burst low on the port side, at the point most likely to do injury to the crew.

Chance jumped from the bowser and stood waiting for the crew to disembark. The marshalling staff put chocks under the wheels and the remaining engines were then stopped. The shadowing fire tender and ambulance had meanwhile closed on to the dispersal.

He watched the crew drop from the rear hatch. There should be seven. The two gunners came first in their bulky clothing, then the bomb-aimer, then a man he did not know. The captain came next, Peter Marek, the New York barber who had volunteered for this duty despite a malfunction of the liver and a chronic distaste for the military life. Drink would kill him if the enemy did not. Then the engineer, then no one. Six only.

Hayden Chance made a quick adjustment to his mind, one that he had made many times in the last winter when casualties had been so numerous he had forgotten the names of the captains as soon as they were lost: he drew a shutter across that part of his mind where pity lay. Death was the great embarrassment of the air war which, like a vulgarity, they had to ignore. He approached the captain, a small hairless man, and used a voice that fell somewhere between concern and flippancy.

'What was it, Peter?'

'Lucky shot,' Marek said. 'Threw us over. Lost all navigation.' He spoke always with minimum of engagement, as if the world had no deeper claim upon him. The shock had gone from his eyes and he seemed unaffected. Well, an alcoholic had made a compact with death.

'It was a good effort getting back,' Chance said, 'particularly with the aircraft in this condition. Hell, I thought you'd left us.'

'Went the wrong way. No navigation.'

'How did you steer?'

'Fires, stars ... '

'You could have used the long runway at Carnaby. That would have been safer.'

'Missed it. Saw only one airfield. This one.'

God, how luck favoured the careless in some vast satire played out against the imperatives of war!

'Sorry about your navigator, Peter.'

'Getting married in two weeks. Local broad. Big tits.'

'A pity.'

'Fragments all round him. Jagged splinter between the legs.' Marek pushed his flying helmet on to the back of his head and released a long breath. 'Thought he was knackered. Thought he was knackered two weeks before his wedding. Jesus!'

'What happened?'

'Shat himself.'

'Was that all?'

'Want any more?'

'Then where is he?'

Marek looked at his Squadron Commander in mute surprise. 'Why, on the can, of course. Been there since we got hammered. Told you — no navigation.'

Chance turned into the grass beside the dispersal and walked a few paces from Marek. He had to bring his mind back from the place where he had sent it. A moment later he came back to the American captain and spoke with soft insistence. 'It was a brilliant piece of flying, Peter, but you were lucky. You should have gone in. Next time it will be different.'

Marek gave the heedless smile of the man who has already beckoned to extinction.

'Well, you're back,' Chance said, giving him a powerful blow in the shoulder. 'This was not the moment to lose you. The Station Commander thinks you can help him with the Poles.'

'Can't help with the Poles,' Marek said. 'I'm not a Pole. Not now.'

'You speak the language, which no one else does.'

'I'm an American, see?'

'Sure you are. But once you were a Pole.'

'A Polack. A discard. A man accursed.'

'That's why you can help.'

'That's why I can't.'

The navigator who was soon to be married joined them a minute later. He was a young South African named Du Toit, and though pale he bore no other mark of the night's mischance. While they waited for the coach, the Squadron Commander circulated his bottle among the errant warriors, wondering why it was that each aircrew possessed a character of its own: like their skipper, these pot-valiant creatures had lost all concern and any night now they would vanish in a group. The coach came then and Chance helped the crew aboard.

To the captain he spoke firmly. 'Peter, you are to be at the main dispersal this afternoon when the Polish squadron flies in. That is the Station Commander's wish.'

The coach was already moving on to the perimeter road. Marek said nothing: he simply looked at his superior with the detachment of a man under final orders from a different authority.

Lord, how did we get so far with this lot? Chance thought, as he walked over the short grass towards the squadron. East and west the armies were pouring into Europe, and by night his own winged force was penetrating further than ever before into the enemy heartland. Six nations served in the squadron he commanded and he himself was a stranger from far off. The displaced, the dispossessed, the riff-raff of Europe — they were closing upon the dark power that had taken possession of the continent. Already the armies advancing from either side were less than a thousand miles apart. It's ending, Chance thought; the Polish squadron will have to get into it quickly if they want to make a showing.

He resumed his seat in the squadron headquarters and looked with disfavour upon the written business awaiting his attention.

The Station Commander allowed himself only three hours of sleep before returning to his office. Now the sky was empty, the air still. It was two-thirty and the Polish squadron was due on the ground in one hour. Count Nikolski was waiting in the Adjutant's office and Armstrong gave him fifteen minutes of his time but with little advantage to either. Nikolski had no interest in operations, and Armstrong received nothing from the Pole but for a fulsome courtesy. Finally he drove the liaison officer away and called instead for Squadron Leader Keeble, the Intelligence Officer, whom he had sent yesterday to Group Headquarters on a private mission.

Vincent Keeble had been the keeper of antiquities at a great national museum only two years earlier. Together with others, he had been drawn into the service when the Air Ministry, with touching modesty, had presumed it necessary to improve the quality of its thought. It was a doubtful initiative. Keeble was strangely shaped and his deportment was slip-shod beyond correction. His face displayed grave scholarship rather than military acumen, but none the less he was polite, attentive and helpful within his means. When he came in he saluted the Station Commander as if he were putting a pistol to his head.

'Ah, Keeble — sit down! We have still a little time. How did they treat you at Group?'

Keeble cleared his throat for the passage of troublesome material. 'They were civil, of course, but distracted by last night's operation. I didn't see the Air Officer Commanding.'

No doubt, Armstrong thought. The AOC was a blunt old hero who would have little time for this apparition.

'But I was able to gain some information from the staff. They were helpful — if otherwise engaged. One officer gave me the whole of his time between telephone calls. I have made some notes.'

'Excellent,' said Armstrong, and smiled his encouragement. He had a liking for Keeble and was in awe of his learning, but time pressed upon him.

'The squadron is newly formed entirely from Polish personnel. They have passed through Operational Conversion Unit and are proficient in the Halifax. They are bringing their own aircraft.'

Armstrong nodded: he knew this already but was too punctilious to say so.

'The Squadron Commander is Prince Karolajczyk of Radom-Striewicz. He is known as Prince Karol.'

'What? A prince?'

'Yes, sir. I have studied his entry in the *Almanach de Gotha*. He is of ancient lineage.'

'I had not known.'

'I was given a list of the officers. I have it here.' Keeble passed the nominal roll to the Station Commander who ran his eye down the unfamiliar names. 'They are, shall I say, of unusual background,' Keeble continued. 'Some flew to the West in September 1939, but many were captive in the Soviet Union until the Polish-Soviet agreement of 1941 when they found their way to Persia and the Near East. They were mainly army officers. A strange migration.'

'Quite so. We in Britain do not know what it is like to lose our nationality. Of course, the Germans behaved with hideous brutality in Poland.'

'There can be few Poles who are not bereaved. Worse still . . .'

'What is worse?'

Keeble hesitated, perhaps unsure how far his brief extended. 'Well, the Poles were a proud nation. The officer corps was old-fashioned and committed to the military virtues. They were defeated by the Germans in seventeen days, and after that there were mass deportations which the army could do nothing to prevent. They are not a people to suffer humiliation.'

'I take your point, Keeble. That I may have a disciplinary problem had not escaped my notice. Still, the Poles will now have an opportunity of attacking Germany which should put them in a better frame of mind. Have you met Nikolski?'

'The liaison officer? No, sir.'

'A strange bird; idiotic, really. I don't know what to make of him. He seems to think the squadron will have greater freedom of action than is obviously the case. I had to speak to him quite sharply.'

Keeble looked into his lap, as if wondering how far to speak his mind. 'Sir, you have read the list of names?'

'I have.'

'It presents a strange feature.'

'What is that?'

'The squadron contains many noblemen. A greater number than I would have thought likely.'

'Well?'

'It goes further. The senior officers have precedence in civil rank over their subordinates.'

Armstrong said, 'You told me they were old-fashioned and this proves your point. Of course, relating civil to military rank has a long history. It was the custom in the British army a hundred years ago, but they got rid of it when they could no longer accept aristocratic incompetence.'

'This unit is an élite, sir. They may be intransigent.'

'My dear chap, I decline to be impressed by plumes and feathers. In any case many of the titles will be discredited. The Poles are here to take part in Main Force operations like any other squadron and that requires no more than a steady hand and common sense. Other military gifts are inappropriate. I assure you they will strike no attitudes at Moreton Valence.'

Clearly the Intelligence Officer was unsatisfied. His hands made circles in the air, giving form to the thoughts he had not expressed.

'You'd better say what you think,' Armstrong said, looking at his watch. 'But please say it quickly.'

Keeble said, 'I am an historian, not a military man. I do not understand the power of discipline which may make anything possible, even the conversion of an ancient élite into a modern bomber squadron. But I would not be doing my job if I did not identify the difficulties. The old Polish army was given to the horse and the sword. They had more in common with eighteenth-century cavalry than with present-day methods of warfare. Their thinking was — how shall I put it? — almost Roman in its intensity and dedication.'

Armstrong smiled as he rose from the table. 'They didn't tell you that at Group,' he said. 'I don't suppose the AOC is well instructed in Roman history. But thank you, Keeble. I appreciate your advice.'

*

20

Silly old buffer, Armstrong thought, as he walked swiftly towards the main dispersal. There were still no aircraft in the sky, but far down the perimeter R for Robert was being towed backwards into the maintenance hangar. Roman dedication, indeed!

But he was disturbed by the advent of the Poles. Having squadrons side by side so different in make-up was not conducive to good order. The unit commanded by Hayden Chance was certainly mixed, but its bad habits were within service experience; Armstrong dealt with the offenders each morning and they were guilty of no more than drunkenness, foul language and the breaking of bounds. The Poles might be given to impulses outside the RAF index. He looked across the airfield at the huts prepared for the Polish squadron, which he could barely see at this distance, and he was thankful for the space that intervened between them and the British lines.

Hayden Chance and the other senior officers were waiting on the apron under the tower, where the Squadron Commander's aircraft would be directed to park. Peter Marek, the Polish-American, had been persuaded to attend. They saluted Armstrong as he approached.

'Glad to have you back,' Armstrong said to Marek. 'I will commend your action to the AOC.'

Marek gave a smile like winter sunlight; he had long since entered a place where there was no commendation, only rebuke.

The tall, absurd figure of Feliks Nikolski could not be assimilated in this group; he was passing from one officer to another as if he were distributing a royal bounty. 'Ah, my dear Commanding Officer, the squadron is late, is it not? Maybe they have become lost. I do not understand such things.'

'The squadron can hardly have become lost between Marston Moor and here,' Armstrong said.

'They hide in the clouds; they do it to surprise you.'

'Nikolski, I have invited Flight Lieutenant Marek to brief the squadron on Group procedure, as he is an experienced captain who speaks the Prince's language.'

'Yes? He speaks the Prince's language? Well . . . '

'I can hear aircraft,' Chance said.

Indeed, when Armstrong listened he too could hear a dull reverberation in the further sky, a continuing bass note which grew in strength as the seconds passed. He could not see the squadron; not yet. The airfield remained empty but for a shimmer of haze over the runway. The sound increased in volume but still he could not give it a direction; it quivered round the horizon as if round the lip of a bowl, drawing his eyes first east, then west. At last he caught sight of a dark smudge above the skyline which might have been a flight of starlings, and he watched it move closer and break into fragments. The sound of the engines swelled until it awoke an answering tremor in the ground. Twenty bombers, up.

Armstrong watched the leading aircraft as it approached on the axis of the main runway, the squadron closing behind it before making a low pass over the airfield and breaking into a landing pattern. They flew overhead in a formless skein and swung into a left-handed orbit.

Armstrong spoke to Chance. 'Fighter tactics. I don't care for theatricals. Nevertheless we will make the squadron welcome.'

'Bloody mad,' said Chance, whose Olympian patience had been tried by this gambit of the Polish squadron.

The landing was not as poorly conducted as Armstrong had feared; the captains responded to the tower's direction, and although the vertical separation was not as exact as he would have wished there was no obvious danger. The Squadron Commander landed first, stopped short at the runway intersection and followed the control vehicle towards the apron. As the aircraft was parked under the guidance of the ground crew, Armstrong saw the name *Snow Princess* inscribed in white letters under the cockpit windows. He waited while the wheels were chocked and the engines cut; then he went forwards to meet Prince Karol at the rear hatch.

He saw a short, substantial man, very dark, with the broad cheeks and narrow chin of the northern Slav. The eyes were so dark he could not tell what lay behind them. The Prince put down his flying gear and saluted Armstrong, moving abruptly, drawing, it seemed, upon a great reserve of energy. He wore the braid of a *pod pulkownik* or lieutenant-colonel in the Polish Air Force, but it was the British habit to translate Polish ranks into the RAF equivalent, and as far as Armstrong was concerned the Prince was a wing commander.

'Welcome, Prince Karol — welcome to Moreton Valence,'

Armstrong said, raising his voice above the sound of the landing squadron.

The Prince held his eye without a word as if weighing his sincerity. Then he slapped Armstrong's sleeve in robust greeting. 'So, we arrive! We make the low pass! You enjoyed the shoot-up, yes?'

'It was unnecessary,' Armstrong said, keeping his voice free from censure, 'and I do not have to tell you that it was against flying regulations. The tower will not have given their permission.'

'Oh, the tower! I do not speak to the tower. Instead I offer you a great spectacle.'

'We will discuss it later, Wing Commander.'

'Quite so. You give me the big rocket. Now I do not care. I greet Group Captain Armstrong, my commanding officer!'

'Er — yes,' said Armstrong, and he introduced Hayden Chance, fellow squadron commander to the Prince. But the Pole's gaze swung back to Armstrong as if to a lode of greater attraction; it was a glance Armstrong recognized, the look of sharp appraisal, when an officer judged the nature of the one man senior to himself and to whom he must account. Armstrong was far from confident. A trace of unease, like a spill of glacial water, had broken within him when the Prince made his low pass over the airfield in defiance of regulations, casting a straw into the wind, testing the Station Commander's authority. No matter what he had said to Keeble he was impressed by nobility, which he saw as part of the natural order of greater validity than military rank. He came himself from a substratum of the middle class and he had gained his education at a grammar school. He struck no attitudes and gave voice to no bizarre opinions because he had not the authority to do so. A prince was different. A prince had ancient privilege.

The Pole approached him again, reading his mind. 'Sir, you must not let my little prank distress you. I do it only once. Afterwards I am very obedient and do everything you tell me. It will be so! See, these are the members of my crew.'

Armstrong greeted the six airmen — older men than he was used to, showing the marks of their captivity, but they dropped their heads in token of obedience.

While he seldom raised his voice, Hayden Chance could command attention by the weight of his presence, and now Armstrong heard him deliver his own soft but considerable reproof. 'Listen to me, stranger! You cannot ignore the tower without risking a collision. Fortunately I had no aircraft in the circuit.'

'I know. The Station Commander is discomposed. I abase myself.'

'Well, take care. I aim to survive the war with as many of my squadron as possible.'

The Prince could not have been angered at this rebuke. In the secret part of his mind, Armstrong had to admit that Chance had the natural leadership he lacked himself, which arose from a strong will modified by sympathy.

Armstrong said now, 'I am sure Prince Karol understands the situation and will not repeat that particular manoeuvre. It was of course contrary to air traffic regulations.' He beckoned Marek forward from his place at the back of the party, and he came slowly, unwillingly. 'Marek, let me introduce you to Wing Commander Prince Karol.'

The Prince did not at once look at the Polish-American barber, but when his eyes were drawn to the pallid face they were held there, the lids narrowing, as though a familiar figure had intruded into a strange landscape.

'Marek will assist you at Moreton Valence,' Armstrong said. 'He has six months' experience of operations and he speaks Polish.'

The Prince seemed to be lost in his study of Marek and he did not reply.

'You will need to be briefed in Group tactics, in local procedures —— '

'It is so? There is need? Count Nikolski is our liaison officer.'

'With respect, Count Nikolski knows nothing of air matters and will be effective only in administrative and social liaison. Marek will act for me in the operational field.'

'Come now! I speak English and French. I pass through the Operational Conversion Unit at Marston Moor. I receive very good marks for my endeavours there.'

'No doubt. But it is my wish there should be an operational link between us and it will be provided by Flight Lieutenant Marek.' He laughed then, keeping his voice in movement. 'We are lucky still to have him. This morning he was ninety minutes overdue.'

24

The pilot who came back from the turbulent dark now stood in front of Prince Karol in a parody of the attention. He said in English, 'Got shot. Shouldn't be here.'

'So? You were lost almost?' The Prince seemed critical of fortune, of the open-handed night that had returned this warrior to vex him. 'It is strange . . . '

He dropped his eyes to the ground. Perhaps like every airman he wondered if the random shell was directed by chance or design. What undisclosed motives were there in the vast dark? Why had Marek come back?

He said, addressing the tarmac, 'It is my Station Commander's wish that Marek should give me his advice. Marek should have died last night but none the less he comes back. Very well! I do not make a contest with fortune. Marek will serve me as aide.'

'I'm glad that's decided,' Armstrong said. 'Pilot Officer Nikolski will show you your quarters at the new site and Marek will brief the captains as soon as convenient. I hope to see you and your officers in the officers' mess for dinner in a few days' time. Please carry on. I shall be in my office if you need me.'

The airfield grew quiet as one by one the incoming Halifaxes were halted at twenty points along the far perimeter and their engines cut. At length there was no sound but for the mowers in the neighbouring hayfields. Armstrong walked quickly away, pausing to look back only once when he reached his headquarters. He could see the short figure of Prince Karol quite clearly. The Squadron Commander had removed his harness and jacket and walked for some distance into the grass. The crew had not followed, respecting his need for privacy.

Armstrong watched as the Prince raised his fist and shook it at the eastern horizon. Alone, and in the broad perspective of the airfield, it looked an absurd gesture, directed at no one unless he meant to condemn the whole continent of Europe which lay in that quarter. Armstrong shrugged and moved on.

It can't last, he thought. Commanding a bomber squadron will be enough to occupy his mind. He must adapt to the routine of the Main Force and fight as we fight. There's nothing else for him to do.

THREE

There was a raid two mornings later, but the Polish airmen had still to establish themselves at Moreton Valence and they did not take part. The RAF squadron was ordered to attack a flying bomb site in the Pas de Calais: a simple raid, to be flown in daylight, involving no penetration of the continent but for a traverse of the sand dunes. At briefing the crews showed a gaiety never present before the long night raids, knowing they would be away for only three and a half hours and that the German defences could not be brought to bear. They would all return; life would be prolonged by at least two days. A gift in a niggard war. Armstrong did not take part himself. A raid on the north-eastern tip of France, when the aircraft would hardly cross the coast and southern England would remain clearly in view, looked so near to cheating he elected to remain at base. As well, perhaps; a little after nine o'clock an aide rang from Group to say that the Air Officer Commanding would visit the station at midday to inspect the Polish squadron.

From the balcony outside the tower Armstrong watched the take-off. It was a morning of brilliant sunlight that might have been put on in celebration of an easy raid. He heard an engine start on the far side of the field; then another. Soon the airfield was ringed with sound and the first Halifax was moving on to the perimeter and taxiing towards the downwind end of the runway. He found it strange to see night bombers launched in the glare of daylight, for their drab colours were in harmony only with the dark. There could be no doubt how far the German defence had weakened when Bomber Command could send these aircraft across the Channel without their favourite cover. The first Halifax took off and pulled slowly away from the ground, the wheels folding, the weight of the bombs making it sluggish in response. He watched it rise and vanish into the light. Thereafter the aircraft left the ground at half-minute intervals until they were all gone.

Armstrong went down from the tower, feeling restless and flat-spirited now that the aircraft were away. The station was empty but for the menials. Outside the airmen's latrine the sanitary party had stopped their wagon to lift aboard the heavy buckets of night soil. Haines was there, wrapped in foul vapours, correcting his error. At Station Headquarters Armstrong met no one but the unlovely Jarvis who would certainly show no interest in the operation; the seat and elbows of his uniform were worn to a shiny patina by his flightless calling. Armstrong worked without relish through the morning's papers. He examined and signed the station messing account. He read and denied an application for redress of complaint from an airman disaffected with Mr Thorpe, the SWO. He signed an order committing Aircraftman Haines to a corrective training establishment for the balance of his detention.

Next he summoned the chief steward from the officers' mess, who was fortunately an elderly flight sergeant with experience of peace-time messing and not a part of war-time utility. 'Flight, I have invited the Polish officers for dinner this evening. I would like to make it a formal occasion — well, within reason. We will wear Number One dress. Grace will be said and toasts given. I will be grateful if you will prepare the best menu you can consistent with our ration scales. We have, I believe, some North African wine . . . ' He remembered the dinners of the past when the candles reached the length of the table and the decorations and medals threw sparks on to the upper walls. It would be nothing like that, of course, but at least he would give the Poles a pleasant evening. A dinner with a touch of style, at which they might feel themselves part of a long tradition, would assuage their bitterness, cool their temper . . . The chief steward went out, bearing his instructions.

Armstrong had one further duty before he met the AOC. He didn't welcome it, but after no more than a moment's reflection he rang the Adjutant and asked him to send in Pilot Officer Lampton-Bell who had been waiting in the outer office. The young man was well turned out in an expensively cut uniform and hand-made shirt. He didn't presume upon their intimate fellowship by greeting Armstrong with other than the customary salute. Armstrong had chosen this moment for the interview because the aircrews were away from the station and would not know that Lampton-Bell had been called before the Old Man.

'Sit down, Simon; I will be brief. It concerns your behaviour on the station . . . '

Once his voice was in movement and following a well-worn path, he found less difficulty in shaping his admonition than he had expected, and Lampton-Bell did not add to his embarrassment by looking other than gravely receptive. ' . . . bound to draw your attention to the speed limit for private vehicles which does not allow you to pass through the domestic site at sixty miles an hour. I've also to complain of the music and voices issuing from your quarters in the early hours of the morning, which have disturbed the older mess members and formed the substance of several complaints. In addition I must remind you that the introduction of young ladies into private rooms is contrary to mess rules and to the prejudice of good order on the unit.' Having recalled to Lampton-Bell's attention that he was the son of an air marshal with a tradition to maintain, Armstrong made it clear he would raise an adverse report if matters did not improve.

The young man with the mask of polite attention listened to the homily without speaking. Perhaps he was nineteen, with a beardless face and features that kept a youthful imprecision. The languor was not contrived but stemmed from ample confidence. He shrugged when Armstrong finished. 'The car's a wreck now anyway —— ' he began.

'That's not an answer, Simon. I don't want to cramp the style of a fellow crew member, because after all I depend upon your fighting spirit. It was madcaps like you who won the Battle of Britain and fought through the worst of the bomber offensive. You're an excellent rear-gunner whom I trust completely. You may also be aware that your father, when your age, was himself a bit of a hell-raiser who more than once was in trouble with his station commander. But I must ask you to moderate your behaviour in the mess and elsewhere.'

A fleeting smile was his only acknowledgement.

'You may go now, Simon,' Armstrong said. 'No one else need know of this interview.'

At five minutes to twelve, Armstrong went out to meet the Air Officer Commanding.

Air Vice-Marshal French had made his name twenty-eight years earlier in single-handed aerial combat over the Ypres salient. Indeed, his name and the silhouette of his Sopwith Pup had been known on either side of the line: Teddy French had been a hero to both nations at a time when heroism could still be recognized above the demands of the conflict. In those days he had the youth and modesty that sat so well with valour, and his war had been conducted high above the foetid entrenchments in a clean, unsullied place.

This morning, when he flew his Percival Proctor into Morton Valence, his landing was not well made. His circuit of the airfield was so tight he remained inside the perimeter, and this obliged him to hammer down near the centre of the runway where only a violent application of the brakes kept the Proctor from continuing on to the grass overrun. A younger man might have managed it; Teddy French had lost the knack of this manoeuvre twenty years ago. Armstrong would have rebuked one of his own pilots for such an abuse of his aircraft and the amenities of the station.

The AOC was directed to park under the tower. When he jumped down from the wing, French made a weaving approach towards the Station Commander as though he were planning an exchange of punches, and indeed he gave Armstrong a powerful blow on the chest. 'Glad to see you, David. Your people had better check the undercarriage after that heavy landing. Want to talk to you.'

Armstrong led him into the operations room, where map displays covered the walls, and they took chairs by the plotting table. French was an old man now and the flesh had withered from his neck and cheek, but the square head and flat nose of the young fighter ace were still clear to see. Portraits of this face, with the years expunged, hung in many of the older messes, and Armstrong knew that no one had ever doubted the heroic quality of Teddy French.

'Boy, have I been put through it by the powers that be!' he

said, rubbing the backs of his hands to rid them of the aircraft's vibration. 'The Poles attract more notice than any other squadron, and Command, the Air Ministry, the Foreign Office — they've all been to see me. You'd think there were no other Allied personnel in the Group.'

'It is certainly an unusual squadron,' Armstrong said.

'So I'm told! So I'm told ninety-six times! Really, David, it makes no difference to me who flies the aircraft so long as they go out and back in proper trim. In this Group we're not doing the funny stuff, like marking the path or attacking pinpoints. Out and back. Coal-heaving. That's all.'

'I'm sure the Poles will adjust themselves to this routine. They are being briefed in detail. I have an American officer who speaks their language —— '

'This man Prince Karol,' French said, following his own thought. 'You have formed an opinion of him? Something firm?'

'I met him only two days ago.'

'I mean, if he had given you cause for anxiety you would of course have taken note of it?'

'Of course.'

'An act of disaffection, perhaps?'

'Sir, I think you'd better tell me what disaffection you expect. It's true the Prince broke flying regulations when the squadron first landed here, but that may have been no more than playfulness. Is there some reason why this squadron should be more disobedient than any other?'

French expelled a draught of air in something like disgust. 'Frankly, old boy, I would not have thought so, but in the last two days I've had to listen to all manner of strange tales. The chap from the Foreign Office was particularly long-winded. He spoke for an hour. Not my thing. Even now I'm not supposed to tell you all that he told me.'

Armstrong said, 'If the squadron's loyalty is in doubt, I should obviously be made aware of it.'

'Loyalty, loyalty — once it was a simple thing!' French said dreamfully. 'In the old days there was no doubting your enemy. His aircraft was painted a different colour and there were large marks on the fuselage to prevent you from making a mistake.'

Armstrong waited patiently until his AOC had returned from the past.

30

'Look, David — I'm no good at politics. I belong to a generation of servicemen whose loyalty was instinctive and who did
not need to climb on to the political dunghill. So do you. That is
our blessing. As I understand it, our government has fallen out
with the Polish government-in-exile, and while they haven't yet
come to blows they've at least taken off their jackets. The trouble is this: when Europe is carved up after the war Britain and
America will be forced to concede large parts of Poland to the
Russians, and naturally enough the Poles regard this as a breach
of faith. As a result, their loyalty to the Allied cause — and by
inference to the Allied commanders — may have been weakened.'

'I see,' said Armstrong. Like his AOC, he had little understanding of politics which he looked upon with suspicion and
distaste. 'I appreciate their indignation, but what can they do?'

'Nothing, I should have thought. They're under orders. Most
of them were soldiers who would not easily rebel against their
commanders. I put this to the Foreign Office chappie, but as he
had no service himself he didn't understand me. He thought all
obligations were political.'

'Prince Karol is a military man,' Armstrong said, but he
lacked certainty.

'Well, yes. I would have called him a noble amateur.'

'But a soldier none the less.'

'David, it's not my purpose to alarm you. I'm sure Karol will
be responsive to your orders. I've told you this story because I
could hardly keep it to myself. Plainly the politicians are frightened of a free-for-all in Europe following the collapse of
Germany, and they believe the Poles must be held in check if
they are not to cut the throat of every German in sight. You
know very well what the Germans have done in Poland. Even
now ——'

The door was open into the sunlight. Armstrong had left it so
because in the operations room the blinds were kept drawn over
the windows. Like every honest man, French had seen no need
to speak in a lowered voice.

'One moment, sir.'

'What is it, David? Christ, have I been insecure?'

Armstrong went to the door and looked out, but he saw no
more than an empty path and a mile away a vehicle moving.

'Please continue, sir.'

'Well, the German position in Poland is now pretty desperate, but they won't leave without a final twist of the knife. Let's look at the map.' A wall display showed the eastern and western battle areas with the main thrusts illustrated by arrows. French prodded the Polish capital with his finger. 'See this, David. The Russian army has reached the Vistula north and south of Warsaw and Rokossovsky's troops have moved up to the eastern suburbs. For the last three days the Soviet radio has been calling for a rising in the city. Yesterday the partisan leader, General Komorowski, ordered his men on to the streets in support of the Russian army and now they are engaging the Germans at every street corner. Splendid effort.'

'And the Germans will not go quietly,' Armstrong said.

French looked at him with the glum stupefaction of the old fighter who, against his will, is obliged to think ill of his enemy. 'It was different last time we fought them. They didn't murder then. Hitler has ordered the complete destruction of Warsaw in reprisal. Can you believe it? The town will be wiped out and the Poles will no longer have a capital. You can see why the politicians fear an outbreak of Polish madness and why you and I must keep this lot in hand.'

A shadow was lying across the doorway. A shadow that did not move.

Armstrong said, 'Who is it? What do you want?'

Pilot Officer Count Nikolski crossed the threshold of the operations room, smiling graciously but failing to salute the AOC. Not by a single movement did Armstrong reveal his disquiet.

'I cannot believe you require my attention at the moment, Count Nikolski,' he said.

The Pole was in no way abashed; he did not fear his Station Commander's displeasure; he was unalterably a civilian. 'It is midday, the sun is hot; if the Air Officer Commanding does not intend to inspect the Polish squadron —— '

Armstrong allowed his anger to raise the pitch of his voice. 'You will remain in my office. The squadron will be inspected when the Air Marshal is ready. You need not wait.'

French stared at the retreating figure, his eyes widening; so might he have appraised a flower of unusual genus whose existence he had not suspected.

Armstrong said, 'I regret the interruption. Nikolski seems to have very little experience of service customs.'

'I wonder if he heard me.'

'I cannot be sure, sir. He may have done.'

'Bloody sauce.'

'He's the liaison officer to Prince Karol. If he heard you, I must believe the Prince will be told.'

The AOC considered this point, then laughed boisterously and stood up. 'So much the better! So much the better, my dear Station Commander! The Prince will know my views and be discouraged from any adventures. Yes, it may be just as well if Count Nikolski *did* hear me.'

Hayden Chance steadied the aircraft on the final approach. He could see the runway receding like a ruler into the distance. He engaged full flap, opened his engines slightly to correct his airspeed and then maintained a constant descent towards the vertical white lines that marked the touchdown point. Steady, he thought; the Halifax could be a bitch to land. A cross-wind was carrying him to starboard and he kicked the rudder pedal to bring the nose towards the wind and keep his alignment. But already he was wide of the runway and making for the grass. Come over, you slut! He gave heavier rudder and a twist of the wheel to regain his line of descent.

He was over the outer circle and into the goose neck. 'Funnel, funnel,' he called to the tower.

The tower gave him permission to land 'Pancake, C Charlie.'

It had been a simple raid. No fighters, no flak, no hazard of the weather. The target had been so near to the sea they had released their bombs while still over the water and turned away without even crossing the French coast; and the flight of the bombs, still following the aircraft's original course, had done the rest; the stick had continued over the beach and the cliff line to fall across the target area. It was not really a raid at all but an excursion in summer weather. It was truancy from war. On the homeward leg Chance had to suppress the excited voices of the crew.

Now he steered from the touchdown point, holding the nose-down attitude. He passed over the fence, the grass overrun and the perimeter road, and when he judged the wheels to be a few feet from the ground he pulled the steering column back into his stomach, kicked the tail straight and reduced the power. The Halifax dropped like a sack of old bones on to the runway. He felt the sudden jolt as the wheels touched and the suspension travelled to the limit of its movement; every joint and spar in the heavy machine squealed a protest. The aircraft bounced, travelled a further twenty yards through the air before touching again. This time he held the tail down, kept the wheels astride the broken white line in the middle of the runway and applied the brakes. Too sharply; the tail rose. He relaxed the brake pressure and then applied it again, slowly, until the aircraft lost the impulsion of flight and was taxiing under reduced engine power. He travelled to the far end of the runway and turned on to the perimeter.

Sod it, he thought. It can be done, but not by me!

At his dispersal point he cut the engines and switched off. When he removed his helmet he found the aircraft filled with silence in which he could hear the crew speaking. Through the cockpit windows he could see the Station Commander's car moving up the perimeter at a slow, distinguished pace, and looking to have come from the Polish site. The car stopped at the dispersal neck and he saw important brass emerging from the rear door.

He hurried the length of the aircraft, steering his bulk past the mid-upper turret and along the cat-walk, and dropped from the tail exit. Air Vice-Marshal French met him forward of the wing, the Station Commander one pace behind him where custom decreed.

In ebullient humour, the AOC said, 'Enjoyed both your landings, Chance. Thanks for the entertainment.'

'I'll never learn,' Chance said.

'Forget it. Mine was worse. Cracked a wheel fork.'

Chance could not trace the origin of the AOC's good spirits, which did not lie in a fractured undercarriage. The Station Commander was wearing his usual garment of quiet reserve. French asked some maladroit questions about the use of Halifaxes in daylight, but his mind was in a different place and Chance knew he had stopped his car to tell a story.

At length he said, smiling largely, 'You can keep a secret? The Station Commander and I have just made damned fools of ourselves.'

'We'll give you a lift to the crew room,' Armstrong said. 'The others can wait for the coach.'

They took seats in the Station Commander's car which Armstrong himself was driving. As they moved away from the dispersal, French said, 'The laugh is on me. The laugh is on the Commander-in-Chief and the Foreign Office. You see, I came down to inspect the Polish squadron and I had meant to use a club. All sorts of important people had told me the Poles were a shower and that the Station Commander and I would have to lick them into shape. Well, we made a blustering entry into the lines, heads down, scowling like furies, and —— '

'And what, sir?'

'Christ, I'd expected a sloppy discipline. I'd expected poor deportment, scant courtesy. I'd expected bottles in the lockers and harlots under the beds. I was preparing a blast for the Squadron Commander. And what do you think we found?'

'I think you'd better tell me, sir.'

'Why, excellence, old boy! Excellence! Blankets folded with a precision I haven't seen since before the war. Lino like glass. We were greeted with a snap the Germans could not have bettered in the days of the Junkers. Heels together, hands at the trouser seam. The Prince has put the fear of God into them and believe me he has created a unit of the highest discipline.'

The AOC's relief was obvious, but Armstrong remained quiet and Chance could not tell what he was thinking.

'We shall have no trouble with this outfit,' French said reflectively. 'Frankly, we'd had doubts about their reliability, but obedience is second nature to a unit with a harsh regime no matter which country they come from. The Prince is a martinet with an old-fashioned sense of obligation and I feel sure he will create a loyal and efficient force.'

They drew up outside the crew room where the airmen were already arriving from the dispersals. The problem seemed to be over, the nightmare of disloyalty forgotten.

Armstrong said, 'Hayden, I've invited the Polish officers for dinner this evening and I'd like you to attend with your senior officers. We will make them feel welcome within our tradition. Seven-thirty for eight o'clock.'

'Oh — sure,' said Chance, whose mind was following a less

sanguine course.

The AOC had lost none of his hopefulness and he beamed at Chance through the car window. 'If you make another landing like that I'll send you back to elementary training — and I'll come with you, by heaven.'

The car moved away towards Station Headquarters where tea would be served in the better china. Chance lifted his shoulders, wondering if French was right. Himself, he lived in a different world from the regulars and had no great belief in the binding power of discipline.

Much later, when he had cleared through interrogation, he saw the AOC's aircraft taking off steeply into a clear sky.

Despite the short notice, the chief steward had done his best with unpromising materials and the dining room in the officers' mess had some of the lost elegance of peace. The table was lit with the intimacy of candlelight. Moreton Valence had no silver, and indeed it had no history but for the formless conflict of the recent winter, but the mess staff had made up for the lack of trophies with displays of roses and with napkins worked into stylish plumes.

Chance waited with the Station Commander for the arrival of Prince Karol and his officers. He felt uneasy in this professional milieu where against his will he found himself moved by the grace of ceremony. Padre Shenstone, a lusty Christian of the regular air force, gave him no comfort with his tales of the service boxing ring; he believed that human nature was given its best shape by the exigencies of combat, and his nose bore the evidence of a powerful blow in the long past.

'The Station Commander is entirely right to welcome the Poles in a formal setting,' the Chaplain said. 'Show them the pattern and they will find themselves a part of it. A pity that none of you wartime fellows has mess kit.'

A pity, Chance thought. Perhaps. He did not know if the Poles could be held in check by a tradition.

'You will stay in the service after the war?' Shenstone asked, his face bright with invitation like an advertisement in primary colours.

Chance had no wish to be offensive and did not reply at once. 'No, Padre,' he said, keeping his voice low. 'I don't belong here.

36

I'm just an amateur dressed up for the occasion.'

The guests arrived with faultless punctuality, led by Prince Karol. The Squadron Commander bowed to Group Captain Armstrong while his officers remained erect and in echelon behind him — like ninepins in a bowling alley, Chance thought; then at a nod from the Prince the officers broke their formation and fanned outward to greet their hosts, and Chance noticed how each officer approached an officer of his own rank. The flight commanders, Count Pakorski and Count Zulka, sought out their counterparts in the RAF squadron and presented themselves with a severe inclining of the head. The RAF officers had seen nothing like this in their brief, makeshift service, and they looked with amused disparagement upon the ritual of a lost tradition.

Into this confluence of officers the stewards brought sherry in utilitarian glasses.

Twenty minutes later the chief steward called them to the table, and they stood behind their places while the Chaplain said grace. Armstrong sat at the head of the table with Prince Karol on his right; Chance was seated on the far side of the Prince.

With the stewards in movement about the table, the Prince turned to Chance, his eyes showing the light of irony. 'This afternoon we are inspected by the AOC,' he said with sombre emphasis. 'He is an old fighting man and thirty years ago he flies all round the Boche. He is the whiskers of the cat. Now he comes into my headquarters making a great deal of noise with his boots.'

'I don't care much for inspections,' Chance said quietly.

'I ask myself, why is it that Teddy French, who once lies upon the wind like a seagull, now comes in like a bullock? I say to myself, does he think the Poles go pee-pee in the corner?'

From the Prince's left, Armstrong said, 'It is simply his manner of inspection, which is shared by many air officers.'

'At once it becomes clear to me! A great hero is too big a man to make faces unless they tell him to. He is obeying his orders. They have said to him, the Poles are a devilish lot from the dark side of Europe; you will go to them and slap their buttocks and then they will behave very nicely.'

'In fact the Air Marshal was knocked sideways by what he saw,' Chance said.

'He was entirely satisfied,' Armstrong endorsed.

'Oh, yes — he is satisfied. All at once he glows like a lamp. When he sees the men scuttle and stamp he is reminded of his old adversaries, the Germans of the past, and he thinks the Poles are true warriors also. He finds himself among friends.'

In unfamiliar country, Chance did not know what to think, though it was true the AOC had been heartened by what he found and perhaps recognized the quality of his old enemy. For himself, he was disturbed and embarrassed by the knightly traditions of Europe which could have no place in the present holocaust.

'The AOC was encouraged by the high standard of conduct,' Armstrong said firmly. 'It was nothing more significant than that. After all, discipline is the same in every country.'

'He sees that we too are military men,' the Prince continued as if the Station Commander had not spoken. 'He knows that such a tradition comes only after generations of training, of trial. He finds we are as good as the Germans and he does not think more about the Polish squadron.'

That much was certain, at least. 'You're damn right,' said Chance, suddenly illuminated.

The candles had burned down half their length before the table was cleared for the loyal toast. At odds with the occasion, restless and bored, Chance had not said much to his neighbours; he saw the need to hold his tongue in a world not his own where each observance was rooted in times past. They could dream their dreams if they wished; they could hang a curtain between themselves and the searing truth if that made their task the easier. The faces at the table had taken on the emphasis of caricature. Padre Shenstone's broken features had all the marks of a pugnacious orthodoxy, while the expression used by Jarvis, the Adjutant, was one of torpid satisfaction with the life that he knew. Only Peter Marek, seated near the foot of the table, was detached from this place in some bitter abstraction of his own.

The toast was proposed by the most junior officer present, Pilot Officer Lampton-Bell, who was Armstrong's rear-gunner and a boy of considerable means. In the candlelight he looked very young, but then all the aircrew were young.

'Gentlemen — the King.'

They stood together and said 'The King', and the candles quivered at the words.

Then Lampton-Bell rose again. Another functionary had to be commended no matter that his country had vanished in the flux of war.

'Gentlemen — the President of the Republic of Poland.'

They drank to this gentleman, and were seated.

The Station Commander had obviously taken pains with the address that followed. He spoke concisely, almost without gesture but with deep conviction. He welcomed the Polish squadron to Moreton Valence and to the comradeship of the mess, and he welcomed them to a place in the Main Force where they would contribute to the defeat of Germany. There was still much strength in the brutal dictatorship which had clothed Europe in darkness, he said, but even now the forces of liberation were advancing towards the enemy frontiers. He dropped his voice. 'Gentlemen, you will have heard that the Russian army is outside Warsaw. You will know that Polish patriots have risen in the city to engage the Germans in fierce combat, and we may hope that the capital of Poland will fall to the Allies in a few days' time. I can think of no better news for our friends this evening — nothing that will give greater strength to their labours — than that Warsaw is at the point of deliverance.'

Prince Karol gave no sign that he affirmed this opinion and simply raised his head to look deeply into the shadows.

'We have seen the Polish squadron to be a unit of high morale and immaculate behaviour on the ground,' Armstrong said in conclusion. 'I have no doubt they will prove a courageous fighting unit in the air. We will drink to the success of their operations and to the fulfilment of their national aims.'

It seemed a worthy sentiment and the Station Commander sat down to unstinted applause. Chance bit into his thumb, having no taste for the approved rhetoric of these years; there would be a victory when one side was exhausted but it would prove nothing, solve nothing. He watched Prince Karol who still looked into the darkness, and he saw the fineness of the head which the candlelight showed him in profile; he saw how the lips were pressed together as if fastened upon an ineffable secret. Then he saw the head lift suddenly, in resolve, in unshakeable pride.

The Prince stood up, and no matter that his figure was short he commanded silence. He spoke without notes, abruptly, guided by a fitful inspiration, and there was no preamble. 'We come from nowhere. We are lost people. If you like, say we are dead people. Shut your eyes and you do not see us! We were swallowed up by the war and sent to dark places where we died, and now we are spirits who cannot rest. No more about that. I say, no more! We follow the same path we followed in life. We are drawn by the same star . . . '

The officers listened with their eyes upon the table, not moving. They were accustomed to a flippant disregard for the war and its consequences and this tone of voice was strange to them. The Prince spoke next of his desire to join in their operations and to strike at the enemy which was a duty he and his officers could not escape. He addressed his words not to them but to the shadows of the ceiling, as if a listener were there — some vengeful spirit whose mood he could not judge but to whom he must make an offering. 'Now we take our place beside you. Too long we have waited. We attack an enemy who has done us injury. It is an enemy we know, whose foul breath we have felt upon our cheek, whose claws have ripped us open. It is an enemy we cannot forget nor forgive. Those of us who are truly of our nation — those who still call themselves Poles — will avenge the injury. We will avenge the injury no matter where it takes us!'

Steady on, Chance thought, wiping away a grimace with his hand. We knock hell out of the Germans because there's a war on and for no other reason. We'd go mad if we took it seriously.

The Prince had little more to say. He had appeased the demon in the shadows, and perhaps he knew he had moved outside the limit of good taste. 'Now I sit down,' he said quietly. 'I say too much. Pay no attention to my madness if it offends you. Afterwards, if you wish, we drink, we play games. I thank you for your comradeship.'

He resumed his seat. Someone clapped, others followed, but the applause was offered more in sympathy than in appreciation. The Station Commander rose from his place soon afterwards and the dinner was over. ·

They adjourned to the ante-room where a bar had been set up and the windows were open to the summer night. The RAF officers were in a mood for gaiety; it was not the habit of the squadrons to give the war too sharp a definition or to hear the evidence of suffering. The destruction of Germany was the job they did, usually concealed in darkness and at a height that separated them from the anguish on the ground. They did not see where the bombs fell. They did not enquire what happened there. Now they were ready for the mess games they had inherited from the peace-time air force and which had been played first on the Canal, at Habbaniya, at Mauripur.

Chance found Armstrong beside him. 'Poor wretch,' the Station Commander said. 'I know he feels badly, but there's no point in making a show of it.'

Somewhere Chance had lost heart and he played no games this evening. Instead he watched the antics of his brother officers as he might have watched the play of marionettes, seeing a show well lighted but one that lacked the power to move him. He did not know why his spirit should have fallen to this low point and from which, try as he might, he could not raise it; that he did not care for the old customs was not the sole reason. A shadow lay across the path, thrown by a figure beyond his sight. The Prince had a strange and savage commitment in this war that frightened him. The aircrews fought in darkness, already close enough to madness, and it would need only a break in their humour to make their work impossible.

He wanted to know what the Poles were about and Marek could tell him. He put down his glass and went in search of the American, but he was not in the ante-room nor in the hall. The outer door was open to the road where some officers were drinking in the pleasant night air, and Chance was about to go outside when Prince Karol and Count Zulka came in together, brushing his arm, wrapped in some purpose of their own which kept them from seeing him. They went into the ante-room and closed the door behind them.

Chance stepped into the road where his eyes were smothered by the darkness. He called, 'Peter, are you there?'

He heard a sound behind him that was not quite a laugh, for there was no humour in it. Marek was standing against the wall as if in need of the support, but Chance did not think he was drunk because Marek had gone beyond drunkenness.

'Peter, listen to me! What are the Poles up to? You must tell me what you know.'

The American's head swung left and right in the darkness and he did not answer.

'Wake, man!' Chance shook Marek by the shoulder and was surprised when he nearly fell. 'Wake! I must speak to you.'

'I cannot tell you about the Poles,' the American said, speaking from some distant eyrie.

'Look — I have to know the truth. I'm not concerned with the traditions of the mess any more than you are; but at dinner the Prince could not contain his anger and he went too far. The idea of taking revenge for injury could be dangerous in Main Force operations, particularly if they were planning a private initiative.'

Marek opened his eyes wide in a struggle to keep awake. 'Ask him, then. Ask him what he intends —— '

'I'm asking you.'

'Why me? I'm a Polack. A man without honour.'

'Christ, you're more likely to tell me than he is. You've been with the Poles for three days and you must have some idea what they're up to. Just now, out here in the dark ——'

'Yes?'

' —— the Prince was speaking to you, where no one could hear him.'

Marek was shaken by private laughter and he pointed to the corner of his mouth. 'See this, brother?'

Chance looked closely in the light from the open door and he could just discern a small globe of dark liquid adhering to the lower lip. 'What is it, Peter? Blood?'

'It's not tomato juice.'

'What happened?'

'He struck me. Then his buddy Zulka weighs in with a cut. Then they go in and you come out.'

'You are telling me the truth? You could have fallen.'

'Sure — I could have fallen.'

'Why would they do that?'

'He hit me because I'm shit, see? He hit me because he's an old Polish aristocrat and I'm nothing but a cheap American Polack. He was telling me to keep out of it.'

Chance looked back at the open door where a band of light lay across the road infringing the blackout. He wanted to enter

42

the mess and ask the Prince what drove him to assault a fellow officer in the dark: what ancient privilege had he claimed when he caught Marek a punishing blow across the mouth? He was about to move on impulse when he recalled the purpose of the evening, which was to receive the Prince into the mess and instruct him in the rudiments of fellowship.

'Peter, you've got to tell me this. What does Prince Karol intend to do with his squadron?'

Marek raised his head until he was looking directly at his superior. He smiled, not at Chance but at some distant satisfaction. 'How should I know? I'm garbage. He doesn't talk to me.'

'But you have a suspicion.'

'No.'

'I'm not easily fooled.'

With his back to the wall, Marek slid downward until he was sitting at Chance's feet in a shapeless jumble; he had collapsed in obstinate indifference to the man that he served.

'Have me court martialled, brother. Have me shot. I'm shit, but once I was a Pole. I won't tell you a thing about the Prince.'

For the next two weeks the Polish captains undertook non-operational sorties to make themselves familiar with Group procedures. They flew navigational exercises and they practised bombing on the Yorkshire range. The Prince was restive but obedient, and Armstrong was satisfied. The two flight commanders, Count Pakorski and Count Zulka, had firm control of their air and ground crews and it was plain they drove them hard. As Station Commander, Armstrong had to review the punishments given by the subordinate commanders and he was surprised by the rigour of their sentences, but he did not interfere, supposing their habit to be different from his own. In particular, the Poles employed the sharpest penalties for an offence hitherto unknown to him: this was translated by Nikolski as 'a lack of patriotic fervour', and it appeared many times in the summary of charges. Stefan Pakorski was an officer who appealed to Armstrong; he was a pleasant-mannered youth with something of the artist in his eyes and finely-drawn mouth; and he was more moderate in his treatment of the airmen than his fellow flight commander. Zulka was a heavy, unresponsive man with a face wiped of expression but for a harsh misanthropy, and Armstrong could not imagine that he was held in much affection. Both officers spoke good English, and once or twice Armstrong had the impression that Pakorski was about to overstep the bounds of formal courtesy and speak to him more intimately; but he did not do so, and Armstrong was disappointed.

In these summer days, when the war had no more than a few months of life, Armstrong was obliged to look into the future. For nearly five years he had not done so: through the dark centre of the war there had been no future but the next perilous hours, and to make a claim upon life had seemed a presumption. Now the chance of his survival had increased and it was possible to imagine a time when one could live through the nights without fear and with the certainty of days to follow. He was frightened of survival; he did not know what he would do in the empty years of peace when life continued to some distant moment of release. He was frightened of the quiet, of the unending time. He had not expected he would need to meet the challenge of peace. In the hubbub of war, when his ears had been stopped by the roar of the engines, he had lost the power of reflection and had grown to rely upon the swift solution of life's problem when the aircraft tipped out of the stream. He was approaching the age when he would be retired from the service, and when he took off the tight-fitting uniform he would also surrender the familiar discipline which had long been his comfort. He did not know what he would do then.

Armstrong had no wife, no children and few close friends. He looked after his ageing mother with patient solicitude. The office of Station Commander did not allow him to form close relationships with his officers, for that would inhibit his power of reproof; he moved in a little bubble of loneliness, knowing that it could only be broken at the expense of his authority — knowing that a break in his authority could lead only to chaos, which he feared more than any other contingency. Yet he wished that Pakorski had spoken to him.

With Prince Karol, Armstrong was conscious of a strong, pain-driven nature in conflict with his own. So far the Prince had shown respect for his rank, deferring to his instructions and keeping in check his obvious impatience; his frustration showed simply in the movements of his hands and the snap of his step. Only once, towards the end of the second week of training, did he indulge in emotional display. Armstrong had told him the AOC would not let the squadron operate for at least another five days. 'It is so?' the Prince exclaimed in angry disbelief. 'He gives us no war to fight? Does he not know the Warsaw insurgents are reaching the end of their strength and that the Russian army has advanced no further than Praga? Mon Dieu, this is insupportable!'

Armstrong forgave him this irregularity, which he put down to his distress, and indeed it was true that Rokossovsky had been unable to relieve the Polish capital. He did not point out that operations conducted in north-west Europe, within the range of the laden Halifax, could not possibly affect the fate of a city on the eastern front; he accepted that the Prince needed to attack the Germans, whose army was now reducing Warsaw stone by stone, to appease his temper, to revenge the injured and dead.

Aircraftman Haines had no other lot in life but to suffer punishment. Every sort of misdemeanour found expression in this ill-favoured airman. If there was a sum of delinquency seeking outlet at Moreton Valence, then Haines took to himself the largest share, and there was advantage in having it so: the identification and punishment of wrong-doing became a simple matter because inevitably Haines was guilty. He carried the station's propensity to offence almost as a private burden. No sooner had Haines returned from detention than he was arraigned before the flight commander charged with malingering, and for this lapse he was awarded seven days' confinement to camp with extra duties. The Station Warrant Officer appointed him to the most fundamental duty on the unit, at the very end of the disposal chain: Haines was to take the buckets of night soil from the sanitary wagon and empty them into the cesspit. There was no more abject labour than this.

The Station Commander was therefore surprised when Haines was brought before him charged with insulting behaviour and the breaking of bounds, for he would not have thought it possible for Haines to get into trouble at the disposal pit. The charge had been preferred by Count Nikolski on the instructions of the Polish Squadron Commander. Haines was marched in under escort by Mr Thorpe, bringing with him a scent of ordure. Nikolski and the Adjutant were already present.

Armstrong read out particulars of the charges, from which it seemed that Haines had trespassed in the grounds of the Polish officers' mess and there caused offence to Prince Karol and to Squadron Leader Count Pakorski. Armstrong asked Nikolski for evidence to support the charges. 'You were present, I assume, and can offer direct evidence that Haines broke bounds and insulted these officers?'

The liaison officer said, 'He offered the deepest insult. It was beyond toleration.'

'Nikolski, I require proof, not innuendo.'

'He was walking on the lawn in the moonlight.'

'Did you see him yourself?'

'I did. So did Prince Karol and Count Pakorski. We were there in the darkness and we were offended.'

'Crossing the lawn need not constitute the breaking of bounds. It would depend upon why he was there. What is the evidence of insult?'

'The man is himself an insult.'

'I must ask you to be precise. The character and bearing of the accused do not of themselves support the charges.'

'He was offensive to the nostrils.'

'Come, now! You must not waste my time.'

'He stumbled and fell. Clearly he was intoxicated. He said words that impugned the good names of the Prince and Count Pakorski.'

'What words?'

'Terrible words.'

'You must tell me exactly.'

'He said, "Excrement and more excrement".'

'I cannot believe that Haines used the word "excrement".'

'Well, no. He employed a coarse vernacular.'

Armstrong controlled his impatience with the liaison officer as best he could. 'Count Nikolski, have you been made aware of the work this man has been doing?'

'He is a dispenser of obnoxious fluids. He is also an xenophobe. When he said these words he certainly intended a description of the Prince and Count Pakorski.'

Armstrong closed his eyes the better to see what happened outside the Polish officers' mess. His imagination showed him nothing but Aircraftman Haines stumbling across the grass in the moonlight. He could not believe that Haines had walked to the mess with the intention of abusing two Polish officers who were unknown to him, but the Prince of course would be quick to anger. As usual, Armstrong was presented with only fragments of evidence — all that remained of an incident now receding in time, passing into obscurity, when an offence might or might not have been committed. The Station Commander's lot. The accused himself had lapsed into a state of trance as if arraigned before a powerful deity, and it was unlikely that he could help; his eyes were fixed upon a vision of implacable judgement, his body sagged under the weight of his delinquency.

'Haines, I want you to tell me, in your own words, exactly what happened. Take your time.'

The accused did not speak, did not move.

'You will not help yourself by remaining silent.'

A shadow of memory passed across his face, but the struggle to give it expression had no result but for a gurgle deep in his system.

Armstrong turned for enlightenment to the SWO. 'Mr Thorpe, can you help me?'

'Well, sir — Aircraftman Haines was on late duty at the disposal pit. The area is subject to blackout.'

'I know that.'

'He suffered a misfortune, sir.'

'What, precisely?'

'I understand that he missed his footing in the darkness.'

'And then?'

Even the Station Warrant Officer, whose duty took him to the lower limits of human experience, found it difficult to describe what happened next.

'Are you telling me that Haines fell into the cesspit?'

'I believe that to be the case, sir. I was not of course present.'

Of course not: such a profound consummation could only be undergone alone and in the dark.

'I see,' Armstrong said.

For all his asperity, Mr Thorpe did not believe wholly in the benefits of punishment; there was in him a largeness of mind that allowed him sometimes to take a moderate course. He said, 'He found himself in an unfortunate situation. I wouldn't be surprised if it affected his mind a bit.'

'I would think it likely,' said Armstrong. 'What happened then?'

'He got out, sir. Somehow.'

'Was there no one near enough to help him?'

'No. The pit is a long way from the nearest building. He crossed two fields, proceeding towards a lighted door which must have been at the Polish officers' mess.'

'Would I be right in supposing that, in walking towards the light, he was going in search of help?'

'I think you would be right, sir.'

Armstrong turned again to the witness. 'Nikolski, had it occurred to you that Haines came for assistance, and that his words simply described the situation from which he had freed himself?'

The Pole was examining the tips of his fingers as if dissatisfied with the manicure. 'Ah — so! No, it did not occur to me. I believe the accused to have meant that all Polish officers were — shall we say? — an effluent.'

'I put it to you now that you were mistaken.'

'But he was plainly intoxicated! He swayed from side to side. He fell. He spoke from a deep antipathy to the foreigner that drink had magnified.'

'And that is your final opinion, notwithstanding what you have heard?'

'It is.'

'Very well. As the accused has no questions, you may wait in my outer office.'

Haines was certainly intoxicated, not with drink but with a terrible miasma. Armstrong required no further evidence.

He said now, using a gentle voice, 'Haines, you have been in a great deal of trouble on this station, but I do not believe you to be guilty of any offence in respect of the Polish officers. I am accordingly dismissing the charges against you. Mr Thorpe, I will be grateful if you will find some other occupation for Haines during his current confinement. I do not wish him sent back to the disposal pit. You may march out.'

As soon as the accused and escort had disappeared, Armstrong thanked the Adjutant and released him. He was disturbed by the charges brought against Haines which no experienced officer should have preferred, and he hoped they did not disclose a habit of irrational behaviour. A moment later Mr Thorpe came back into the room from the passage, not wholly at his ease.

'Yes, Mr Thorpe?'

'A moment of your time, sir. If you please, sir.'

'Of course. Please take a seat.'

It was unusual for the SWO to be less than confident, but for a moment he could not find his voice, or perhaps he was uncertain of his message. Finally he said, 'Last night when Haines was brought to the guardroom he told me what happened at the Polish mess. I didn't press him, sir. That would have been improper when charges were pending against him, but you know how it is when you have charged a man many times — he begins to tell you his troubles.'

Armstrong nodded, aware of the bond that joined the defaulting airman with the NCO who contrived his punishment. 'Well, what did he say?'

'Something I didn't understand.'

'I think you'd better tell me.'

The SWO was silent, bound by the custom that did not allow him to describe the behaviour of senior officers.

'Mr Thorpe, I will be obliged if you will speak freely, as a matter of duty.'

'As you wish, sir. He told me this.' Then, in a voice that betrayed his discomfort, Mr Thorpe described how Haines had approached the mess in darkness from an unexpected quarter and how at first he had not been seen. He had collapsed on to his hands and knees at the limit of his strength, but he had seen that the Polish officers were engaged in some sort of ceremony in the moonlight. The officers were drawn up outside the door, not exactly for a parade but certainly for a formal occasion. Haines had watched Prince Karol approach Squadron Leader Pakorski and throw something on the ground before him. The other officers didn't stop him: indeed, they were standing at attention as if they had been called to witness an act of sombre ritual. It was only when the officers had been dismissed and were returning to the mess that Haines had been seen and arrested. 'That was his story, sir. I thought you would wish to know.'

Armstrong felt as though he had been pricked by a blade of ice, but he did not let his composure slip; he was alarmed because a powerful influence was in movement at Moreton Valence and one that did not originate from him. 'Did Haines say anything else?' he asked.

'No, sir.'

'Of course, he is a confirmed liar.'

'I don't think he was lying on this occasion.'

'Maybe not.'

No, Haines was not lying, for his imagination was not large enough to invent such a story.

50

'Very well, Mr Thorpe. You were correct to give me this information. Please keep it to yourself for the time being.'

The SWO went out leaving the Station Commander to his disquiet. He paced the small office from end to end, halting at last by the window where perhaps the long view would relax his mind, but his fear could not be eased. A confrontation had taken place between the Prince and one of his flight commanders. A challenge had been offered and a challenge could only be resolved in conflict. He couldn't think why the youthful Pakorski, the most modern-minded of the Poles, should have taken part in this proceeding, nor why the Prince should provoke a breach of discipline of the most serious kind. Finally he shrugged his shoulders at the absurdity of it and went out to inspect the kitchens.

There was no raid that night; the aircrews were standing down. Armstrong went early to bed where he lay watching the moon rise behind the window and thinking of the story that Haines had told. An odd witness to such a scene. Later he must have slept, for the moon had gone from the window and the room had darkened. Something had wakened him but he couldn't tell what. Then the telephone rang again and he felt for it in the darkness. What message could there be at this late hour when the squadrons were at rest?

'Station Commander,' he said.

He could not identify the voice with certainty. A courteous voice, with a Polish inflection — a voice that barely lifted above a whisper. The speaker apologized for the late call and then paused in embarrassment.

'What is it?' Armstrong asked.

'I must tell you the boy was innocent.'

'What boy?'

'I do not know his name. A man of many troubles.'

'You are speaking of Haines, the defaulter?'

'I saw only a dark figure. He was guilty of nothing more than a lack of circumspection. He entered at a moment of dedication and his condition was — may I say it? — inappropriate.'

It was a pleasant voice. Someone in the Polish camp had regard for the Station Commander's authority and Armstrong was heartened.

He said now, 'Will you tell me your name?'

'It will be better if I do not.'

'I know it, I think.'

'Then it need not be spoken.'

'I can tell you that I dismissed the case against Haines,' Armstrong said. 'I believed the charges to be mistaken.'

'They were conceived in anger. I am glad you found him innocent.'

'I appreciate your concern.'

'Not all of us live in the past, sir.'

'I do not understand why you have called me so late,' Armstrong said.

'I might have no opportunity tomorrow.'

Armstrong was drawn to the speaker, whose voice had the warmth of friendship. This man had been moved to speak to him notwithstanding the difference in their rank and nationality. In the dark, in these bare quarters, Armstrong felt a sudden break in his loneliness.

'Listen,' he said with quiet urgency, 'I am concerned for your safety. I do not like what I have heard. There are dangers enough ——— '

'You cannot help me, sir.'

'I have authority here.'

The speaker paused, too polite to offer a contradiction. Then he said, 'There are differences between the Poles which can only be settled by themselves. Old differences. I recommend that you do not concern yourself. The matter will be resolved very soon.'

'I don't want to see you hurt. The Prince is a dangerous man.'

'So he is; but there is no other way.'

'You cannot expect me to agree with you. This is an RAF station governed by British standards of conduct. I will intervene if you wish.'

'No, sir. There is nothing you can do. I bid you good night.'

Armstrong held the still live telephone in his hand, aware that the moment for decisive action was passing, aware that his power was incomplete.

'Count Pakorski, you must know that I forbid any form of conflict between officers,' he said, raising his voice.

'You are kind, sir. I regret my disobedience.'

Nothing more: Armstrong was holding a dead telephone. He

52

replaced the instrument and lay still, looking at the night sky behind the window panes. He was frightened by the sense of unalterable commitment that seemed to reside in every Polish mind. He did not believe in predestination, which he saw to be no more than an ugly superstition it was certainly his duty to resist. He was concerned for the young nobleman who, even in the toils of a sombre destiny, had spoken to him in friendship.

He closed his eyes and beckoned sleep. There was nothing he could do; nothing. Whatever witchery had sway in these dark hours must work itself out to an end. Then, dragging his mind from the folds of sleep, he recalled that he wes Station Commander with a duty to dispel faulty notions and to preserve the good order of Moreton Valence. Pakorski had said the matter would soon be resolved and that could mean that even now the Poles were in defiance of his instructions.

He got up, pulled on his battledress and went out into the soft night air.

The airfield was reduced in size and importance in the moonlight, and the bombers at their dispersals were little more than shadows — dark symbols of the mid-century that would vanish in a year. He took his car from the parking bay and drove slowly round the perimeter towards the Polish site. The hooded lights revealed no one but for a sentry with a torch under the control tower and, further on, an airman with a girl close to the wire. He stopped the car well short of the site and went forward on foot, by a path that led away from the airfield and in the direction of the officers' mess: he was following the same path that Haines had used when he stumbled towards the light in the hope that someone would help him. Once he halted. Not a sound. Nothing but a sky of enormous height, silent now, and the outline of Nissen huts close at hand. He went on again, quietly, until he was within fifty yards of the mess and overlooking the entrance, where he stopped and waited.

He waited while the moon rode onward in the vast sky and the dew fell upon his cheek. He did not know what he expected to happen; perhaps nothing. But he did not want to see an injury done to Pakorski when he might prevent it. He did not want an outbreak of violence at Moreton Valence when the nights contained violence enough already.

Voices now. Voices speaking a language he did not understand. A band of light had opened at the entrance and perhaps a dozen officers had come out into the moonlight. There was no laughter. He strained his eyes through the moon-softened darkness but could not see what they were doing. He edged closer, to a place where a hedge made a wandering inscription across his sight and offered some concealment; he was now within twenty yards of the Poles and able to discern their separate shapes.

Two figures had detached themselves from the group to stand facing one another in silence. A salute of some sort was exchanged. Then, as if they were dancing in measured steps, they slowly revolved, keeping a space between them; they might have been joined by a cord which kept them always at the same distance apart. From his place in the larger darkness he watched a dance of strict formality. He was mesmerized by the slow movement, his mind dulled to a point where this play of shadows was no more than an antique ritual he had no power to check. A while later — how long, he could not have said — the figures flowed together and he heard the ring of metal and saw the gleam of the blades as one swordsman made a savage thrust which the other parried; and thereafter the conflict swayed from side to side in the darkness, the blades showing now and again like the dance of fireflies. Armstrong did not move. He could now distinguish the shorter figure of Prince Karol, who fought with an extravagant energy that made up for his lack of reach. Stefan Pakorski, the more stylish in movement, held a defensive blade as if he had no heart for more, and certainly he was in the greater danger.

Well, what should he do? For the time being, bereft of will, he was inclined to let them fight it out now that the conflict was joined. Whatever argument divided the Poles might as well be resolved here in the seclusion of darkness. And if there was risk, so what? Every night there were dangers more acute. Then, as he watched, with an upward stroke the moonlight clearly defined, the Prince broke the younger man's guard and Armstrong saw that Pakorski was injured. The Prince had gained a mastery he would be quick to exploit. The Station Commander shook himself awake, wondering why he had stood so long in silence when a scandalous breach of station discipline was in progress before his eyes. He broke through the hedge and approached the duellists in a mood of guarded fury.

'A dangerous game, Prince Karol,' he said. 'In twenty-eight years of service I have never seen a duel between officers.'

The swordsmen disengaged, astonished at the sudden appearance of the Station Commander.

Armstrong took the sword from the Prince's hand and felt the sharpened edge and the point. He said, 'I shall require an explanation of this extraordinary conduct.'

Finding no words, the Prince shrugged his shoulders.

Armstrong called Pakorski to his side and examined the wounded arm. He said tersely, 'Squadron Leader, you are to report to sick quarters immediately. An officer will accompany you. That is an order.'

'Come, sir!' Prince Karol exclaimed, his speech restored. 'You are too serious. We make a battle because you do not let us fight the enemy. In the Polish army we practise regularly with the foil.'

'You take me for a fool,' Armstrong said with the fluency of anger. 'This is not a foil but an épée, and the edge has not been blunted. You were fighting without guards and your opponent is wounded. It is one o'clock in the morning.'

'I do not understand who has sent you here.'

'An airman sent me. An airman falsely charged.'

'You have interfered in a dispute between Polish officers, who have their own traditions.'

'You cannot rob me of my authority, Prince Karol. I am responsible for the good order of the station and have every right to interfere, particularly when I know the dispute to have been inspired by yourself. We are here to fight the enemy, not each other . . . ' But to rebuke a senior officer in the presence of his subordinates was contrary to the service code, and Armstrong could not continue. When in doubt, apply the convention, usually that was best. 'You will report to me in writing. I shall need to know the origin of this absurd spectacle and to be given an assurance it will not happen again. My further action will depend upon your explanation.'

'You must return my sword,' the Prince said.

Armstrong still held the weapon in his hand. He would have been entitled to take it with him, but to disarm an officer in time of war, and that officer a prince of uncertain temper, he saw to be folly. He did not hand it back; he thrust it into the ground a yard from the Prince's feet, where it swayed back and forth like a finger wagged in reproof.

Then Armstrong turned on his heel and went back the way he had come.

FIVE

The Polish squadron was brought to readiness for operations the next morning. Armstrong sent notification to Prince Karol with the hope that the promise of action would do something to soften his ill-humour. He did not know what to make of last night's encounter, although he was sure the conflict was not just an archaic sport but the symbol of a real division in the Polish squadron. The Prince could not tolerate a dissident voice, particularly when that voice belonged to one of his flight commanders and himself of noble birth; he had to revive an ancient custom of the Polish army to decide the issue and there could be little doubt that he had won his point. Armstrong could not imagine what cause was at stake because, to his mind, the war allowed no differences of opinion. Their purpose was to defeat the Germans and no other aim was possible. Of course, Pakorski was the least traditional of the Poles with a mind belonging to the twentieth century, and it was easy to imagine that he could have fallen out with Prince Karol. He had accepted a challenge, and he had lost. Armstrong could not imagine what penalty he had now to serve.

For himself, he needed to refresh his mind after the night's excursion, to return to the cool sanity of the air; so when he had cleared his desk of business, after the midday meal, he called the operations room and asked what aircraft were available for flight. R for Robert had returned to the RAF squadron after major repair and was ready for test. She was the Halifax brought home by Peter Marek no matter that the wing and forward cabin were severely damaged. That night the navigator, shortly to marry, had escaped emasculation by a miracle. An aircraft of strange omen. Armstrong took his flying kit from the locker and went into the sunlight, where he took note of the still air and the trace of cirrus at thirty thousand feet.

As he stepped into his car an officer approached him with an ill-managed salute: Squadron Leader Keeble, the Intelligence Officer, who plainly desired his attention.

Armstrong spoke upon impulse. 'A lovely afternoon, Keeble. Will you join me in the air?'

The Keeper of Antiquities looked at him as if he had given voice to an heretical opinion. 'If you wish it, sir. I have never flown in an aeroplane.'

'Then it's time that you did. We'll find you some gear.'

Armstrong drove to the crew room where he picked up Marek's navigator, engineer and wireless operator — the minimum complement for a non-operational flight — and found Keeble a harness and parachute. In this equipment the old scholar looked like a martyr trussed for burning and hardly more enthusiastic. 'I had come to see you on a matter of intelligence,' he said, the note of vexation only just audible. 'Certain information has been brought to my attention which I must share with you.'

'Later, Keeble,' Armstrong said, suppressing his smile. 'The navigator must instruct you in the use of a parachute.'

'There is need? I had not expected —— '

'There is always need.'

Clearly Keeble had given no thought to suspension in space, but with a certain abstracted dignity he turned his mind to the problem of descent. 'I see. You jump through the bottom of the aeroplane and, having fallen some distance towards the earth, you pull this metal ring. Thereafter it is a matter of wind and gravity in mutual influence. Station Commander, I believe my information to be urgent.'

'You may tell me about it in the air.'

Armstrong took a keen pleasure in the sensations of flight which in a life of austere dedication had supplied the single beauty. He had flown since he was a young man: Harts in Iraq, over the grey and rose desert; Furies on the Canal; the Battle, the Blenheim, the Wellington in the early years of the war. Now he lifted the Halifax from the runway and felt the smooth upward surge as the wheels disengaged and the aircraft was borne upon the compliant air. He climbed into the lower sky, his spirit freshening. The shadows swung on the cockpit floor as the aircraft turned, seeking her course, climbing away from Moreton Valence and the problems of his command.

At six thousand feet he levelled out and tested the hydraulic systems — wheels, flaps, bomb-doors. He feathered each engine in turn, watching the blades slow and stop, using the trim tabs to take the weight off the rudder bars. For twenty minutes he gave the whole of his mind to the movements of the aircraft, letting his instinct tell him how the systems were operating. This Halifax was different from the one he flew usually; it had a quicker response, a greater buoyancy, as if possessed of a stronger will to live. He recalled the last flight it had made, when under Peter Marek it had returned from the Ruhr with damage sufficient to destroy it but had somehow found the home base and there landed with dry tanks. That night the navigator at least should have died. The same boy was sitting below him in the forward cabin, doing nothing, because there was no need for navigation when the towers of York Minster remained firmly in view — a quiet, fair-haired South African whose name Armstrong tried hard to remember.

He switched on the microphone in his oxygen mask. 'Pilot to navigator. Better than your last trip, I think. You are lucky to be here.'

The navigator joined the intercom and Armstrong could hear his breath, like the rustle of tissue, in his earphones; and the same moment the boy's name came to him — Flying Officer Du Toit.

'Yes, sir. Thank you, sir.'

'I believe you are to be married soon.'

A pause, while the sound of his breath continued.

'Yes, sir.'

'We'll drink to that,' Armstrong said.

The boy made no reply and Armstrong forgot him almost at once.

He turned the aircraft south, towards the Humber, confident that she was flying normally. The river gleamed through the haze. Moreton Valence was to the north of the estuary and his eyes picked out the familiar pattern of runways after a moment's search. He began to descend.

He spoke next to Keeble. The elderly scholar sat on the strap seat beside him in some paralysis of the spirit, but he started into sudden life when he heard his name on the intercom. 'You had something to tell me, Keeble.'

The Intelligence officer was speaking, but Armstrong could hear none of it.

'Try that switch,' he said.

Keeble became audible then, his voice magnified to a painful level. 'Switch? It is necessary to press this switch?'

'It activates the microphone.'

'But you are beside me!'

'Nevertheless I can't hear you.'

'Then am I to assume my message was lost?'

'I'm afraid so. Say it again.'

While Keeble reassembled his mind, Armstrong held a course a little to the west of the airfield, from which he would pass into a left-handed orbit. He knew that Keeble was going to say something that mattered.

'Late this morning I received a call from the Intelligence Officer at Command,' Keeble said with laborious clarity. 'You can hear me? I am not speaking to myself?'

'Please continue.'

'A Halifax was reported over the Welsh coast soon after dawn.'

'Well?'

'It was flying low.'

'Can you say why this is important?'

'Command checked with the operations staff and the flight was not planned. As far as they were concerned there should have been no Halifaxes in the area.'

Armstrong slightly increased his rate of descent. Events had moved on. A wayward Halifax had been sighted over the Welsh coast.

'I do not understand why this has been dealt with by Intelligence,' he said, keeping his eyes upon Moreton Valence. 'It is surely an operational matter.'

'I believe not. The aircraft behaved unusually.'

'In what way?'

'It approached Bardsey Island at an exceptionally low level.'

'Childish antics,' Armstrong said, pushing the subject away from him, finding a satisfactory answer. 'This happens all the time.'

60

'It dropped two sacks of straw, which fell close to a derelict building.'

'Good heavens! What did they do that for?'

'The area is remote and it was only by chance the aircraft was seen.'

'Well, what do they expect me to do about it?' Armstrong asked. 'I doubt if it will be possible to trace the aircraft.'

Keeble still spoke with tedious emphasis. 'Sir, the squadron has been identified. The aircraft passed close to the lighthouse and the keeper read the fuselage markings.'

Armstrong trimmed the Halifax into a better attitude, taking no less than his usual care. Now he knew that he could not dismiss the matter. 'Squadron Leader, I will be grateful if you will complete your report after we have landed.'

He did not want the crew to hear what came next, for there was no reason why an act of penance should be known by junior personnel. God, it was only thirteen hours since the Prince had outfought his flight commander and imposed his will upon the dissenting faction!

He landed the Halifax and taxied to the dispersal, where he switched off the engines and signed the air test report. The aircraft which so nearly had been lost could now return to squadron service. He took off his helmet, released the restraining harness and made his way out of the aircraft. Once on the tarmac he drew the Intelligence Officer aside.

'Keeble, you need not tell me the Halifax belonged to the Polish squadron. It is obvious from the way the incident was reported.'

Keeble nodded; then he spoke as if there were still a need for exact articulation. 'There were only three aircraft from the Polish squadron in the air during the early hours of this morning and the operations officer has checked their flight plans. Two were on cross-country exercises in the north of Scotland. The third has an incomplete record.'

Armstrong exhaled a long deep breath. 'And it was this aircraft, of course, that flew low over Bardsey Island and dropped two sacks of straw.'

'I have identified the captain, sir.'

'No doubt. No doubt.'

'His name will surprise you.'

'I think not, Keeble. I am no longer capable of surprise. The captain was Squadron Leader Count Stefan Pakorski.'

Hayden Chance was drinking too much, but he knew he would not be required for operations before morning. The back bar at the Haymakers' Inn was crowded to suffocation with the members of his squadron, men wearing the same battledress but of different ranks and nationalities. In the last four years of extravagant war the aircrews had founded a new tradition in the British services, when of their own accord they had abandoned the use of rank and made a mockery of the old regime. No longer was the aircraft captain necessarily the senior crew member. There were no parades and no inspections. The aircrews were privileged people for as long as they lasted. This evening they crowded the Haymakers' in the knowledge that there would be no charges for drunkenness and that the gate would be opened for the last man home.

Their host was a young South African Chance hardly knew, and but for his escape from injury in the last night raid Chance would not have known him now: he would have been part of the shifting population of young men who manned the squadrons and who, but for the war, would barely have left school. Flying Officer Du Toit was to be married next day to a girl from the village of Moreton Valence — the girl, it seemed, who now displayed a gaudy face and well-used body at the centre of the room.

Chance lifted his heavy frame from the chair and went in search of the boy's captain. He didn't like the look of things. He found Peter Marek fast in a corner speaking to no one. 'Tell me about Du Toit,' he said.

Marek shrugged, keeping his eyes upon the turbulent crowd as though he watched a dance; Du Toit belonged in the greater world from which Marek had long ago taken his leave.

'Come on, Peter. Maybe you've signed off, but this boy hasn't. Where does he come from?'

'How should I know? Cape Town, I think. His father's in the wine business.'

'A wealthy family?'

'Why don't you ask him yourself? Six vineyards, I think he said. The boy was educated in Europe. He should have been knackered that night when the cabin blew in.'

Chance put his hand on Marek's shoulder and spoke into his ear. 'What about this girl, Peter? Give me the story.'

'Big tits. Boy, have you seen them? More than you can hold in two hands.'

'How do you know?'

'The whole squadron knows.'

'You mean she's a tramp.'

'Whore. Big whore.'

'Hell, man — you're his captain,' Chance said, suddenly angered. 'It was your job to steer him away from her.'

With a certain dignity, Marek turned towards Chance, his eyes showing a proud detachment.

'You were in a position to prevent this from happening,' Chance continued, 'but you have ducked the responsibility and done nothing.'

'Listen: she's an airman's dream. Big tits. Hot belly. Sump well lubricated with axle grease. She's a great big marvellous whore. Why should I talk him out of that?'

'But he's going to marry her, for Christ's sake!'

Marek's eyes kept their long focus and Chance knew him to be trapped by the poetry of whoredom. 'Should have been knackered,' he said. 'He should have been knackered that night when the side came in and the splinter went between his legs. Instead he came all the way back in the dark; he was given another week, another month. Why was that? Why?'

'You'd better tell me, Peter.'

'Boy, he came back, nuts and all, to the Great Whore!'

'And after that, when the war's over?'

'There's nothing after the Great Whore.'

Chance knew he would get no further with Marek, who had ventured even farther out into the dark sea than the rest of them. But they were all adrift in perilous water. In these days there was no past and no future and the aircrews simply didn't care. Even Chance found it difficult to picture the wife he had left in British Columbia, and the faces of his two children had lost their vividness: all, all lay behind the images of war. A movement in the crowd brought Padre Shenstone to his elbow.

'Padre, have you talked to him?' he asked. 'Does he know what he's doing?'

'I talked to him, yes. I explained to him the difficulties of a war-time marriage, but he took these things very lightly.'

'You mean he doesn't expect to survive.'

'I gained that impression. It is, of course, a common conviction amongst the aircrews which leads to much impulsive behaviour.'

'You're wasting your time, brother,' Marek said.

All right, he was wasting his time, but he was sickened by the fatalism of war which even the Padre shared. Using his weight, he pressed his way through the shifting crowd until he found Du Toit. The boy was so young he barely grew a beard. Chance took him by the arm, propelled him out of the bar and into a yard where there was little but darkness and the stench of a nearby urinal.

'See here,' he said softly. 'I want to say just one thing, and you can ignore it if you wish. Never assume that you're a dead man. Now tell me why you have to marry that girl.'

The boy said nothing.

'OK, she's built for the bedroom, but what happens after that? Are you aiming to take her home?'

'No, sir. I can't take her home.'

'So you'll live here?'

'I hadn't thought about it.'

'Well, isn't it about bloody time you did think about it?'

Du Toit shook his head, smiling faintly. Like others in aircrew he had lost the power to look forward; like them, he believed himself in the last days of his life when there was nothing to do but drain the bottle. Chance himself wanted to live and to return to his own country, and he knew he must not yield to the comfort of oblivion.

'One thing is certain,' he said with the emphasis of deep conviction. 'If you give up the thought of living, you increase the odds against you. If you count yourself already lost, you might as well put a pistol to your head. Now tell me what you want me to do. If you'd like to be posted away until this thing blows over I'll arrange it and nobody need know how it happened.'

But Du Toit would not abandon the luxury of an imminent release and he did not look up.

Man, you're asking for it,' Chance said, as he went back into the brilliant light of the bar.

'Yes, David, I heard you,' the AOC said, his voice distorted by the scrambler mechanism but still recognizably his own. 'I get the story. Bloody strange, if you ask me.'

'I felt obliged to tell you, sir,' Armstrong said.

'Indeed you did; but I shouldn't worry overmuch. Tomorrow morning they'll be in the thick of it and that should be enough to keep them occupied. There's a nasty one coming. Of course, they have much in common with the German officers. Last time round the Germans were often cutting each other's ears off and this naturally saved us the trouble. It's part of their spirit.'

'The unauthorized flight still concerns me, sir.'

'A gesture, a demonstration of nerve. He lost the bout and had to beat up Bardsey Island to show his metal. They have an exaggerated élan.'

'I fancy it was more than that.'

'Maybe; but I doubt it. Have the Prince in and ask him what the hell goes on. I give you the authority to deal with it. But — take care, David.'

'Of what, sir?'

French paused, surprising Armstrong, for he was not usually reflective. 'Well, of cutting them back too far. Frankly I admire their offensive spirit; it's part of the old order and there's a lot to be said for it. I could use a foil once. But make it plain to Prince Karol that I won't put up with any deliberate disobedience of orders.'

The familiar voice was gone, leaving Armstrong with his discomfort. He called Jarvis and asked him to summon Prince Karol to the Station Commander's office, and as he waited he ran over the words he might use to convey his displeasure. When the Prince came in, Armstrong kept him standing.

'Wing Commander, first of all it is my duty to warn your squadron for operations tomorrow morning. The target will be announced later today and we may assume the raid will involve some penetration of the continent in daylight and that the defences will be effective. I am sorry that you have been denied offensive action for so long.'

The Prince stiffened, and Armstrong saw that he was smiling secretly, as if amused that the war's imperative had at last brought him face to face with those who murdered his country.

'I must remind you that the raid will be in support of strategic objectives, a part of Main Force operations; it will not be a private vendetta against the German people.'

The Prince opened his hands, as if to release his innermost sympathies. 'The bombs fall. The Germans are killed. It is as one, is it not?'

'Our task is to reduce the German economy, not particularly to destroy life. Well, that is the declared aim. You will brief your squadron accordingly.'

The Prince paced the narrow carpet, trying to find the words he needed, words to describe the shapeless torment that had possession of him and his people. He said, with his voice a little out of shape, 'Attend me, sir! You are an old regular officer with no knowledge of Europe. Before the war you serve in India, in the Middle East, where you build bridges and smack the naked black bottoms. So it is! But you do not know what is happening in your own continent; you do not know what madness is creeping through Europe, madness like a black beast —— '

'Prince, I have twice fought the Germans; I have been engaged in this war since the beginning —— '

'You fight as you would play chequers. For you it is a war of calculated risk, a strategic offensive. You have not felt the bitter wind that blows off the snows. You have not seen the black beast —— '

'Come now! I must ask you to remember your military tradition. It does not allow these superlatives, any more than mine does.'

The Prince came to a halt. 'My tradition? What is my tradition? I will tell you, sir. My tradition is one of invasion and occupation. Even now there are two armies in my country. Very soon —— '

'Very soon your country will be free,' Armstrong said curtly, disliking the emotional colour that had so far disfigured their conversation.

'It is so?'

Prince Karol held the Station Commander in a steady gaze, but as ever Armstrong could not tell what thought was passing behind those black, empty eyes — eyes that for all he knew contained some of the madness the Prince had described. Then he saw the jaw snap shut and he knew that the Prince would not speak his thought aloud.

Armstrong folded his hands as if this would compose his weary mind. 'One thing more. I have received no report from you in respect of the incident two nights ago when Squadron Leader Pakorski was injured. I do not expect my instructions to be ignored.'

The Prince, who a moment ago had been stiff with mute dignity, now brought his heels together and bowed his head in deference. 'My dear Group Captain, I do not think you are serious when you ask me to make a report. We play only a game. I am instructing Pakorski in the use of a sword when all of a sudden — voilà! — the Station Commander arises from the hedge.'

'I must tell you that I was wholly serious. What is more, I shall need to know why it was that Count Pakorski, within hours of his injury, was dispatched on a low-level exercise over Bardsey Island when he should have been resting in sick quarters.'

Armstrong could only admire the strength of purpose which allowed the Prince to master his shock so quickly; he did no more than turn wondering eyes towards his superior. Then he said softly, intimately, 'Ah, the young Count — he is an impetuous man!'

'You must tell me what happened.'

'It was nothing. A demonstration of strength, a flourish of hurt pride.'

'Why did you let him go?'

'He had to redeem himself. He was faulted at sword-play.'

'That is ridiculous.'

'You do not understand the Poles, my friend.'

'Will you tell me what it is that divides yourself and Count Pakorski?'

'What would divide us?'

'Listen. First you offer a challenge to Pakorski and fight him with a sharpened weapon. Then, when he is injured and humbled, you send him on a dangerous exercise which could have led to the loss of his life. That is not sport as I know it. Obviously you have a need to dominate him.'

Prince Karol did not at once deny it. He said, in a voice so private he might have been speaking to himself. 'No, it was not sport! I do not know the meaning of sport. Pakorski had offended me.'

67

To tempt his confidence, Armstrong kept his voice equally low. 'Was that why you tried to destroy him?'

'I did not try to destroy him; I love him as my son. But the offence had to be expiated.'

'You have not told me the cause of your dispute.'

The Prince raised his head, perhaps startled that he had said so much, and Armstrong realized he would get no answer to his question. He did not know how to continue. He believed Prince Karol to be in breach of air force law, but he knew it would be difficult to frame charges against him for what could be described as an exercise in discipline. In any case the trial of an Allied officer would be politically impossible: the AOC, who regarded the whole thing as a commendable flight of the spirit, would not recommend the C-in-C to take it up with the Polish Air Force. Armstrong had to rely on his own persuasiveness.

He said, choosing his words with slow deliberation, 'Prince Karol, we are military men. We trained in different schools but we acknowledge the overriding need for obedience and for frankness in discussion. Your squadron is going into action for the first time and it will only succeed if you have a firm regard for RAF operational control. I will overlook your conflict with Count Pakorski which may have been within the Polish tradition. The flight at low-level over Bardsey Island, which was a wide departure from exercise procedure, was not only disobedient but pointless and foolhardy. You placed the aircraft at hazard for no purpose. I realize that Polish officers are driven by compulsions that are unknown to me, but I must now seek an assurance of your loyalty.' He paused, embarrassed by the emotional appeal he was obliged to make. 'Will you give me your word, as a fellow officer, that in future you will be guided wholly by me? I see this as a primary obligation.'

He could not believe that a Polish nobleman, bound by the practice of the old Europe, would give a pledge he did not intend to keep, and indeed Prince Karol quartered the room in his search for an answer, plainly disturbed by this challenge to his fidelity. At length he returned to Armstrong wearing a troubled face.

'My friend, for you there is only one obligation. That is the abiding good fortune of the English and the source of their strength. I tell you they are blessed beyond all other people in

Europe. I wish very much that I am Englishman and that I acknowledge one king, one commander and one cause: how happy I am then! But it is not so for a Polish officer. No! We are divided just as our country has been divided. Do not force me to an undertaking I cannot keep.'

This made no sense to a man who found peace in submission. In genuine bewilderment, Armstrong said, 'But the matter is so simple! You have only to accept the authority of your superiors in what is, after all, a common cause. They have a claim upon you that you cannot deny.'

'My superiors — they are so concerned?' the Prince asked. Then, dropping his eyes in gloomy recollection, 'Yes, they are! They fear an outbreak of Polish madness. You are told to keep me in check while my capital burns and the last stones are ground into dust.'

It took Armstrong a moment to recall his conversation with the AOC, when a shadow had lain across the door, making no movement. 'I see. Nikolski has told you of what the AOC said. He should not have listened.'

'It makes no difference. It is not difficult to guess how the Poles are regarded.'

'Prince Karol, will you affirm your loyalty?'

For the first time the Prince's face showed distress unrelieved, and he closed his eyes as if he were trying to suppress a deep hurt. A moment later, with more grace than Armstrong would have thought possible in so short a man, he skirted the table and laid a hand on the Station Commander's shoulder, in comfort, in sympathy.

'It grieves me to offer you so little consolation, my friend,' he said. 'You are a fine officer; and when the war is over I take you to Poland and there we hunt the deer and the wild boar together. But now it is war and there are strange duties resting upon us. I cannot do what you ask.'

The briefing room was too small to contain both squadrons comfortably and many of the aircrews were obliged to stand at the back. The squadron commanders, Prince Karolajczyk of Radom-Striewicz and Hayden Chance of British Columbia, sat at the front on either side of the gangway, and according to their nationality the other captains and crews had taken places behind them. The tin hut was filled with a ripple of voices.

On the wall behind the dais a map of north-west Europe displayed the flight plan for the day's operation: red tape marked the route to be followed by the Main Force on the outward and rearward legs, the defended areas were shown in black, and the directions in which supporting squadrons would make diversionary attacks were indicated by arrows. A fan-shaped outline covering the Channel and parts of the Low Countries marked the limits of fighter cover. The outward path lay south-east over the North Sea, crossed the Dutch coast south of Den Helder, passed through the flat-lands north of the Waal and terminated over the railway yards at Münster: it was the deepest penetration so far by RAF heavy bombers in daylight. The route back was northward over the soft unguarded coast of Friesland.

Squadron Leader Count Stefan Pakorski tried to centre his mind upon the briefing given, knowing the pattern of operations, the depth of the defence, the speed and direction of the winds to matter as much to him as to any other captain: he kept his eyes upon the map and his ear attuned to the brisk voices of the briefing officers. He heard — but did not hear — the details of tactics, intelligence and weather as each specialist gave his account of the morning's hazard; he listened, a ghostly nostalgia filling his mind, to the small sounds in the body of the hut, the

70

scratch of a pencil, a whispered conference, the continuing murmur of anticipation. The Station Commander was speaking now, welcoming the Polish squadron to the community of the Main Force, wishing them luck.

The briefing was over and his navigator, a sombre, older man, was shaking him awake and pointing to the open door where the sun threw a ramp of light into the room. Pakorski got up and moved with the current of airmen towards the exit. The laceration of his forearm, where the Prince had caught him with an upward stroke of the blade, was still remotely painful like a memory that could not be extinguished. In the sudden glare outside the door Pakorski closed his eyes and shook his head to dispel the giddiness. The firm hand was still at his elbow, but when he opened his eyes again, and his sight cleared, he found himself looking into the spare features of the Station Commander — a face showing all the calm of a single allegiance.

Armstrong was speaking, holding Pakorski with a look of concern, '. . . the arm, it no longer troubles you? I had not expected you to be fit for operational duty for a day or two. Well, if the medical officer has given you clearance . . . '

'I am quite all right,' Pakorski said.

'I will withdraw you on my own account if you don't feel up to it.'

'There is no need.'

The navigator, Sergeant Jawornik, was pressing his elbow to bring the conversation to a close; but he spoke little English and Pakorski doubted if he could follow the Station Commander's words or taste the anxiety that lay behind them.

'Take it easy, then. Nothing rash. Keep well within the stream.'

Pakorski's eyes had filled and he knew that his distress must show; he knew also that this quiet, unknown man had a mind lying close to his own, moved by the same influence, following the same courses; they were like birds borne upon the same streams of air.

'I will be careful,' he said.

Armstrong turned away from him, no doubt to spare him embarrassment, and he addressed his voice to some vision of his own as the airmen pressed past him on their way to the crew room. 'Nevertheless, it may be I should prevent you from flying.

You have been under stress. The Prince is a single-minded man and he may have brought you into action too soon.'

Pakorski was shy of leave-taking which seemed to him the saddest of all exchanges. He said, as Jawornik's hand tightened upon his arm, 'It will be better if I go, for there has been trouble enough. I thank you for your consideration.'

'You must tell me what is wrong,' Armstrong said with sudden force. 'Sergeant, release him!'

'Nothing is wrong. There is no alternative but to fly. Goodbye, sir.'

Already he was ten paces away from the man who could save him, joining the file of airmen walking across the tarmac to the crew room. He did not look back. He simply brushed away Jawornik's hand with a certain proud disdain and continued on his way alone.

A flying jacket of leather and fleece was not the garment for a day late in August, when the sun was burning in the stubble outside the wire. As Hayden Chance emerged from the crew room carrying his safety equipment he felt the heat of the morning. He waited with his crew members for the coach: better, of course, to be in movement, to have his hand upon the living controls, to be caught in the relentless progress of the bomber stream when the only way back was through the smoke of the target area. Peter Marek came out behind him, leading his file of miscreants. They looked like the seven dwarfs. A shower in anybody's opinion. Yesterday afternoon Chance had attended the navigator's wedding in the village of Moreton Valence.

He watched the American approach and knew he would not raise his eyes. He said, 'Tell me, Peter, how did he go?'

Marek would have passed him in silence if Chance had not tripped him with his flying boot.

'Five times, he tells me. I don't believe it. I don't know how he went.'

'Was it worth it, I wonder?'

Marek put down his kit and turned to Chance, his face showing no expression but for a sullen independence of spirit. 'One night in the dark with the Great Whore? Of course it was worth it.'

'Where is he now?'

'Not with me.'

'What do you mean?'

'Swapped him with another captain.'

Chance was astonished, for the integrity of an aircrew was normally complete and a transfer in any case required his authority. 'Man, you can't do that! If you wanted to exchange Du Toit, you should have made an application through the flight commander.'

'Had no time. He's at short odds. I won't take him with me today.'

'I don't get you, Peter.'

'Look — he's laid himself on the line. There's nothing after the Great Whore, nothing but the great chop.'

'You must be mad,' Chance said; but within the air war he had seen the workings of irony and he did not laugh.

The coach travelled down the perimeter road, stopping at each dispersal to set down the seven members of an aircrew: A for Able, B for Baker, C for Charlie ... Chance dismounted in his turn and stood idly by the silent machine, waiting for the allotted moment when he would embark the crew and start the engines. The bomb-doors hung open and he could see the weapons chosen for this sortie — the short, blunt high-explosive bombs that would crater the railway yards and the canisters of incendiaries that would fall in a wider arc and fire the environs. The airfield was quiet. The sun beat on the tarmac and a bee searched the grasses at the dispersal's edge.

At length Chance ordered the crew aboard and started the engines: port outer, port inner, starboard inner, starboard outer ... He felt better for this activity and for the noise that smothered even the movement of thought. His nineteenth operation in the current tour and his fifty-third in all; he didn't know how far he was pressing his luck. As the war drew to a close it was possible to think he might be alive at the end and these perilous days no more than a sombre memory. He wanted to live. He had the taste of summer upon his lips.

He signalled for the chocks to be withdrawn from under the wheels and taxied out towards the main runway.

The aircraft that would compose the bomber stream drew together over the coast on a south-easterly course. The Hali-

faxes from Yorkshire were already in a loose assemblage —
separately navigated but kept together by their common flight
plan. Soon they were joined by Lancasters that came in high on
the starboard quarter to increase the aircraft density; they had
started six minutes later from fields in Lincoln and now they
took the upper places in the stream. From his place in the middle
of the force, Group Captain Armstrong could see aircraft above
him and below him and reaching forward to the horizon; from
the rear turret Lampton-Bell could see later waves stretching
back to the coast. The bomber stream moved towards the continent in the glare of daylight, holding the same direction, keeping
the same pace. An armada of laden aircraft fifty miles long. The
Main Force in being.

Armstrong did not count their number but he knew the raid to
be a maximum effort. He kept his Halifax level at twenty thousand feet, the required height, and watched his companions trying for a better altitude. In a force of this size the dangers arose
not only from the enemy shell but from the fall of the bombs
which sometimes crippled aircraft low in the formation. There
was a clear advantage in a place high in the stream. The Lancasters had the best of it; their superior power took them high above
the plodding Halifaxes. He looked up and down for aircraft of
the Polish squadron which should be somewhere abreast of himself, and those he could identify from their markings were keeping a good discipline, flying straight and level along the path
towards the Dutch coast. Once a Halifax drew close to him high
on the bow, the sunlight catching the turrets, and he recognized
the *Snow Princess*. Well, justice was served.

Beneath him the sea, with a painting of cloud shadow. After
forty minutes, so high he could barely see them, the fighter
escort kept its rendezvous and followed the Main Force towards
the enemy coast. The light flashed upon their wings. They were a
temporary comfort, keeping the bombers company only
through the outward defences of the continent; for then they
would be at the limit of their endurance and forced to retire to
their airfields in the south of England.

A long stain on the horizon with a whiff of cloud above it — a
mark of greater substance than the cloud shadow — was now visible to Armstrong as he narrowed his eyes against the glare. The
coast of Holland had no feature but for its drabness; a single

wave of the sea could wash over this abject place. For a moment he felt nothing but a slight tightening of the muscles in the stomach wall and a sensation of unease at approaching this place, not in the folds of darkness but in the brilliance of midday. The night bombers were bereft of their protection. They had come without their overgarment.

'Ten minutes to the coast,' he said. 'Quiet now.'

The voices on the intercom stilled; the only words spoken were crisp imperatives.

Sergeant Lacey, the mid-upper gunner, kept his turret in slow revolution as he looked both forward and aft, and to him both coasts were visible. The waterway between them was swept of ships. The bomber stream made a ragged bridge from one side to the other, the leading aircraft already penetrating the continent, the rearmost barely clear of the English coast. Far ahead and beyond his sight the pathfinders would be almost into Germany carrying the coloured flares that would identify the target and bring the Main Force to the aiming point; and among them was the Master Bomber who would direct the attack from low level. The diversionary squadrons would be on their separate courses, feinting towards German cities, drawing the enemy fire. Meanwhile the Main Force continued its solemn progress across the most disputed waterway in the world and into that corner of Europe where every conqueror had found it necessary to concentrate his power.

The enemy coast passed under the aircraft nose, under the wing, and in a minute it was visible from the rear turret. Armstrong saw the stream narrowing as the outlying captains sought for places near the centre of the pack. An aircraft detached from the force could fall more easily to the enemy fighters. The ranks closed and the density thickened. Now there was the hazard of collision as the heavy unresponsive machines were drawn into a tighter procession and their shadows fell one upon the other. A random shell might take one aircraft out of the stream: of necessity a collision took two. The gunners told Armstrong of movements in the blind parts of the sky and he made changes in his path to keep the aircraft clear of the fatal impact. Below him, under the haze, the light sparkled in the canals and ditches of Holland.

'Twenty-eight minutes to the target. Hold this heading,' the navigator said. He was the only crew member with a full occupation.

Twenty-eight minutes. Armstrong wondered if he could live so long. He tried counting, but he was counting at twice the speed of the clock; he tried watching the passage of the ground under the leading edge of the wing but at this altitude there was a barely noticeable movement. As in childish dreams time had stopped, there was an arrest of the heart, and try as he might he could not make time flow again. Nothing in his life could match this experience but for the fantasies of the nursery when, long ago, he had been touched by the horror of eternity.

He kept his eyes upon an aircraft high above the stream, higher even than the Lancasters, following the same heading as the Main Force but separate from it. There was a joker in every pack. The square fins and blunt wing tips showed the aircraft to be a Halifax. What would take a Halifax so high, when his own machine was groaning at the limit of her climb? The problem had not force enough to cut through to his intelligence and in a moment he had forgotten it: but in the mid-upper turret Sergeant Lacey had seen the aircraft and made a mark in his memory.

Ten minutes later Armstrong could see a broad serpentine river forward of the starboard wing tip — a river swinging away south to become lost in the haze. He suppressed the tremor in his hands and forced himself to breathe evenly. He had not seen the Rhine before, though in the dark he had passed it many times and its configuration was engraved in his memory. Beyond the river and its northward axis lay the greatest concentration of anti-aircraft guns this war had seen, guns pulled back from the lost territories in the east and the west and now forming a barrage in front of the Ruhr and the north German plain. And indeed, far ahead where the pathfinders were making their first approach, he could just discern a darkening of the sky as if a veil had been drawn across the path.

He kept his voice level. 'Navigator, I can see what must be the target at five degress on the starboard bow. This course will take us too far to the north.'

'Correct as necessary,' the navigator said.

The veil thickened to a deeper grey as the guns found the height and bearing of the approaching force. Armstrong steered for the centre of the curtain. After a while he could see the separate shellbursts, each a black dot that hung in the air until erased by the wind; he was flying into a wall of smoke that was still some distance off but which, like every aircraft in the stream, he must penetrate to gain the release point.

He said, 'Stand by for flak, intense and accurate. Gunners watch the tail. Bomb-aimer, take us in, if you please.'

Hayden Chance, ninety seconds in front of the Station Commander, was already inside the flak curtain. Beyond the smoke he could see where the pathfinders had laid red and green markers across the target. The first aircraft had already passed the aiming point and their bombs were in flight, but Chance was still short by two minutes. He heard the voice of the Master Bomber whose task it was to orbit the target at low level, enduring the rain of bombs and incendiaries from high above him, and to correct the aim of the incoming aircraft: 'Master Bomber to Main Force. Go for the greens. Don't undershoot. That's it. Keep them coming, chaps ... ' Chance opened the bomb-doors and steered for the centre of the green flares. From all over the sky the aircraft were converging upon the same aiming point, narrowing the stream to its greatest density. Black stains were opening on either side of the cockpit canopy. Once they sprang close to him and he heard the explosions, like the banging of an attic door, and the splinters striking the aircraft skin. A Lancaster on the port bow swung unnaturally from her course, turned belly up and collided with a second aircraft a little way below it; then both were wrapped in orange flame and making a long, slow, tumbling fall towards the ground.

Take is easy, Chance told himself. It wasn't you.

He kept control of his limbs and held the aircraft to the path. He listened for the bomb-aimer's instructions. Already he could see a lighter sky on the far side of the target ...

The bomb-aimer, lying in the nose with a clear view forward and down, had already pressed the selector switch which armed the bombs and had taken the release mechanism into his right hand. A glance at the bomb-sight showed him that the aircraft was drifting to the right of the green markers.

'Left, left,' he said, and felt the aircraft swing to the left as the captain applied heavy rudder.

'Steady,' he said.

He watched the bomb-sight — a narrow pane of glass upon which a graticule, shaped like a slender dagger, was illuminated: he saw the dagger creeping across the urban landscape towards the markers. The target was coming into his vision but obscured now by the grey smoke that was drifting away south. He saw the bombs bursting in straight lines across the marked area as though they were crossing it out with heavy strokes. With an airman's detachment he saw the sticks going wide, flung carelessly into the environs, enlarging the area from which the smoke was drawn. He could no longer tell where the railway yards lay because the smoke covered the town and the green flares had been extinguished. He heard the Master Bomber calling in the pathfinders to re-mark the target, but he could not wait: the dagger had reached the centre of the smoke.

He pressed the release button, felt the tremor in the aircraft frame as the bombs were released in sequence: he felt the great upward surge of the lightened machine and he knew the relief that came when the target was past.

'Bombs gone,' he said.

In the cockpit Hayden Chance closed the bomb-doors and started a slow turn to the north and to the sea.

Over the sea on the rearward leg the stream broke up as the aircraft steered independently for their airfields. There were bombers in every part of the sky. The Lancasters turned away westward to the Lincolnshire bases and they would be the first home. The squat, unlovely Halifaxes — the ragged crows of the Main Force — clung to their original north-westerly course towards a landfall at Flamborough Head.

The Station Commander allowed himself a few minutes of celebration. He engaged the automatic pilot, released his Sutton harness and stretched his arms. He was alive, and the sunlight played upon him like a blessing. He knew the aircraft to have been holed over the target but none of the systems seemed to have been affected. He knew the bombers had largely missed their aim. He had seen the two aircraft collide far ahead of him, and he had watched the fireball falling away from their altitude, but the position in the sky made it unlikely that the aircraft were from Moreton Valence. He closed his mind to the casualties and searched the horizon for the familiar landfall . . .

Hayden Chance still held his position ahead of the Station Commander and he had Flamborough Head firmly in view at about ten degrees to the right of his flight path. He was steering visually now and not by the direction indicator, and though it was forbidden he had slightly increased his air speed to bring himself early into the circuit at Moreton Valence with a place near the bottom of the stack: with aircraft of the Polish squadron also trying to land, the last man home would probably be in orbit for an hour. The fuselage was full of strange air currents and the taste of dust was in his mouth; these arose because the aircraft was holed fore and aft of the mid-upper turret; but none of the crew was hurt and the systems responded normally. He took off his helmet, giving himself a respite from the voices, letting the sun bathe his temples with its reassurance of life renewed. He savoured the minutes one by one as the aircraft flew itself home and the Yorkshire coast gained in detail . . .

Behind both Hayden Chance and the Station Commander, a long way off course to the northward, a Halifax captain urged his gunners to stay watchful. He knew that enemy fighters would fall upon an errant aircraft if they could. He was not certain of his position. He applied a compass bearing that should take him towards the Humber, but as he did not know the speed and direction of the wind he could not be certain how much to off-set for drift. His navigator could not help him. He lay in the rest position aft of the main spar where the bomb-aimer had carried him. He lay with his head resting on a parachute which made a pillow of sorts. It was not the enemy that had killed him; his skull had been crushed when an incendiary bomb, falling from an aircraft far above, flung in sour jest, had penetrated the nose forward of the wireless position and found the exact mark. The captain could not think of him now, though he knew him to have married only yesterday; his task was to bring the aircraft back with the remaining crew members no matter that the nose was damaged and he did not know the path.

SEVEN

The Air Officer Commanding did not care to dine alone. At Garfield Manor, where the Group had set up its wartime headquarters, he would avoid the company of his Senior Air Staff Officer if that could be done without offence, for Air Commodore Pratt had a lugubrious tongue that French found damaging to his appetite. He sought instead the company of younger men, officers with recent battle experience and with whom he could refresh his spirit. Those who wore no wings, those who managed the administration of the Group, were not sought out by the Air Vice-Marshal and in fact he could barely see them; though too courteous to say so, their lack of heroism seemed to him a moral disablement that placed them in a secondary order. The AOC was indeed fortunate that his life had contained two terrible wars and that he had been able to play a significant part in both of them. His table in the dining room was often resonant with epic. This evening, when he was about to rise from an excellent dinner, the duty officer came in to ask for his presence in the operations room.

He arrived in the underground chamber level with Air Commodore Pratt, who had also been summoned. His good humour lapsed at the sight of his second-in-command and he wondered why it had been necessary for them both to appear, but he greeted him affably enough. 'Evening, Stanley. Can't think what they've got for us at this hour.'

Pratt did not smile; that effort would have exhausted his small reserve of charity; instead he turned his long grey face to his superior to acknowledge that he had spoken but without committing himself to an opinion. French knew that Pratt, like their Commander-in-Chief far away in High Wycombe, believed in the systematic destruction of German cities as the technique most likely to shorten the war, and that he would set forth this doctrine with an abundance of supporting detail and a tedious rectitude. For himself, French had an imperfect grasp of strategy, and he found the present policy justified only in the sense that the Germans had started it and could not rightly complain if they were now the victims of their own invention. If they were consumed in their own fires, then justice was satisfied; he saw no need to give the policy the mask of strategic necessity. He did not like Pratt, nor the sound of his voice; he withheld his assent from saturation bombing not only because it did not fit his notion of combat but more especially because it had found an advocate in the Senior Air Staff Officer.

The duty operations officer, Wing Commander Dancy, met them under the display board which still showed the plan of the morning's raid. He was a young pilot resting between operational tours, of a type the AOC found entirely comprehensible.

'Well?' said French, feeling a slight discomfort in his digestive system.

'I don't know what to make of these, sir.' Dancy held a number of signals in his hand and his face bore the expression of an honest pilot who cannot believe that anything of worth has an origin on paper. 'They concern the losses from the Münster operation.'

'Remarkably small, if you ask me, with flak of that intensity,' French said. He looked at the tally of loss and damage shown on a separate panel. Seven aircraft were missing from the Group and twenty-two had suffered moderate to severe damage. One crew member had been brought home dead and two others were injured. Sixteen aircraft had landed away from base.

Pratt, who could never speak to an inferior without whetting the edge of his voice, said now, 'What is your point? You have brought us here at some inconvenience.'

'My point is this, sir. From the interrogation reports it is clear that four of the missing aircraft crashed in the target area and that two more ditched somewhere off the Dutch coast. The seventh aircraft cannot be accounted for.'

French suppressed his indignation with an effort. He could not understand why he had been summoned in haste from the dinner table to be appraised of the obvious. 'My dear chap, what of it? That you can account for six out of the seven aircraft is a piece of sheer good fortune.'

'Command have expressed an interest in the missing Halifax.'

'Very good. I appreciate their concern. But what do they think I can do about it?'

'They have asked us to determine where it went.'

'Well, tell them it went the way of all missing aircraft — into the ground, into the sea, into Valhalla. It's not possible to say where it went.'

Pratt said, 'I think we'd better know why Command are interested in the fate of this particular aircraft. Their request is unusual.'

'They have now seen an interrogation report originating in this Group,' Dancy said, 'in which a mid-upper gunner mentioned a Halifax flying at unusually high altitude. He was able to read part of the fuselage marking which tended to confirm that this aircraft and the one wholly missing were the same. An aircraft at high altitude was also mentioned by a number of other captains.'

'There's no problem as I see it,' French said. 'The captain had departed from the flight plan by exceeding the given altitude, and not surprisingly a fighter got him.'

'The combat was not seen by anybody in the Main Force.'

'Stranger things have happened, my lad.'

Pratt said, taking the opposite course from the AOC as a matter of habit, 'Is that true? It was broad daylight with maximum visibility, and there were five thousand alert men in the stream. Surely someone would have seen what happened?'

Dancy was not given to the solution of mysteries and could only add to the problem. 'I do not understand how a Halifax got to a height of twenty-five thousand feet.'

'Pure indiscipline,' the AOC said.

Pratt shook his head slowly, the simplest method of contradicting his commander without actual impertinence. 'The Halifaxes had an all-up weight of more than sixty thousand pounds at take-off. That would give them an absolute ceiling of twenty-two thousand feet. It is difficult to see how any aircraft could have gained the altitude stated.'

'Oh, freak conditions, an exceptional machine . . . ' The AOC saw no point in clouding the issue when there was enough of a problem already.

'They could not have increased the ceiling by three thousand feet. Unless —— '

'Unless, what, Stanley?'

' —— unless the aircraft was carrying a smaller load.'

'Not possible, old boy. All aircraft in the Group were carrying the same fuel and armament.'

Pratt spoke with the softness of tone that goes with an insubordinate spirit. 'There has to be an explanation, sir.'

'Naturally. I don't doubt it.' French had raised his voice as far as he could in front of an officer junior to Pratt. 'As we all know, to every phenomenon of flight there has to be an explanation. To which squadron did the missing aircraft belong?'

Dancy said, 'To the Polish squadron, sir.'

'Ah!'

He didn't like the sound of it. If the Polish squadron was playing tricks the politicians would be all over the Group in next to no time. He said evenly, 'We cannot be sure the aircraft was correctly identified. In operational conditions all manner of mistakes are made. I do not accept that the missing aircraft was necessarily from the Polish squadron.'

'Nevertheless we should know the name of the pilot,' Pratt said, making plain his contrary opinion.

'Can it matter? Their names are unpronounceable in any case. Dancy, you'd better get through to the Station Commander at Moreton Valence and see what help he can give you; then make a signal to Command. If as I suspect the answer's a lemon, you may say so. I see no reason for encouraging Foreign Office interest in a matter where we cannot certainly establish the facts. And now, my dear Stanley, I am returning to the mess . . . '

Group Captain Armstrong had not been to the mess that evening. He did not care to become part of the strenuous party that usually followed a bad raid with losses. He went once to his headquarters to receive a call from the operations officer at Group, but he could not answer the question put to him. He did not know what became of the missing aircraft. It had simply vanished like a hundred others — it had flown into the void — and the crew would be listed as missing until in time they were presumed to have died. He had nowhere to go but to his quarters where the empty rooms gave him no comfort. At nine o'clock he listened to the news and heard the Münster raid reported as a brilliant success for Bomber Command, but it had not been that: the flak had broken their nerve too soon and the bombs had flown in every direction but the right one. Better to have called it a shambles. In disgust, he turned off the wireless and sat looking through the open window at the boundary fence and the woodland beyond.

He sat there as the light failed. He had not strength enough to rise. He was conscious of weakness, but he could not bring his mind back from the place where it had fallen. He was breaking a convention which Clausewitz should surely have added to his Principles of War, but then the grim old Prussian could not have conceived that a commander would trouble his mind with a single casualty. In particular Armstrong's memory would not relinquish the picture of two men walking away from him, and of himself watching them, doing nothing, no matter that he had the power to intervene. He must count it a failure in command.

Finally he broke from his weakness. So what? A young officer was lost who might otherwise have been saved, but probably he would have gone soon anyway and then the book would have been squared. He was of a type that always died. Armstrong jumped up and went out into the dusk. He crossed the boundary fence and walked between the trees until he was a mile from the camp, feeling the better for the exercise.

Then he leant against a tree, his head upon his arm, his eyes probing the shadows.

'Stefan . . . '

He could not have said how long he stayed there, but when he raised his head the darkness had crept towards him and he did not know which way he had come. He listened for the sounds of the airfield that would give him his bearing, and sure enough he heard the starting of an aircraft engine at a long distance behind him. He followed the sound back to his quarters where the light was still burning and it was possible to believe he had never left the narrow empty rooms.

He slept then. The bed was hard and comfortless but Armstrong had known nothing else in twenty-eight years of service. At two o'clock he was wakened by a knock at the outer door and as he rose he realized the knocking had continued for some time.

He had not known how much the day's mishap had tired him. He put on his dressing-gown and opened the door.

'Who is it? What do you want?'

A young voice said, 'Orderly Officer. I tried the phone, sir, but you didn't answer.'

The light was flooding over the grass, infringing the blackout. 'You'd better come in,' Armstrong said.

In the hard light of the sitting room he saw the Orderly Officer to be Lampton-Bell, his own rear-gunner.

'I'm sorry, Simon; I didn't recognize you in the dark.'

Notwithstanding the wide difference in their ranks, Armstrong never quite forgot that his rear-gunner came from a family superior to his own. He had an amiable disregard for consequences that Armstrong had to admire.

'The AOC has been trying to reach you, sir. He will be grateful if you will phone him.'

'What, now? This minute?'

'That's what he said. He was wakened himself and was not in a good temper.'

'Very well, Simon. I'll use this telephone. You'd better stand by in case I need you.'

While he waited for the call to come through, Armstrong lost sight of the young rear-gunner as he wondered what further wretchedness was now to unfold. Then the phone rang, breaking into his tired mind.

The AOC was indeed out of sorts, and Armstrong held the phone an inch from his ear as the Air Vice-Marshal gave vent to his complaint. 'Listen, David. As far as I'm concerned there's no one left at Bomber Command with complete sanity. Once they get an idea into their heads they're not open to reason. I've told them what I feel. Of course, they're being got at by the politicians and they haven't the guts to send them packing.'

'Can you tell me what has happened, sir?'

'They're obsessed with that bloody Halifax.'

'But I've already told Wing Commander Dancy that I can't help in that respect. I've no idea what became of it. I believe I saw it at one moment — well, that is my recollection — but I may have been mistaken.'

The voice on the telephone still had the colouring of grievance. 'Oh, we know what happened to the aircraft, old boy.

Command have a report of a Halifax coming down in Scotland which is probably the same machine. Hence the excitement.'

Armstrong turned to the wall, so that Lampton-Bell should not see his face.

'David — are you there?'

'Yes, sir; I am here. Can you tell me if any of the crew has survived?'

'I can't, but it seems doubtful. The aircraft went into hard terrain and hasn't yet been found. That's why I want you to go there.'

'Me, sir? Is that necessary?'

'Normally I wouldn't waste your time as the recovery people are capable of dealing with it, but Command want a senior officer present — one conversant with the political implications.'

'I'm sorry, sir, but I haven't understood you. What are the political implications?'

'Well, they seem to think the aircraft may not have been carrying a normal load — that it may have been engaged in a private venture. My fellow Pratt supports this view and has identified the pilot as the young madman who made a low pass over Bardsey Island. You know — unreliable. I confess that it seems far-fetched to me, but with the C-in-C on my neck I can't take chances. You'd better go there, find the wreckage and see what you think.'

'I see,' Armstrong said. 'Very good, sir.'

'First light, if you please. The search is being mounted from Lossiemouth. Flying Training Command have told the Station Commander to expect you and that you are to lead the search. If you find anything interesting, you are to impose a security screen until you have reported to me. That's it, David. Good hunting.'

Armstrong replaced the phone and stood looking at the bare wall. He had attended more than once at the point of impact and he knew the sort of thing that he would find there.

Lampton-Bell still stood in the doorway. When a moment had passed, he asked, 'Is there anything more I can do, sir?'

'What? Yes, Simon. Bring the crew to the tower at six o'clock tomorrow morning with kit for three days. Tell the navigator to lay a course for Lossiemouth.'

The young rear-gunner waited, uncertain if he had received

his final instructions. Armstrong looked up and saw him again.

'That's all. Our destination is in confidence. You may go now.'

Lampton-Bell turned to leave, but before he had opened the door Armstrong said, 'How old are you, Simon?'

'Nineteen, sir.'

'How many operations have you flown?'

'Twenty-one. And two wash-outs that didn't count.'

'That's a fair number. I'll have you taken off, if you wish.'

The boy stared at him. 'But I haven't completed my tour, sir!'

'You haven't?' Armstrong was suddenly very tired. 'No, I suppose you haven't. I was forgetting the rules. Forgive me.'

He bade Lampton-Bell good night, and when he had gone he sat looking at the back of the door until, after a while, he remembered that the night was passing and that tomorrow he had a duty to perform. He lay down and tried to sleep.

South of Kylorne the ground rose steeply and the burn they had followed for the last hour became narrow and fast. Whether this thread of peat-stained water finally joined the Spey or the Deveron Armstrong could not have said, but now it led them by a natural stair to six hundred feet. On either side of the burn the Kylorne Forest, planted more than forty years ago and now of commanding height, stretched for a score of miles along the northern face of the hills, a forest of spruce and fir of such density there was sparse light under the branches and Armstrong could see nothing beyond fifty yards.

He kept himself to the climb, his mind's eye showing him nothing but the shape of the country as the map had disclosed it; this was a problem of systematic elimination which should bring them to the correct position in the end. The radio direction-finding stations had plotted the aircraft as it crossed the coast transmitting a distress signal, and three good bearings had been taken at the moment when the transmission ceased: transferred to the chart, these bearings had intersected cleanly at a point about a mile beyond the limit of the timber, but Armstrong knew that bearings taken upon an aircraft at low level and in mountainous terrain could be inexact and that the impact point could be wide by several miles. A light aircraft had searched the area that morning but made no sighting. Armstrong had therefore divided his men — five in the recovery party and six from his aircrew — into three groups and sent them into the area on different paths. He himself would search the point of intersection. If the Halifax was in open ground above the timber line the task should not be too difficult; if it was in the trees they might never find it.

He was accompanied by Warrant Officer Barnes, second-in-charge of the recovery party, an old-stamp NCO with little to say; by Lampton-Bell and two other from his aircrew. Mostly they walked in silence. After an hour the burn vanished into a bog and they continued up a fire-break towards the upper edge of the forest. Once Armstrong called Lampton-Bell to his side.

'Simon, our duty takes us to strange places. I imagine you have not been at a point of impact before.'

'No, sir.'

'It is — well, a place one would wish to avoid. You may see things you would not wish to see. At such times I find it helpful to remind myself that I belong to a disciplined service.'

The boy nodded, but none the less he went eagerly up the path ahead of the party. His imagination had not shown him the likely scene. Armstrong bent to the incline, keeping to a pace that would not exhaust the party too soon. It was summer, and at this high latitude there would be many hours of daylight in which to search the hillsides. He kept his mind upon practical things. If they found the aircraft, then it was possible that fire would have destroyed all evidence of where it had been and for what purpose it had been used, and he would never know what had brought it back so far north.

Where the forest ended the rocks began and the air chilled. Armstrong continued up the ridge for half an hour until he gained a height from which he could observe a wide segment of the hillside. He took binoculars and searched the ground above and below him. He did not expect to find the aircraft here; had it come down in open ground the light aircraft would surely have seen it; but he completed a careful search of the terrain before replacing the binoculars in the case.

'Mr Barnes, I can draw only one conclusion,' he said. 'The aircraft is in the forest, which means that it will be fragmented and probably difficult to see. I cannot think that we will find it from the ground. We will return to Lossiemouth and resume the air search.'

He could not believe the other parties would have fared better than themselves. He felt a sense of reprieve that lightened his spirit. They would not find the Halifax today, and it was possible they would never find it. He started down the incline towards the trees that were wrapped like a blanket round the bowl of the hill, making for a division in the forest which must be the firebreak, but when he entered the trees he stopped, uncertain if this was the path they had used before. It looked the same, it descended at the same gradient and there was the same depth of shadow under the trees. The map told him that whichever path they took would join the burn and bring them ultimately to the Kylorne road; so Armstrong continued down through the trees at a steady pace. From Kylorne he would telephone to Lossiemouth and ask them to resume the air search, this time concentrating on the forest, particularly where the ground rose steeply over the ridges.

No, this was not the same track. The trees were taller and the light was excluded even from the path. They walked silently, as if in obedience to a law of the forest, Armstrong listening for the sound of the burn that would tell him they were on the right heading. As yet he could hear nothing but the sound of their footsteps. This might have been another forest altogether with heavier shadow and colder airs. A part of his mind followed an independent course, but uneasily. He stopped on the path, guided by an instinct he did not question but which drew its strength from twenty-eight years of fellowship with the behaviour of aircraft.

This was the place. Within fifty yards of where they stood the Halifax and all its crew were lying.

He tried to drive the impression from his mind, but it stayed, like a dream's fearful image retained upon waking. He looked left and right into the trees, seeing nothing but for the accumulations of shadow. Warrant Officer Barnes halted beside him; and he didn't ridicule an airman's fancy.

'It is here, Mr Barnes. We will radiate from the path. Use your whistle if you find it.'

He went leftward himself and could not have said why. He was frightened but he did not falter in his step. He had stood by in silence while Stefan was led away, and he saw it as fitting that he should now attend at the place where his flight had ended. He followed a line of fir trees until he was beyond sight of the other searchers. Three paces further and, at his feet, he saw the top-most crown of a tree — nothing more than a spray of leaf no bigger than his hand. The next tree was severed perhaps five feet from the top; the one after that was cut still lower; and thereafter for as far as he could see, like a row of organ pipes, the broken trees descended in height until the last was little more than a stump.

He blew his whistle.

Of the wings and the greater part of the tail they could see nothing and Armstrong knew they would be yards back where the trees had ripped them from the aircraft body. The fuselage had continued forward, opening the ground like a ploughshare, and it had come to rest only where the nose had struck buried rock. It looked like a shabby garment flung down carelessly. There had been no fire, no doubt because the aircraft was low on fuel and the main tanks had been shed with the wings before the final impact. Armstrong judged the aircraft to have been flying east to west and to have come down in a shallow glide. He did not look for the crew. Not at first.

He said, 'Simon, I want you to go down to Kylorne. Make your best pace. Tell Lossiemouth to send the recovery vehicles and a minimum of fourteen men with seven stretchers. At once, if you please!'

Along the path scored by the aircraft the contents of bomb-bay were spread. It was a strange cargo. The first hamper had sprung open, but three others had retained their bindings of sacking and straw and were more or less complete. Probably there were others covered by the loose earth or trapped under the fuselage. They would have lain on the bomb-doors and spilled out only when the bottom of the eircraft was torn off. Armstrong cleared the debris from the first hamper and pressed the lid fully open, calling Warrant Officer Barnes to witness what it contained. In his professional mind he was already assembling evidence for the court of enquiry.

'See, Mr Barnes, the length to which desperate men will go! They had not a chance of getting these goods to their destination.'

Packed neatly within the hamper and cushioned against shock were an assortment of bandages, simple medicines and preserved food which probably they had acquired from the shops of York. He did not examine the hamper to the bottom but closed the lid with a contemptuous gesture.

'What does it mean?' the Warrant Officer asked, whose experience in the ruins of aircraft contained nothing like this.

'A pathetic escapade. Nothing more. I must ask you to keep these things to yourself.'

Then Armstrong, using his whistle, summoned the two members of his crew who were searching for the wings a hundred yards back.

'Mr Barnes and I will now enter the fuselage,' he said curtly. 'I do not wish you to follow. You are to continue looking for the detached parts of the aircraft which may be at a considerable distance. If you find the rear turret you are not to open it. Carry on!'

He beckoned Warrant Officer Barnes and together they approached the foundered aircraft.

'Amateurs,' he said, containing his dread. 'Nice boys, but not up to this. Here we have a job for regular personnel.'

Garfield Manor was not looking its best. The present tenants had respected the panelling in the old hall, and most of the pictures still hung in their ancestral places, but the armed services had a gift for turning even the most elegant premises into a featureless waste and the manor had now the anonymity of any military headquarters. The Air Officer Commanding occupied the library, but he had not disturbed any of the volumes. This morning he was accompanied by Air Commodore Pratt and a shapeless gentleman who had collapsed into a chair as if his bone structure had insufficient strength to keep him upright — a Mr Shane-Gould of the Eastern European desk at the Foreign Office. To Armstrong, the body of any civilian had always too many joints in it. He saw a man with a loose lower lip, defective vision and a brow swollen with abstruse scholarship. Armstrong did not adapt his manner to fit this unusual company: in giving an account of his discovery at Kylorne he kept to simple fact and excluded his own conjecture. Mr Shane-Gould listened with his eyes closed and acknowledged each point with a tiny spasm of the lower torso.

When he had completed his account, Shane-Gould did not stir and Armstrong wondered if he was sleeping. The AOC glared at the visitor with barely concealed impatience.

'I do not think the Station Commander can tell us any more,' he said. 'The interpretation of these events is scarcely a military matter.'

Shane-Gould had opened his eyes and turned them towards Armstrong, but it was the sightless gaze of a man who lacks all interest in his surroundings. 'Nevertheless, Air Marshal, it will be helpful if the Group Captain discloses his opinion.'

92

'Really?' In his discomfort French had worked a paperclip to the point of fracture. 'Politics are not our business, and I do not see how uninformed speculation can be of assistance.'

As if he hadn't spoken, Shane-Gould said, 'Well, Group Captain?'

'I would not wish to embarrass my AOC by giving an opinion he does not share.'

'Of course! You have a duty not to do so. However, the opinion of the local commander is naturally of value and I am sure the Air Marshal will overlook the irregularity.' He spoke fluently but without commitment, as if engaging only a small part of his mind. Evidently he was bored by the military ethic.

With the air of a generous man drawing on his last reserves, French said, 'You may speak up, David.'

Pratt had sucked in his mouth almost to vanishing point, so deep was his absorption. Armstrong guessed him to be the architect of this meeting, which obviously the AOC had not welcomed, but so far he had not advanced his point of view.

Choosing his words with caution, Armstrong said, 'I understand that the Russian army has been unable to break through to the Polish capital and that the partisans are at the point of defeat. I believe that Count Pakorksi attempted a relief of Warsaw. It was a futile gesture, certain to fail, but I can think of no other explanation.'

Shane-Gould nodded, showing no surprise. 'Could the aircraft have gone there and back?'

'No, sir. The city is far beyond the radius of action of the Halifax. They could have flown there on a one-way passage if, as I suppose, they carried little weight and maximum fuel. We found the remnants of an overload tank in the forward part of the bomb-bay which suggests that a long flight was planned.'

'A strange adventure,' the AOC said, 'if that indeed was their purpose.'

'It must have been,' said Pratt, with the humility of tone of one who had read the evidence correctly in the first place. 'Nothing else would explain the dummy run over Bardsey Island which was obviously a rehearsal. Of course, the bandages and sticking plaster weighed next to nothing and that would account for the height they were able to attain.'

'I suppose so,' said French, but with little grace. He had been outmanoeuvred by his deputy and was entitled to his displeasure.

Armstrong said quietly, 'I understand their motive, but they destroyed an aircraft in what was obviously a hopeless undertaking.'

Shane-Gould was not interested in the by-play of the two air officers; he kept his impaired vision upon Armstrong. 'Let us assume that you are right, Group Captain. Pakorski intended to relieve the insurgents in Warsaw even though it could be no more than a token gesture. However, the aircraft did not reach its destination and instead came down in Scotland hours after it left the bomber force. It still carried the supplies destined for the partisans. Where had it been? What went wrong?'

'I cannot be certain where the aircraft had been,' Armstrong said, his mind entering the place where the hurt was greatest. 'We found parts of the navigator's chart but the plot was complete only as far as Münster. There was a six-hour interval between the time when it must have left the stream and the transmission of the distress signal from a position near Moray Firth. I believe they accompanied the stream as far as the target, which allowed them to penetrate the continental defences without additional risk, and then flew an easterly course towards Warsaw, which was six hundred miles away across defended territory. It was preposterous, of course ——'

'Quite, quite. But they might have got there.'

'I think it most unlikely. A single aircraft, flying slowly in daylight, would have drawn the attention of every fighter in the area.'

'Then put it this way. Was there the slightest chance they could have reached Warsaw?'

'There was just a chance.'

'And having got there, could they have made an effective drop?'

'I doubt it. The Halifax is not designed for this work. The hampers were resting on the inside of the bomb-doors and would have dropped when the doors were opened, which is a method we have used for scattering leaflets. They would probably have flown in low, extended the flaps and undercarriage to reduce the ground speed, and then opened the doors when they believed themselves in the right area. They had tried this manoeuvre over

94

the Welsh coast. Almost certainly the hampers would have gone wide or been destroyed on impact.'

Shane-Gould's lower jaw was in constant small movement as though he were consuming the evidence with a certain distaste; he didn't seem surprised that an aircraft should embark on a fool's errand across Europe. He said swiftly, 'I am sure you are right in these assumptions, Group Captain. In your opinion, what caused the crew to turn back?'

'Who can say?' French broke in. 'The Station Commander can only speculate.'

'Nevertheless I find his guesswork illuminating.'

'I think the answer lies in the character of Count Pakorski,' Armstrong said. He spoke shyly, because the memory of Pakorski had filled his mind in the last hours. 'He was a brave man, but I don't think he shared the fatalism of Prince Karol or was convinced of the need for the operation. He was prepared to work with us. Once — well, he seemed on the point of speaking to me intimately, and had he done so I believe I could have prevented him from throwing his life away. I can visualize what happened. If it was to succeed, the operation required total commitment, but if the captain was infirm of purpose he would have been diverted from his course very quickly. I do not know what first turned him to the north. Perhaps it was the defences at Hanover. When we found it, the aircraft had been hit many times by cannon and machine-gun fire and a large part of its own ammunition had been used. Pakorski himself had been wounded more than once. At any rate, he was forced more and more from his line of flight until he was at a position far to the north from which he could no longer reach Warsaw but had a slender chance of reaching Scotland. So he came back, defying his instructions not to return; but he couldn't keep the damaged aircraft in the air even though there was just enough fuel in the tanks to take him into Lossiemouth or Milltown.'

Armstrong paused, and Shane-Gould raised his eyebrows in enquiry. 'There was something more?' he asked.

'I believe that Count Pakorski wanted to live.'

'That is a common emotion, surely?'

'Where the Poles are concerned, I am uncertain.'

'Can you say why Prince Karolajczyk employed an irresolute officer for this task?'

'Not with any confidence; but I think he found it necessary to demonstrate his mastery of the squadron. Pakorski was known to dissent from the Polish line. The Prince challenged him to prove his point at sword-play, and it must have been understood between them that, if he lost, he would accept the Prince's authority and make the flight. I am sure Pakorski regarded this as binding upon his conscience.'

Air Vice-Marshal French was reluctant to accept any evidence for which there was no proof. While Armstrong was speaking, he had tossed his head from side to side as he weighed each point and found it wanting. He said now, 'I can see no alternative but to convene a court of enquiry at which the ascertainable facts can be set down. I cannot believe it will be a satisfactory process but we must try to separate fact from fancy. To impugn the character of a fine commander like Prince Karol when we have nothing to go on but a headful of supposition and innuendo seems improper to me.'

Air Commodore Pratt had remained as still as judgement while the AOC was speaking. Then he said, 'I would have thought we had enough evidence at our disposal to call him to account. The flight broke every rule in the book ——'

'He is an outstanding officer,' said French shortly. 'While I deplore disobedience, I cannot help admiring the unbreakable spirit of the Poles. The concept required courage of the highest order.'

Pratt gave a smile like vanishing sunlight, and by so doing revealed his inner motive: it was his task to modify the bombast, to protect the purity of their aim. The Group was in being to destroy systematically the industrial cities of Germany and not to sponsor a forlorn sacrifice.

'At any rate, it was an enterprise of some interest,' Shane-Gould said, with a lack of ardour that implied the opposite. He responded to different pressures. He took off his spectacles and wiped them as if this would improve the clarity of his thought. 'Gentlemen, I am obliged to put one factor before you which may seem irrelevant in the military context but which is necessary to the picture as a whole. An attempt to relieve the Warsaw insurgents, should it become known, would seriously encumber His Majesty's Government in its dealing with the Soviet Union. Regrettable, but true. For three weeks we and the US government have been trying to persuade the Soviet Union to go to the assistance of General Komorowski and his irregular forces. The Russians have sixty airfields in easy range of Warsaw and more than two thousand machines, and Marshal Rokossovsky is on the Vistula with a large army. But, no matter that they called for the uprising, the Soviets have done nothing to sustain it.'

French said, 'Can this be true? I do not understand their motives.'

'Their motives are simple, Air Marshal. They are allowing the Germans to destroy the Polish élite, and already there have been a great many casualties. They never intended the rising to succeed because they wish to set up a government of their own complexion. Rokossovsky has been halted deliberately and they have declined to mount airborne relief. When we requested landing rights for Allied aircraft operating from Italy, these were denied and the insurgents dismissed as criminal adventurers. It is easy to see why Prince Karol found it necessary to intervene.'

'Do you mean the Russians intend to do nothing?' the AOC asked, his mind opening slowly to this contingency.

'They will aid the insurgents only when they have been effectively destroyed. In about a fortnight they will probably allow flights by Allied aircraft and make some gestures of their own, but by then the partisans will be dead or dispersed. The Russian army will postpone the capture of Warsaw until the Germans have razed it. Our Foreign Secretary will then deny that any delay has taken place and praise Marshal Stalin for his initiative. You understand — this will be necessary to preserve the alliance.'

The AOC did not look as if he perfectly understood; he inflated his cheeks in amazement and allowed the air to escape in a slow draught.

'It follows that a flight to Warsaw at a time of sensitive negotiations could give rise to Soviet complaint,' Shane-Gould continued, 'particularly as the aircraft could only have landed in Soviet-held territory. For this reason I must request that knowledge of the affair be strictly limited. There can be no court of enquiry. All evidence of the misadventure should be destroyed. The bodies should be buried in Scotland without ceremony of any kind ... Yes, Group Captain?'

Armstrong hesitated. 'I had hoped to bring the crew to Moreton Valence for military honours,' he said. 'In my opinion there should be some recognition of their sacrifice.'

'I cannot give Foreign Office support to that intention.'

'Then I would wish to be present when the bodies are interred in Scotland.'

'I would prefer not.'

Air Commodore Pratt, the guardian of Group integrity, still maintained his glacial calm. 'I do not see how we can ignore the disobedience of Prince Karol, who is undoubtedly guilty of an offence in service law. We must surely require some reckoning ___,'

Shane-Gould laced his fingers together as if he were placing a final lock on the military animus. 'I appreciate that these things are within service jurisdiction, but I must advise against any measure that admits to the enterprise. I would like your permission, Air Marshal, for the Prince to be dealt with by a member of my department. I will be grateful if otherwise you will take steps to eliminate every trace of the operation which, as far as we are concerned, simply did not happen. The aircraft should be listed as missing and the bodies should be — well, lost.' He looked from one officer to another with those dim-sighted eyes which kept him in isolation from their community. He knew they must comply.

The AOC stood up. A fine figure, Armstrong thought, with his white hair and mark of heroism.

'I will do as you ask, Mr Shane-Gould,' he said. 'The operation will be expunged from the record and the bodies buried in an unmarked grave. I can do no less. I can do no less, no matter that the Russians have been guilty of a hideous confidence trick with human lives as the forfeit. But — if it matters to your department, which by your own testimony seems doubtful — I believe that an act of courage can never be effaced and that one day Count Pakorski and his fellow airmen will come back into our view.'

He summoned an aide and, with a minimum of ceremony, Mr Shane-Gould was shown out.

NINE

That autumn the raids increased in their depth and in their danger and the squadrons recalled the summer as a time of easy winnings: then they had raided along the French coast and into the Low Countries in bright weather and it had been possible to complete a tour of operations in four months. Not so now. The armies had taken the Channel coast and the heavy bombers had resumed their former route across the Rhine and into the heartland of Germany, and the crews would be at this business all winter. The great daylight raids continued as Bomber Command struck at the oil plants. Gelsenkirchen repeated the disaster at Münster. But when at the end of October the weather worsened and the nights grew longer the Halifaxes returned to their proper role of raiding by night. Cologne, Düsseldorf, Dortmund ... the menial task for which the old work horse was best suited. In these operations the Polish squadron joined with exemplary obedience and a high degree of accuracy, and Armstrong had to admit the quality of their airmanship. On instructions from his AOC, Armstrong had erased all account of his findings in the Kylorne Forest and obliged those who were with him to forget what they had seen. Now the Poles fought with an angry commitment that made them formidable. They had not deviated from the business in hand even when Komorowski and his patriots had been forced to capitulate and the Germans had torn down Warsaw stone by stone, the Russian army watching from across the Vistula. Amid the ruins lay the countless dead. The weather thickened as the winter advanced and at Christmas the snow lay across the airfield and a heavy fog obliterated the huts and hangars at Moreton Valence. The last winter of the war was as cold as malice.

On Christmas day, the Station Commander was invited to

dine in the Polish mess. He sat between Prince Karol and Count Zulka, and they treated him with courteous attention and kept his glass filled. The dinner was conducted with greater formality than was usual in an RAF mess; the voices were restrained, the laughter subdued. They did not throw paper darts or play tug of war with the napkins. Still, it was Christmas and the Prince had softened his manner and allowed himself to smile.

'For you, the war will soon be over,' he said, after the toasts had been given. 'In the summer it ends for Britain and you fly no more. You are happy then.'

'Will it not end for Poland as well?' Armstrong asked.

'My friend, the war in Poland has continued many centuries and it does not stop now. My country is won and lost on the gaming tables of Europe more times than any other. The Kingdom, the Congress, the Republic — each has passed away at a fall of the dice, and the next throw will bring us a new master.'

Armstrong could find no answer to this melancholy; and indeed, when he looked round the walls where the swords and trophies of an old aristocracy were displayed, it was difficult to see what future these officers could expect. A banner hung with pride on the end wall showed a white lily on a black field, a motif that was repeated on the squadron aircraft; he did not know the exact meaning but certainly it bound the Prince and his followers to an old, lost order.

Armstrong said, 'Then you will make your home in England, where you have earned a welcome.'

'You are kind, Group Captain, but the nature of our oath makes it difficult for us to perceive an end to the war.'

'Your obligation will surely be at an end when the enemy is beaten.'

The Prince smiled, it might have been at the notion that the struggle could ever cease. 'The armistice will not set us free.'

Zulka nodded. A sombre man, he had taken no part in the conversation that evening. 'We are ghosts,' he said. 'We are ghosts with no resting place!'

At the foot of the table where the light faded, an officer lifted his head and looked towards Zulka as if he had caught the words. A strange head, which Armstrong was certain he had not seen before — a cranium devoid of hair, a face without expression but marked by a long scar which ran from ear to lip and told of some unspecified violence. Not recent, Armstrong guessed; the wound had silvered and become part of the face and it was difficult to imagine how this man had looked before he was disfigured. He wore army uniform and his place on the lower table suggested that he was of junior rank.

'There is an officer at table I have not met,' Armstrong said. He was surprised, because officers were required to call upon him when they arrived.

The Prince followed the direction of his gaze. 'Captain Wolkow,' he said, but he offered nothing more.

'And who is he?'

'A visitor, a friend.'

This officer wore his scar where all could see it; the others, wounded no less, kept theirs hidden.

'From where does he come?' Armstrong pursued.

The Prince opened his hands to imply that he came out of the mist like the rest of them. 'He brings us news,' was all he said.

When they rose from the table and adjourned to the anteroom, Armstrong kept his eyes on the strange soldier; a spare man, short even amongst the Poles, the cast of his face fixed for ever by the passage of a blade or bullet. Armstrong was disturbed by the presence on his station of an officer he did not know.

Later, when it was possible for him to leave the group of senior officers, he said to Zulka, 'I will now meet Captain Wolkow, if you will be so kind.'

Zulka didn't comply at once. 'He speaks no English,' he said after a while. 'He has reached this country — only lately.'

'Then you will be good enough to interpret for me.'

No officer could decline a service so plainly required by his Station Commander and Zulka brought the stranger forward. 'Sir, I present Wladyslaw Wolkow, captain of the Polish army.'

Wolkow made a short bow. No, there was nothing to be learned from this face which seemed to have been paralysed at the moment of wounding. The eyes were empty, the mouth drawn closed by what might have been a habit of reticence; a face from which the past had been wiped away. Armstrong could not tell if he was young or old. Now that he could see it more clearly, he was certain the scar marked the path of a bullet which had flown from somewhere behind the ear to a point above the upper lip, leaving a deep, white furrow.

'The Captain conveys his duty,' Zulka said. 'He regrets that he is unable to speak your language.'

'None the less he is welcome at Moreton Valence. What is his unit?'

'He has no unit. He arrived only recently.'

'By which route did he reach here?'

The question was put to Wolkow who gave a short reply.

'From the Middle East. Before that he is a long time displaced.'

Armstrong did not follow this line of enquiry which led back into the Polish agony, but nevertheless he was entitled to know what Wolkow was doing at Moreton Valence. 'I am happy the Captain has found his way to liberty. Can he tell me the purpose of his visit to this station?'

He found Prince Karol at his side, perhaps disturbed by these questions. 'He comes to see me because we are old friends. He is passing this way.'

The untruth of this statement must have been apparent to everyone present: no one 'passed by' Moreton Valence which was on no direct route and deep in empty country. To correct his error, the Prince said, 'You must understand, we have little knowledge of many of our comrades and Wolkow comes to tell us what he knows.'

At once Armstrong was ashamed for having pressed his point so hard, for underlying every enquiry was the suffering of people dispossessed.

'Wolkow comes to us with news — news we have not heard,' the Prince repeated, raising his head in stoic pride. 'He comes from far away and he tells us where our comrades are.'

Concealed in the fog twenty yards from the Polish mess was a single figure who did not move. A squat man with a rounded back and splayed feet. His cap was at an improper angle and the buttons on his greatcoat were fastened in the wrong sequence. He could hear voices from the ante-room and he could see where the light spilled at the edges of the blackout curtains. From across the airfield the sound of raucous music reached him from the airmen's mess, but the fog had smothered it almost to vanishing point and he no longer listened. He had forgotten it was

Christmas; his mind recalled only an injury done to him which the passage of time had magnified into an open wound and a need for recompense. Even in the bitter cold the prospect of a reckoning kept his blood in movement.

After a time spent in contemplation of the building where he had been misused, Aircraftman Haines approached the nearest window and put his eye to a wedge of light where the curtain hung aslant; he saw the officers in conversation, the Station Commander speaking to a hairless man in a uniform different from the rest. And, yes, the tall bum boy who had told malicious lies was present in the room. Haines pressed his nails into the palms of his hands, as yet unaware of what indemnity he required from these bearers of false witness; he felt a formless anger that could only be appeased by action of some sort. He moved along the face of the building wondering where to effect damage and of what kind. He moved in a glow of anticipation because the possibilities were so wide; he was a giant whom anger had freed from restraint and who might now use his strength in sweet retaliation. He came to another window where he could see a small segment of the room beyond, and here mess servants in white coats were clearing coffee cups srom the table and sweeping the floor. A kitchen-hand himself, he recognized the dining hall from which the officers had lately withdrawn leaving their debris for the attention of others. A room with strange trophies: swords, relics of the chase, photographs of unknown leaders. High on the wall beyond the foot of the table, in a place of manifest honour, he saw a black banner with a white device placed centrally — a device he could not recognize but which he assumed to be of high solemnity to the Poles.

The banner did not at once become the object of his disfavour. Aircraftman Haines was not a quick thinker. It was only when he had watched the room for some minutes and seen the stewards complete their task that his attention was drawn wholly to this emblem. Now he knew that nothing else would quite do as an object for his indignation. Take it, burn it? It did not matter so long as it was despoiled. He felt a keen pleasure at having devised the perfect retort. He skirted the building, his instinct leading him to the kitchen parts where he found the entrance to the dustbin locker. More than once he had used this small space as a hiding place; the sour smell of refuse had underlain his days.

He knew the kitchen staff would leave the mess as soon as their work was done, leaving only the barmen waiting on the mess members, and sure enough the clatter from the tin-room ceased ten minutes later and he heard the staff leaving by the back door. There would be no one in the kitchen now and in the dining room the lights would be out.

He crept from the locker and stood for a time outside the back door, shielded by the fog, his mind alight with a sense of denouement. He entered the kitchen, from where he could hear a throb of voices in the ante-room; he passed soundlessly through the pantry and found the service door into the dining hall. Here the voices were louder and there was a brush-stroke of light under the ante-room door where shadows passed forward and back. In the darkness he followed the wall towards the place where the banner was displayed, and when he was beneath it he reached up with his fingers until he held the lower fringe in his grasp. He took a deep breath, summoning his strength for an act of settlement the Poles would clearly understand.

Armstrong kept his voice at a steady trot. With this strange people it was necessary to stick to the trivial if you did not wish to be drawn into the dark glades of the past. He paid no heed to a sound like the breaking of a thousand wine glasses in a neighbouring room; in a mess not his own it would be impolite to draw attention to a domestic mischance. He stuck to his theme, while from the corner of his eye he saw the Prince send Nikolski to enquire the nature of the disaster. The door into the ante-room was opened and behind it the light sprang on. Armstrong turned his back upon the sight of Nikolski standing in the doorway in frozen silhouette as he did not wish to concede that anything was amiss.

Count Zulka, to whom Armstrong was speaking, could not be described as a good man at a party. He said little, and such words as he offered revealed a mind of immovable gravity. He was looking across Armstrong's shoulder in the direction of the dining room and there was nothing in his eyes or the set of his mouth to suggest what he was thinking. Armstrong knew that the voices in the room had stopped and that he alone kept to the conversational path. A moment later Prince Karol laid a hand upon his arm.

'Forgive me, sir — an accident, a misfortune. Nikolski will conduct you into the bar where you will be equally comfortable. Here there is a matter for us to attend to. Zulka, you will come with me.'

As a guest he could make no comment, ask no questions, and he went with Nikolski into the bar where they were soon joined by other Poles. He could not think what kept his hosts from the party, but Nikolski knew — of this he was certain. His flippancy was reduced in scale and his silences had lengthened.

Perhaps it was fifteen minutes before the Prince came into the bar with Count Zulka. He had retained his courtesy, but his eyes were harassed and sad, and for once his movements were lacking in decisiveness. The mask of severity Zulka always wore had if anything increased in emphasis. The Prince said, 'Come, sir, I will fill your glass! We do not forget that it is Christmas and that we are comrades.'

Armstrong said tentatively, 'I have enjoyed the hospitality of your mess, Prince Karol. If you are preoccupied ——'

'Oh, it is nothing! An evil spirit, a hobgoblin who crosses our path. We have dealt with him.' But the matter still troubled his mind and he raised his shoulders in something like despair. 'We had no asset but our pride, sir. Our army is defeated. Our capital is lost, torn brick from brick and ground into the dust. Our fellowship of officers is scattered and tonight we learn from Wolkow how many of them fare. But we had our pride — our emblem!'

'I do not understand you. What has happened to your emblem?'

'A sacrilegious hand was laid upon it.'

'Whose hand?'

'No one. A troll.'

'Let me say this, Prince Karol. If an insult has been offered to the Polish officers I will punish the offender very severely.'

'There is no need — no need.'

'I would have said there was every need.'

'A punishment has been imposed, and it was fitting.'

It was not possible for Armstrong to say more, though he did not like the sound of an informal penalty; the evidence should have been examined and a charge preferred. But it was Christmas night and the Poles had entertained him at dinner.

He took his leave soon afterwards and went out into the thick night. A strange evening: he did not know what to make of it. The image of Captain Wolkow and his terrible wound stayed in his mind to perplex and frighten him. It was bitterly cold and nothing penetrated the fog which lay at a depth of fifty feet over the airfield. He walked towards his car, stopping once to taste the air and listen to the silence. When these winter days were over the conflict would end and the squadrons would disband. What would the Poles do then? Where would they go? He did not know: they carried a sum of dudgeon the peace would not dispel. He got into his car and drove carefully through the fog towards the main camp.

'Keeble,' he said, 'you can do me a service. No, nothing outside your experience, so you needn't look so alarmed. I can think of no one better qualified for this work, which falls — by only a small extension of your terms of reference — under the heading of intelligence. I shall require your absolute discretion.'

The Intelligence Officer nodded. It was morning, but still the fog lay tight against the window panes and in the Station Commander's office the lights were burning.

'You will have noticed the emblem that decorates the Polish aircraft. No, not the red and white checks carried on the rear fuselage; those are their national colours and an agreed marking. I mean the little white lily set upon a black background that is borne under the cockpit canopy. Last night, when I was dining with the officers, I noticed the same emblem in a place of honour on the mess wall and I am interested to know what the symbol means.'

Keeble looked at Armstrong with forbearance; so might he have rebuked a junior who sought elucidation of the obvious. 'Can you not ask them, sir?'

'I would prefer not to.'

'The white lily has of course been used as an armorial device by many houses in Europe.'

'I don't doubt it; but I would like to know why it is of significance to a Polish squadron in Bomber Command. As far as I am aware it is not an approved crest and does not relate to the Polish government in exile. I am sure you will be able to trace the origin.'

Keeble went out through the Adjutant's office, but a moment later he came back to offer the salute he had omitted.

'Thank you, Keeble,' Armstrong said. 'I am touched by your attention to custom.'

The light grew hardly at all as the day advanced. No chance of getting squadrons up in this foul weather; even the MT had stopped. In the Ardennes Von Rundstedt had broken the Allied line and was driving towards Dinant and Liège, but in England the Main Force had been grounded for a week. Armstrong worked in his office and by midday he had disposed of the accumulated business. He rang for the Adjutant.

'You may take those files away, Jarvis. If you have nothing else for me, I will go over to the Met Section. Sometime there must be a break in the weather.'

Jarvis turned to his tray where a clerk had just dropped a buff-coloured form. 'I have only this, sir. It does not require your immediate attention.'

'What is it?'

'An absentee report.'

'I'd better see it.'

He took the form under the light and read the single page. It was nothing; just a fragment of paper in the great volume of business that passed through his office. A kitchen-hand had not reported for the first working parade and was presumed absent without leave. Very well; it had happened a hundred times before. He was about to return the paper when the airman's name caught his eye.

'Haines — I might have known it! As this airman has a history of absence, you'd better inform the service police.'

'His kit is still in barracks, sir.'

'Even so, we can't be certain he intends to return.'

Jarvis shrugged, and flung the paper on to a pile of others awaiting attention. He contrived a mirthless smile. 'It will save us a great deal of trouble if Haines has deserted,' he said.

'Maybe so. But I cannot overlook an absentee, even where I might wish to. Haines, was there ever an airman worse than you!' Now that the habitual offender had taken himself off, Armstrong knew that he would miss him if he failed to return; there would be no standard of frightfulness against which to measure other defaulters and the station would have lost a vital dimension. 'Please tell the police I would like Haines apprehended and returned. He cannot have gone far in weather like this.'

Outside the fog rubbed his cheek and the cold clutched at his lungs as he walked towards the tower. The snow was a week old and beaten hard and grey. At the Met Section in the base of the tower he studied the charts and saw how the fog lay over the whole of northern Europe and would not break for twenty-four hours. He returned into the fog and started back towards headquarters, but in a minute he had lost his direction. He stopped, listened. Nothing moved on the station but for some uncertain footsteps on his right. There were no lights to guide him; he was contained within a perpetual twilight. He started again, hoping to strike a landmark, but nothing broke through the wall of the fog except for a tentative figure who came into his vision from the right hand and was clearly lost like himself.

'My dear Keeble,' Armstrong said, 'I presume you were coming to see me.'

'I was, but I missed my way.'

Armstrong looked left and right, wondering if this little recess in the fog was the best place for a conference. He was certain that no one was near.

'Well, here I am! Tell me what you have discovered.'

Keeble moved his feet awkwardly as if dissatisfied with his researches. 'I cannot be sure of the precise meaning of the white lily, which is not an approved marking and seems to have been devised privately by the squadron. I can only speculate . . . '

'I have asked for nothing more.'

Armstrong could hear footsteps behind him now, but their voices were smothered by the fog and would not carry.

'The white lily was the emblem of the French monarchy until the Revolution, when it was adopted as a badge by the royalist counter-revolutionaries. But that is very distant; there are more recent uses.' He paused, reluctant to go further.

'And what are they?' Armstrong asked.

'Believe me, sir, we are in danger of making a false premise, but the white lily gave rise to the term "white party" for those who opposed the revolutionary movements both in France and Russia. You will recall the wars of the Red and White armies in Russia following the Great War: at that time Polish units assisted the White Army in the Ukraine and were active even when that army was defeated. They fought with desperate courage; many noblemen were among them.'

'Are you suggesting there may be a link between the Polish squadron and the interventionists of 1919?'

'There is no evidence to suggest it beyond the white lily they have painted on their aircraft, which could have another meaning.'

'And the black background?'

An unnecessary question, for Armstrong could himself infer that a black field meant 'until death'. He was arrested by a footfall close at hand and knew that someone was moving just beyond his vision. They were not alone in the fog.

Armstrong said, 'Thank you, Keeble. I think your deductions are probably right. I wish their colours had not been violated.'

Even as he spoke — rashly, it seemed — the footsteps in the hard snow came to a halt, as though someone had been taken by the same thought.

'Who is there?' Armstrong said.

No reply — just a laugh in the enfolding mist.

'Tell me who you are!'

'It does not matter who I am,' said a strong, resonant voice. Every impaired syllable was familiar to Armstrong. 'Call me the commander of the White Squadron, the captain of the *Snow Princess*. Your aide has worked well.'

He said no more and Armstrong heard his footsteps receding into the fog.

TEN

When the fog lifted the raids resumed. Cologne, Hamburg, Stuttgart. Night raids upon the brick and bone of the German nation. Hayden Chance didn't know what to make of it, outsider as he was, though obviously the shifting aim of Bomber Command in the last year had arisen from their failure to accept the nature of the weapon they had made. The Main Force was a blunt instrument. It had no subtlety in the business of destruction and could not limit the area in which the bombs fell. The policy of saturation bombing was adopted when it was already in being and because the Main Force could do nothing else. After all, the bombers were in need of employment. In March, Air Commodore Pratt, that exponent of the method, gave a lecture at Moreton Valence to explain that a military objective comprised the whole town because the residential areas were part of the productive effort; but the aircrews listened with scant attention; they had accepted the true role of Bomber Command months before when they had seen the great fires lighting the undersides of the clouds. Chance wondered why he didn't care. When the Germans razed Warsaw he felt a guarded fury, but these cities were no less in ruin. He wondered if there was need for either, because already the Germans had lost and we had won. Of course, the aircrews didn't care because they were detached from the ground and often enough the bombs simply vanished into the dark, into the cloud; if they saw the town it was in miniature, the bombbursts as trivial as raindrops, the engines obliterating every sound.

Flying eastward, the darkness came quickly; it was like diving into an approaching wave. From the cockpit windows Hayden

Chance could see how the wing tips vanished as the light weakened and how far ahead the first stars were showing. Now that the nights had shortened, the bombers took off in daylight and found the cover of darkness only at the enemy coast. Below him a carpet of cloud concealed the ground and reached forward into Germany — the friendly bank of cumulus which suppressed the searchlights and within which an aircraft and its crew could take refuge. This guilty fellowship with the clouds was at the heart of the air war, for the presence of cloud made bombing inexact but increased the odds on survival; the aircrews therefore hoped secretly for cloud. Well, tonight the clouds were there, unbroken as far as Chance could see — the familiar overcoat he had not sought but counted a secret blessing no matter what it did to the flight of the bombs.

No point in throwing his life away now. It was April, Eisenhower was on the lower Elbe and yesterday the Russians had entered Stettin; the frontiers of Germany had drawn inward and soon the country would collapse. There was nothing left to die for. At a word from the navigator, he changed course on to a leg that would take them far across the German plain to Neustrelitz, a town opposing the Russian drive into Pomerania and which, as a gesture of co-operation, they were bidden to destroy.

The darkness increased until there was a shine upon it. He could just see the upper surface of the clouds which the starlight painted with a timid brush. The aircraft in the bomber stream had vanished from his view but he knew them still to be there, his fellow travellers in the dark. A tiny effusion of cold light on the starboard bow marked the place where the moon would rise out of the clouds. Nearer at hand the luminous dials of the instrument were in continuous small movement and, in the nose below him, a soft amber light was spreading from the navigation table. He checked the compass and direction indicator which showed a mean course a little to the south of due east, but with its heavy load the aircraft was swinging left and right in an endless yaw. Still, they were going in the direction of Neustrelitz, whose destruction would assist the Russians in their occupation of eastern Germany.

He could see the navigator, Flying Officer Tom Woodward, but no other member of the crew. It was a community of voices, so intimate they did not need to speak their names. Tonight that community was broken by a strange voice because the rear-gunner had been replaced that afternoon when he had fallen sick, and although he knew the replacement well enough Chance was uneasy at having him aboard; it upset the balance of the crew worked out over many months of comradeship. A strange thing, the aircrew — a random grouping of seven men that grew so tight a single change could break it. With an interloper aboard, who knew what might happen?

He had to mend this rent in the fabric. He switched on his microphone and said, 'Rear-gunner, you're very quiet. Hope you're still with us.'

'I'm still with you, skipper.'

'What can you see?'

'Not much.'

Indeed, looking westward from the tail, there was nothing to catch the gunner's eyes but for a softening of the darkness where the cloud lay; there was a pallid star, and another, at a great height above his head; and if he looked left and right to the limit of his vision, just forward of the beam, he could see the square fins of the tail assembly where the rudders were in movement. He was contained in a bubble of perspex at the extreme limit of the aircraft; here it was as cold as in northern seas and his breath froze into an icicle where it escaped from the oxygen mask.

No, this crew was not the same as his own: Pilot Officer Lampton-Bell was accustomed to the strict procedures followed by the Station Commander, and the haphazard methods adopted by this captain were strange to him. He was not at ease. He did not recognize the voices on the intercom and this turret was not his own. He was used to the loneliness of the tail position, where he was separated by fifty-five feet from the intimacy of the cockpit and the forward cabin, but tonight there was the added strangeness of an unfamiliar aircraft. He elevated the guns and saw the four barrels rising towards the vertical. He turned up the gunsight illumination until he could just see the circular graticule superimposed on the grey sky. In the whole hemisphere visible from the rear turret there were no fixed objects but for the illusive stars. He chose the least dim and fixed the aim of the four Brownings exactly upon it, holding it within the graticule as the tail weaved back and forth in the slipstream; he placed his thumb upon the firing button and took the first pressure. A simple thing, to put out that distant light!

A minute later, complying with an old discipline, he resumed his searching of the enemy sky for the fighter aircraft that could be there. He ran his eyes from beam to beam, starting in the high position and finishing in the underlying cloud. Over enemy territory the tremor in his nerves made it possible for him to miss even an obvious intrusion into his sky; with nothing on which to rest his eyes, he could not tell if their focus was long or short and an aircraft could swing towards the tail without being seen.

Beam to beam, high to low. The long watchfulness at the tail guns induced a mesmeric sleep from which Lampton-Bell awoke with a clap of the heart and a sensation of nakedness. He struggled to stay awake. With Armstrong he was kept alert by a bond of affectionate discipline; not so with this crew of strangers. Beam to beam, high to low. An hour of this and his fancy was painting the enemy upon the clouds. There were movements at the edge of his vision — diving, swinging movements — as his eyes created hostile shapes on the dull surface of the sky, shapes that vanished as soon as he brought the guns to bear. With an effort he dispelled the phantom aircraft and told himself that the sky was empty except for his own guns and the far off, immovable stars.

Lampton-Bell was tough, tougher than even his own captain knew; his forbears had been fighting men for many generations and he did not find it strange that he should occupy the most vulnerable position in a Halifax at the age of nineteen. This was an hereditary duty. He had not liked Armstrong at first and had not wanted to fly with him; he had thought him too austere for friendship; but over the months a mutual trust and dependence had grown between them. A friendship across many ranks did not happen outside aircrew, but of course the aircrews had done away with differences in age and degree: it was a friendship that made no claim upon the past or the future but belonged simply to the minute and to the experience of flight. Armstrong had not wanted him to fly tonight, but he had yielded when no other gunner could be found.

Now Lampton-Bell rotated the turret, searching the great space behind the tail, seeing nothing.

*

The navigator, Flying Officer Tom Woodward, had turned down his lamp when they passed the enemy coast and now there was just enough light for him to read the charts. On his right where the curtains parted he could see the bomb-aimer outlined against the perspex nose of the aircraft; to his left the wireless operator sat in deep shadow. Here in the forward cabin there was greater intimacy than elsewhere in the fuselage and the heating was sufficient to keep his breath from freezing. The point of his pencil hung over the plotting chart at what he believed to be the aircraft's present position, which was some fifty miles east of the Weser and well beyond the ground held by the Allied armies. As usual in hostile air, his mind worked stiffly and his concentration was easily broken. He was nearly certain the pencil point marked their true position because earlier the radar had given him two good fixes from which he had computed a reliable wind-speed and direction. Now of course the radar could not help him; they had flown beyond the effective range of the transmitting stations in the south of England and the screen was hatched by enemy interference. Though a long way short of the target, they were 'on course' and somewhere in the dark centre of Europe. At the scale of the chart they moved forward at a barely perceptible pace. Each time he laid off the distance flown they had made hardly any progress along the pencil line that joined the last turning point to the target.

Like most aircrew, Woodward had not bothered to put on the bulky outer flying suit and instead wore only the quilted lining under his parachute harness and stuffed into his boots. His hands were always frozen because he could not do his work in gloves. Now the cold had penetrated to his body and he wanted to urinate, but this meant leaving the table and walking the length of the aircraft to the Elsan bucket in the tail. After five minutes he could postpone the visit no longer. He did not announce his intention on the intercom; he didn't want the crew to say that Woodward was pissing himself again; he simply disconnected his intercom plug and oxygen tube, stood up and started on the long journey aft. He climbed the three steps into the cockpit where he caught a glimpse of the night sky beyond the canopy. Chance saw him, of course, and knew the nature of his errand, but the captain just punched him in the shoulder and sent him rearward. He passed the engineer at his panel, and paused for a moment under the astrodome to project his head above the level of the fuselage and look round at the featureless sky, but even the subdued light of the navigation table had destroyed his night vision and he could see nothing beyond the wings and the beating engines. He ducked down again and continued his journey, passing the oxygen cylinders and climbing over the main spar into the rest position. Here he was behind the engines and the noise increased; he could hear the spars creaking as the Halifax, bearing its burden, continued the long flight eastward. He stepped over the smaller rear spar, skirted the mid-upper turret, where he could just see the lower half of the seated gunner, and balanced along the catwalk that took him over the radar scanner and to the Elsan position just aft of the rear entrance. Beyond this point there were only the ammunition tracks feeding the rear turret and the hatch leading to the turret itself.

He arrived breathless and light-headed. Without oxygen, the walk had consumed the whole of his strength. He found the oxygen terminal, connected his mask and felt the pulsating flow of rich air in his mouth and nose. His mind cleared and his strength returned. He plugged his helmet into the local intercom point and rejoined the circle of voices in time to hear the engineer saying, 'Tom's gone aft again, the pissy bugger!' And Chance: 'Hush, now! Hush!'

He released the straps of his parachute harness and unbuttoned the inner flying suit. Then he opened his fly and felt the searing cold of the rear fuselage invading his loins as he urinated into the bucket. The movements of the aircraft, accentuated here in the tail, caused the stream to travel in a haphazard pattern all round the Elsan and across the lip and on to the aircraft floor. He prayed the aircraft would not be attacked while he was thus engaged: it was a secret fear of his that the machine would be ripped by enemy fire and himself blown into oblivion with an undone fly.

When he had finished he went back the way he had come, thumping the engineer as he passed. At the navigation table he resumed the air plot. They were approaching the tenth meridian east of Greenwich where the wireless operator must take countermeasures.

*

Flight Sergeant Ramsey, the wireless operator, had done little so far. The bomber stream observed a radio silence on the outward journey, for even a brief transmission would have revealed the presence of these intruders to those who listened on the aircraft frequencies. He had tuned the receiver every thirty minutes to the Group transmitter back on the Yorkshire moors, and he had heard the routine broadcast which as yet contained no message for these birds of passage. The signal grew weaker as the range increased. Ramsey — a man under twenty, only two years out of school — had an obsessive fear that he would miss a recall signal and that his aircraft alone would continue into the dangerous void when the rest of the stream had turned home. It would be easy enough, for the frequencies were congested with the hubbub of war, one signal overlapping another and the German transmitters jamming wide segments of the wave band, and from this entanglement of sound he had to pick up the thin thread of morse intended for his ear.

Behind his head a shuttered lamp threw a single beam of light on to the face of the receiver; the transmitter was a shadow above. At his left hand a small square window showed him a fragment of sky and, if he looked to the rear, the two port engines, each with an issue of flame from the exhaust manifold. His was the best position in the aircraft; there was a womb-like security in this dark corner where the warm air accumulated and there was so little vision of the scene outside. Ramsey had received the last Group broadcast and now sat waiting for Woodward to tell him when to employ defensive measures.

At a word from the navigator, he opened the chute beside him, heard the roar of the slipstream and felt the warmth being sucked from the cabin. Stacked at the foot of the cockpit stair were the parcels of tin foil which, when broadcast upon the air, confused the enemy radar by creating numerous responses; by this device one aircraft could be made to look like ten. Once a minute he dropped a packet of foil down the chute and heard it ripped away by the wind. Better to be employed than idle. From this moment the passage of time was marked by a regular activity, and with each discharge of foil he knew there was a minute less to endure in this dark place where the menace increased with each mile of penetration.

*

The moon, the bombers' moon. From the cockpit Hayden Chance saw the moon break free of the clouds at his own height and rise slowly, the face enlarging, to a position on the starboard bow. The cockpit was filled with ghostly light. Outside, the boundaries of his vision fell back until he was flying in a great moonlit dome, the walls of which were broken by stars. And — yes! — a Halifax passed over the face of the moon, reminding him that he was not alone — that through the last murky hours his fellow captains had been out there in the dark, keeping him company, seeking the same destination. Moments later a silent aircraft, as big as a whale, passed slowly from left to right above him and vanished on the port beam. The sky which hitherto had seemed as empty as the polar night was crowded with aircraft bound by a common intention. But in this busy world there was a place for others beside themselves. The enemy's vision had also lengthened when the moon threw her opulent beams upon the bomber stream. Far away off the port wing tip — so far it might have been in another world — he could see a long red incision in the blue-black curtain that marked the passage of an aircraft on fire; it continued with them for a long, long minute before it fell away from their height. He did not report what he had seen, neither did the mid-upper gunner who could hardly have missed it.

Forty more minutes in the luminous dark before they could expect to see the target. An odd thing to die in the last days of the war. Chance laughed grimly at his own predicament: he was a stranger from far off who did not believe the war would settle much, or that it had a purpose beyond the easement of savage tempers, but none the less he had fought through it to the last. He applied no moral justification to the business of war; in his mind the dead were equally dead whether they died in concentration camps or amid the rubble of Hamburg and Cologne; war was a delirium in which the instinct for violence found joyful expression. He would fly until the last day, the man who had no faith in war, who saw nothing in victory but the exhaustion of one partner in the shared lunacy. Ride on, simpleton! Yet, even in this tiny world of shattering noise, he had the sensations of peace in his limbs, the taste of it upon his lips. Peace and a cessation from madness were only weeks away. He wanted to return to the lumber forests of British Columbia and to recover the family he had left there — he wanted to return to the dimension of sanity and to let the recollection of these days become submerged in his memory.

Of course, they had failed. They had laboured in vain and their failure was now evident. From the windows Chance could see the last of the night bombers engaged on a final exercise in futility. The Germans had not been defeated from the air; their will to fight had been sharpened, not blunted, under indiscriminate attack. He knew it now. The airmen knew it, though their commanders did not. They were taking part in the last episode in a mistaken offensive, launched in error and continued in perversity by those who could not admit that their weapon was ineffective. Well, so be it; the bomber stream moved under its own momentum across the field of cloud, passing the Elbe unseen and forcing on towards the thirteenth meridian, where the target lay.

They didn't speak. Chance could hear only the shallow breathing of his companions. To speak disengaged the attention, giving the shadowing forces an advantage in the ebb and flow of the long battle: they did not tempt the ill-mannered spirits that attended upon the bomber stream by letting their minds wander. As the hours passed, the shape of their adversary lost definition and became simply an ominous presence in the closer sky — a spectre of the nursery, a giant of uncertain temper living just beyond their sight. They rode into Germany upon tip-toe while the phantoms of the dark kept pace.

The enemy fighter, diving from high on the port quarter, was visible for perhaps three seconds from the mid-upper guns, but the attack was so quick the gunner had not time enough to bring the guns to bear before the Fokker Wolf had disappeared into the blind area under the aircraft belly. Hayden Chance caught the gunner's gasp of surprise on the intercom but saw nothing himself.

'What was it?' he asked sharply.

'A fighter made a downward pass.'

'Did he get off a burst?'

'I don't know. I think so.'

'Engineer, check for damage. Gunners, open fire as you bear.'

A moment later there was no need to identify where the damage was sustained. The port inner engine was losing revolutions and setting up an unfamiliar vibration. He applied starboard rudder to correct the yaw and keep the aircraft from going off course. From the window he could see a ribbon of smoke escaping from the engine gills and flowing over the upper surface of the wing.

Fire. Fire close to the inboard petrol tank. Shit.

He looked back for the engineer, but at the same moment the engineer came forward, colliding with his face.

'Engine fire,' said Chance. 'Cut the fuel. I'm going to feather.'

He stopped the engine and operated the nacelle fire extinguisher. The smoke lessened but a narrow plume continued from the gills. He trimmed the aircraft for asymmetric flight and opened the three remaining engines to bring the airspeed back to that of the stream.

'Shit,' he said. He took a deep breath to check the beating of his heart. 'Gunners, what do you see?'

'Nothing,' said the mid-upper.

'Nothing,' said the tail.

Was that all, then? Was the fighter at the end of his endurance, getting in a random burst as he dived towards the ground and replenishment? Chance looked at the clock and saw that the target was still fifteen minutes away.

'Engineer, what other damage?'

'Holes in the port wing and in the fuselage. Some loss of fuel.'

'What about the port outer?'

'A bit rough.'

He overcame the shaking in his hands and feet and compelled his mind to serve him. He knew it would be safer to continue within the stream than to return across Germany, solo and lame, a target for every fighter, in the hope of putting down in southern England or somewhere behind the Allied front line. From the target the route was north to the Baltic and then back across Denmark to the Yorkshire coast, which meant a flight of at least four hours on three engines and perhaps with diminishing fuel; but that route offered the better chance.

'I'll continue on three,' he said. 'Watch the fuel consumption. Damned if I'm flying alone.'

Yes, he was going home; the war was nearly over and he was not going to become part of the debris. He took firm hold of the wheel and willed the machine to stay airborne.

He said without reflection, 'Gunners, listen! Any aircraft on a converging course is an enemy. Let him have it. If you hit one of our own aircraft, that's just too bad.'

He felt a rising enthusiasm for life that excited him and put strength into his limbs. There was sweetness in simply drawing breath. He'd keep the old lady in the air. He'd cross the North Sea to a friendly shore.

'Bomb-aimer, I want the bombs away first time no matter what you can see. I'm not going round again with the aircraft in this condition. Got it?'

Indeed, it was unlikely the bomb-aimer would see the target, for the cloud was without a break and the pathfinders would have to lay sky markers. The fighter had not reappeared, so he had either returned to base or fastened his attention on some other aircraft. His spirit lifted as the minutes passed and he was still in flight. For no reason he could think of, Chance was suddenly happy.

Seven minutes later Chance saw the first of the sky markers — red flares borne upon parachutes and sinking towards the upper surface of the cloud. As they fell they separated. The pathfinders had reached the target to find it obscured and they had put down these markers using radar ground scanners. The Main Force would aim at the flares and the trajectory of the bombs would carry them onward in the direction of the target. It was a device only a little better than dropping the bombs upon navigational dead reckoning; but in any case the crews were briefed, when they could not find the target, to aim their bombs at any inhabited area provided it was inside Germany. A second cluster of flares fell a long way from the first. They would be lucky to hit the town and luckier still to hit the target. Far to the south there were searchlights breaking through rents in the clouds and showing where the German capital was again under Mosquito attack.

He switched the radio-telephone on to the frequency used by the Master Bomber, and he heard that official speaking in the unmistakable accent of Bomber Command and with the 'end of term' spirit that was affecting the whole force. 'Well, there you are, chaps — the best we can do. The greens are better placed than the reds, but I don't think it matters much. Drop your loads and bugger off. See you at the party . . . '

Further markers were breaking out, and when Chance reached the area they were all over the sky. The defenders were firing flak through the clouds and the orange bursts were added to the red and green of the flares. He had flown into a great lighted cathedral whose upper arches vanished in shadow.

He opened the bomb doors and felt the sudden chill as the slipstream penetrated the fuselage through the inspection panels.

'Go for the middle,' he told the bomb-aimer. 'Nothing else for it.'

A moment later the bomb-aimer launched the bombs on their long flight down through the clouds in the approximate direction of Neustrelitz. Chance closed the doors, glad to be separated from four tons of high explosive, his mind turning to the journey home.

The route continued easterly for twenty miles, then swung north towards the sea.

He was going home; there was darkness enough to cover his retreat.

Going home.

In the ensuing minute, by a mistake so small no one but himself would notice it — or perhaps guided by an underlying imperative of the war — Chance became party to a secret he was not meant to share. The night contained a purpose other than their own. The voice of the Master Bomber had faded as they left the target and now Chance reached for the button to turn off the radio; but instead his finger struck a second button which opened a normally unused frequency. Another voice was speaking here above the clouds. A voice close to him. A voice he seemed to recognize. He found it difficult to believe there could be a second intention in the perilous dark; for who had the strength for anything more, when the war was ending and they had only to get themselves back across the North Sea to survive into times of peace?

He heard the clear instruction: 'The White Squadron will bear zero-eight-two degrees. Distance sixty-three miles. Close upon the *Snow Princess. Jeszcze Polska Nie Zginela!*'

He could not bring his mind to bear upon this diversion from the Main Force; he had troubles enough keeping his own aircraft on the planned course. If the Poles were mad, it wouldn't add much to the volume of insanity washing across Europe as the continent broke apart. But ten minutes later he remembered what he had heard.

'Navigator, what lies sixty-three miles from the target at zero-eight-two degrees?'

He waited while Woodward applied the protractor and dividers to the plotting chart.

'Stettin,' he said, 'exactly.'

'You don't say! How does it bear from our present position?'

'About twenty miles on the starboard beam.'

Well, let it be. He could not concern himself with what happened in a remote corner of Europe at a time of convulsion.

Nevertheless, a minute later he said, 'Mid-upper, watch the starboard beam and report what you see.'

He looked himself through the right-hand window, but his view was incomplete and he saw just the engine cowlings and the broken cloud beyond. Whatever caprice of history was taking place off the starboard wing was hidden from him.

The mid-upper was speaking now. 'There are searchlights aft of the beam. Some flak. Must be a raid.'

He wanted to see it for himself, this insult to the rule of war; he engaged the automatic pilot and went back to the astrodome where he looked along the surface of the wing. At a hand's breadth into the rearward quadrant he could see searchlights penetrating the cloud breaks and darts of flak at the point of intersection. He was impressed by the effrontery of it, no matter that his mind was numbed by the violence of recent years.

'Holy cow,' he said in the seclusion of his mind.

He regained his seat and took the aircraft back into his hands, wondering how much it mattered. There was a ventilation of temper all over Europe and Asia as restraints were released and accounts were satisfied. Such things happened when a war ended. He could not imagine what the Station Commander would say when he heard of it; he pictured the grave and kindly face of the Old Man, where obedience had inscribed deep lines of resignation, when the tale was told to him. How would he judge the renegade captains who had turned from the path to attack a target of their own? Perhaps it would be better to say nothing and allow the secret he had learned by chance to lose itself in the throes of victory.

*

The engineer hit him on the shoulder to attract his attention and Chance realized he had been speaking for some time.

'Yes? What is it?'

The engineer's voice had lost its usual character, but he spoke quietly. 'A substantial fuel loss from the port tank,' he said.

'What endurance have we got?'

'About three hours, if it doesn't worsen.'

'Shit,' said Chance. 'Navigator, will that get us home?'

'No, not by any route.'

'Shit.'

Well, the news he bore might in any case perish if he came down in the pastures of Denmark or in the North Sea.

'All positions are to be ready to bale out.' he said 'But not yet. Not over Germany.'

If they had to abandon their aircraft they would do so over Denmark and not where they might be torn to pieces by a maddened people. The land below them lay in the path of armies advancing from east and west. Denmark, an hour ahead, gave them their greatest chance.

He was losing height. A dead engine and another without full power had increased the drag and caused him to drop away from his ceiling. He watched the altimeter as the hands continued to unwind like a clock running backwards. He doubted if they could fly for even an hour if this continued.

He said inwardly, Steady, baby! Don't let us down now.

He thought again of the White Squadron that by this time must have turned north-east and rejoined the stream. Likely enough their secret mission would never be revealed if he did not return to tell the story. Who could determine the nationality of the machines flying in from the west when the air was thick with aircraft? Who would know which hand had launched the attack? Let them be, he thought. It was no business of his. He was an outsider who did not believe in war's justification but saw it instead as a common tragedy.

Then, unbidden, the calm and obedient face of the Old Man appeared before his mind's eye — a man whose life had been given to a practice of the military virtue, to the acceptance of authority, to a quiet pride in the motives of his country and his service. Even Chance had to admit that, when the world split asunder, there was merit in an unaltering loyalty. If he had to

123

make a choice, he stood with the Old Man and not with the White Squadron. Armstrong would be angered and hurt, but he had a right to know that a unit from his station had broken faith with him. He should be told, but Chance might not reach home to tell him.

'Wireless operator,' Chance said, 'are you within signalling distance of base?'

Sergeant Ramsey came on to the intercom a moment later. 'Yes, at extreme range.'

'Could you get a short message through?'

'If I break radio silence.'

Chance looked at his airspeed and altitude and judged that he was now at the rear of the stream and much lower than the force. If he used the transmitter he would betray his position and invite the attention of predatory fighters, which he had not the engine power to evade.

Hell, he thought. I can't speak to him.

Yet he was witness to an unparalleled act of indiscipline.

He had not meant to become obsessed by the figure of his commander, but now he felt as if Armstrong watched his every movement, not critically but with eyes that were filled with disappointment. Armstrong was a man to whom one spoke the truth, and failure to tell the truth amounted to falsehood.

The altimeter showed that Chance had lost another thousand feet. God, was he too caught by the beauty of obedience?

'Ramsey, come up here!' he said suddenly, violently. 'Bring a signal pad.'

When Ramsey appeared at his side, Chance took the pad, scribbled some words across it: *Exclusive for Station Commander Moreton Valence. Suspect Polish squadron attacked Russian forward positions at Stettin. Recommend you investigate as my return doubtful. Adios.*

'Encode that and get it off,' he said. 'Waste no time, as I don't know how long I can hold her.'

Pilot Officer Lampton-Bell — the stranger at the rear guns — saw the fighter high on the port quarter only a second or two before it was also seen from the mid-upper turret. He had time enough to warn the captain and to elevate the guns before the fighter started a long curve of pursuit from the quarter to the stern position. He saw the slim wing and the radial engine of the Fokker Wolf 190, but whether this was the same aircraft as before he could not have said. He kept the circular gunsight ahead of the fighter and slowly reduced the angle of incidence as the aircraft approached the tail. When it closed to three hundred yards he pressed the firing button, felt the violent hammering of the four Brownings and saw the tracer bending away to his right. At the same time the captain put the Halifax into a left-handed corkscrew designed to increase the fighter's rate of turn, and in this manoeuvre he was helped by the lack of power in his port engines which allowed him to bank inside the curving path followed by the fighter. Lampton-Bell continued the burst until the Fokker Wolf broke away downward.

He knew his own aircraft had not been hit. He cleared a stoppage in the lower left-hand Browning by drawing back the breech block until it was retained in the cocked position. His fear had left him at the moment the guns fired and he was impatient to engage the fighter again.

The captain said, 'Where is he now?'

'Climbing to port,' said the mid-upper guns.

'Try to keep him on the port side.'

Of course, if he attacked from starboard they could not hope to evade him; the lack of power in the port engines would prevent them from making a tight turn in that direction. Lampton-Bell rotated the turret as far as it would go on the port side but could not see the fighter; in that area his view was blocked by the large square fin and he could only wait for the fighter to return into his arc of fire. He heard the mid-upper guns firing, and a moment later he saw the tracer coming into his sight high up and plainly wide of the mark. With that degree of panic, the mid-upper guns would never be brought to bear. Lampton-Bell waited calmly for the Fokker Wolf to reappear. He drew upon an instinct for battle that was part of his endowment as he kept the gunsight at that point beyond the trailing edge of the rudder, where he expected the aircraft to enter his vision.

The second attack came exactly upon that line of sight, and as soon as the fighter was clearly etched against the darker sky he gave a short burst at extreme range. Not a chance of doing him damage over that distance, but the pilot would know that he was observed and that the bomber was still dangerous. As he made his approach, Lampton-Bell got in a sustained burst without stoppages, and he saw his own tracer passing close to the fighter and burning out in the sky beyond. He heard the chatter of the mid-upper guns, but the turret was firing all round the clock and Lampton-Bell knew that the moment belonged to him, the stranger, the fighting man. The attacking aircraft levelled out two hundred yards astern and he saw but did not hear the repeated discharge of the cannon: it was as if he watched his adversary and saw his lips moving in savage abuse but did not catch the words. He kept his thumb upon the firing button as the range narrowed.

'Breaking to starboard,' he said.

In the cockpit Hayden Chance heard a cannon shell striking somewhere amidships and at the same moment the mid-upper guns ceased firing. He could not think of it now; from the sound of it the guns had been ineffective anyway. He ordered the engineer into the astrodome to report the position of the fighter, and he learnt that it was high on the starboard quarter, just where he least wanted it.

Dive.

Dive for cover.

When in doubt, put the nose down. Nothing else for it. Here the clouds made a tattered blanket without much comfort, but none the less he put the aircraft into a steep descent and held it there despite the mounting airspeed. They fell like a stone towards the bank of clouds. A one-way passage, Chance thought, because he could never climb back to where he had been. He entered the topmost fold of the cloud at eight thousand feet, but after some miles of this seclusion he broke into a vast empty arena where there was no cover. Below him were the coal-dark waters of the Baltic with a scatter of islands showing dimly. If they were found in this barren place they would have no hope of bailing out, and he did not think he could ditch the machine in darkness and with little power on the port side.

No place for an outsider.

Then he heard the firm but youthful voice of Lampton-Bell addressing him from the rear guns. 'He's still there — starboard quarter up.'

This was it; he could not escape an attack from that side but must endure a raking of cannon fire. Lampton-Bell would have to fight it out from the one effective turret. Call it an even match, because the stranger in the tail had proved himself to be formidable.

Chance said, 'You're on your own, boy. Do your best.'

But the words were smothered by a vehement exchange of fire. He heard the rear guns making their defence, but louder was the sound of the shells striking home. He could not tell how many times they were hit but the smoke was filling the cockpit and stinging his eyes. The engineer had fallen somewhere behind him. He saw the fighter for an instant as it passed them, carried by the momentum of its attack, but he knew that Lampton-Bell had destroyed it: it was just a ball of feathers at the start of a long-downward trajectory.

He fought to maintain level flight, but the nose kept dropping as if with tiredness. There was nothing below him but a sea that gleamed like gun-metal and offered no deliverance. An island showed dimly ahead of him, like a promise he had not strength enough to grasp. He was going down in the manner of all lost air-crews, and in the company of men already dead, and he could not arrest their fall.

Down, down. The seconds grew in length until each was as vast as an hour. His thought slowed, and then stopped against an insurmountable obstacle.

He heard the scream of the wind outside the cockpit canopy and saw the dark surface of the water rising towards him.

It was a long way down to the sea . . .

ELEVEN

Flight Lieutenant Jarvis, the Adjutant, paused in the doorway and then advanced on the balls of his feet, supposing the Station Commander to be asleep at his desk. It was no uncommon thing in these rough days to find a pilot sleeping. When he drew closer, he saw that Armstrong was not asleep but staring into his lap where his hands were tightly fastened. He did not respond when Jarvis spoke to him; he simply drew his eyelids together, squeezing a ball of moisture in the corner of one eye to the point where it overlapped the brim. At length he slowly raised his head.

'Yes, Jarvis?'

'Pilot Officer Edwards is here, sir.'

'Edwards?'

'The young man who will serve you as rear-gunner.'

'Indeed? So soon? Well, ask him to come in.'

Jarvis was halfway to the door when Armstrong stopped him.

'I have a paper to clear first. I will use the bell.'

The Adjutant went out, shaking his head. He had urged the Station Commander to take leave a month ago but he had declined, saying that he would wait until the war was over. Anyone could see that he was suffering from operational fatigue. Seated in the outer office was a spruce young officer whose boyish features were not yet in their final moulding. His type was repeated a hundred times on the squadrons and Jarvis would not know him when they met again. To him, the aircrews were all alike, faceless young men with whom he was not engaged.

On his desk lay a draft casualty signal awaiting his clearance. He took it up and ran his eye down the column of detail. A missing Halifax: nothing exceptional in that but for the rank of the captain. He made a correction, signed his name to authorize release and placed it with the outward traffic.

The bell rang and Jarvis conducted Pilot Officer Edwards into the Station Commander's office. Armstrong stood to greet him; he was erect and unsmiling. He barely looked at Edwards and did not invite him to be seated.

He said, 'I understand you are joining me as rear-gunner. As you know, Lampton-Bell flew last night with the Squadron Commander and did not return.'

'I look forward to joining you,' the young man affirmed, who could say no less.

'What? Very well. Of course, the war is almost over.'

Edwards was ill at ease in the sombre presence of the Station Commander and he tried the sunlit path. 'I hope it will last long enough for me to get into it, sir.'

'I beg your pardon?' Armstrong had not responded to this warmth and instead looked at Edwards as if he had expressed an insubordinate opinion. 'I very much hope that it does not. There is no point in continuing the war a minute longer than is necessary. We are already wasting lives. You may go now.'

In the outer office Edwards released his breath in a long draught. He asked Jarvis if the Station Commander was usually like that.

But the Adjutant was engaged with his menial duties and did not look up. 'He is tired; probably his stomach is upset; with the loss of the Squadron Commander his work has been doubled.' He was not concerned with the susceptibilities of young officers, all of whom should be suppressed in his opinion.

Edwards went out, but before the door had closed behind him, it was thrown open again with a flourish of authority and Jarvis looked up in vexation. The Station Warrant Officer stood in front of his desk, asking to see the Station Commander.

'He is — preoccupied,' Jarvis said. 'Can it not wait until tomorrow? With the loss of the Squadron Commander ——'

'Today, sir, if you please.'

'In what connection?'

'Personal.'

The decision was finely balanced. The Old Man was clearly out of sorts, but the senior airman had a right of access to him which the Adjutant could not deny. And it was true that Armstrong had a liking for the SWO, whom he seemed to regard as the only other professional on the station.

'I'll see,' Jarvis said; and he made a tentative entrance into the Station Commander's office. 'Mr Thorpe wishes to see you, sir.'

'Mr Thorpe?' The expression of severity that Armstrong had used all morning weakened a little. 'It is — kind of Mr Thorpe to call. Ask him in, Jarvis.'

When the SWO was ushered in, he paused on the threshold and Jarvis saw that his eyes had joined those of the Station Commander. Something passed between them but Jarvis could not have said what it was: they lived in the old regular air force, admitting obligations that everyone else had forgotten, following the same patterns of thought. He resumed his work until, a minute later, Mr Thorpe rejoined him in the outer office.

The SWO stopped at the Adjutant's desk and spoke in a voice roughened by years in barracks. 'The boy's kit will be in my personal custody until required by the committee of adjustment. It is the Station Commander's wish.'

'Oh, really? Then you'd better take it before the fatigue party gets there.'

'I've already taken it.'

'Without an instruction, Mr Thorpe?'

The SWO nodded and went out, and Jarvis closed his eyes to banish the vision of faultiness. A departure from routine usually ended in confusion. Still, if the Old Man wanted it so. . . .

His ear, alert for any sound of movement from the inner office, caught the scrape of the chair as Armstrong rose from his desk. A moment later he came into the Adjutant's office carrying his cap and gloves.

'I shall take a short walk, Jarvis, as I am in need of exercise.'

'Very good, sir. You have an appointment in the operations room at eleven-thirty.'

'I am aware of it. I shall go there directly.'

The Adjutant was disquieted. The possibility of error multiplied when the Station Commander was at large on the unit: decisions were unrecorded, channels were broken, the administration went all out of shape.

He lay back in his chair in a semblance of exhaustion, heaving with small anxieties, as the brisk step receded along the passage outside.

Armstrong walked to the perimeter and stood looking at the airfield. The wind had freshened and cloud shadows were moving over the grass at a dizzy pace. He saw the outline of Moreton Valence — the hangars, the square water-tower, the accretion of huts — and he drew some comfort from the unlovely scene; for to stand here in the centre of the station was like wearing an old, familiar garment; there were no faces that were unknown to him, no sounds he could not identify. Of course, his command of Moreton Valence was nearly over. The station would have only a few more weeks in being because the service would have no need for the place once the war had ended. It was made from inferior brick. It was built for a task and the task was accomplished. When the squadrons disbanded there would be no one here and in time the huts would fall down. But while it remained he could find some easement in these rude buildings which had been his home for two years of war.

The station was quiet but for the running of an engine outside the maintenance hangar. He tried not to sink into bitterness. A commander could only do his job if he kept his mind cleared of emotional debris. He never discussed casualties, and he saw the need to impose this embargo even in the privacy of his mind. This morning he had to keep a steady nerve, a steady voice. He could not relax his standard of discipline at the moment of victory no matter what others did; he could only apply the rules that had served him throughout his life and which he knew to be best.

At eleven-thirty exactly, he went to the operations room, drew the blinds closed and sent the staff beyond earshot. He sought out the chart he needed and laid it on the map table. From his inner pocket he took out the signal he had decoded that morning and placed it beside the map. Then he waited, forcing his breath to come evenly, keeping his mind empty but for the evidence before him.

The Prince did not exactly smile. When he raised his eyes to Armstrong's face they were marked with strange humour, while about his mouth, deeply incised, the lines of satisfaction were both grim and jubilant. He did not speak. Whatever thought was in his mind was contained by a fierce pride and his lips stayed closed. He nodded once in silent affirmation, keeping his eyes upon Armstrong's face. Nothing more. Nothing to explain or excuse the most outrageous act of the war. He was a noble-man of exalted privilege who recognized no motives more com-pelling than his own and acted with the power and justification of an old, vanished kingdom. He might even have been asking for Armstrong's complicity.

'Your silence is unacceptable to me,' Armstrong said, when a minute had passed.

Prince Karol brought his heels together in sudden considera-tion for his commanding officer. 'Sir, I have offended you! I offer such apology as I can.'

'An apology is hardly appropriate. This is a most serious mat-ter. In deference to your rank, I have sent the staff away and you may speak freely. So far only I have seen this signal, but it will be my duty to show it to the Air Officer Commanding unless you can persuade me it is untrue.'

The Prince raised his shoulders. 'True, untrue — how much does it matter?'

'In my judgement, a great deal.'

'Come now! The war has devastated two continents; there are millions dead.'

'That would not excuse an operation of this sort.'

He must have seen the anger in Armstrong's face, for he did not pursue his point. He said without strength, 'In battle many errors are made.'

'So they are, Prince Karol; but were it not an error it would be an unprecedented crime of war.'

The Prince looked sharply at his Station Commander, as if accepting for the first time that he was serious. Then he used his softest voice. 'You are angry, my friend. Aye, so! These things are difficult for you to comprehend.'

'My feelings are unimportant,' Armstrong said firmly. 'The offence was done to others, not to me. I will let you know pre-cisely what I think, as I do not want you to be under any illusions as to the seriousness of your position: I believe that your squa-dron deliberately overflew the target and attacked the Russian positions in Stettin. That is to say, you engaged not the enemy but an ally. You must have been aware that the Russian army had taken Stettin the day before and were concentrating there for a further offensive. The town was full of men and vehicles. If so, you were guilty not so much of disobedience as of murder.'

Not for the first time he had the impression that the Prince was sustained by a powerful drug that gave the world an illusory colour. He did not seem afraid. He could not have guessed what political consequences would flow from his action if news of the raid became public, nor have foreseen the inevitable verdict of the court martial. He was intoxicated by his own delinquency.

'Well, what of it? The White Squadron flies in to clobber the Bear. Smash, bang! It is a great spectacle.'

'You admit, then, that you attacked friendly forces, in defiance of the rules of war?'

'Never have I lied to you, my dear commander. I attack Stettin, where the Russians are. I do not care a jot for your rules of war.'

'That is an astonishing admission. You cannot realize what might happen internationally if your aircraft were identified.'

'We fly out of the darkness like avenging angels. Nobody sees us but the ghosts of our comrades.'

Armstrong kept to the path of reason no matter how hopeless that might be. 'Prince Karol, I must tell you that I care for the rules of war and for the good faith of my country. I believe that in times of conflict there must still be law, and that those who are in breach of the law must account for their actions. I could understand — though not approve — what led the young Count Pakorski to attempt a relief of Warsaw when his countrymen were denied assistance. However mistaken he may have been, his was an act of gallantry in support of aligned forces and I remember him with admiration and respect. Your action is entirely different. I accept that you have no love for the Russians after their treatment of the insurgents: it is natural enough. But I cannot accept that you have the smallest justification for attacking them in total disregard for the military obligations of this country and for the course of the war as whole.'

'We had our reasons,' the Prince said, not in defiance but in sombre introspection; he had lost his gaiety now. 'We are not of this country; we came from elsewhere.'

'The aircraft were under British control and bore British markings.'

'The aircraft are so much tin and rubber.'

'They may not be used illegally. That degrades not only the Polish Air Force but this country — my country — as well.'

Prince Karol bent over the table and placed his hands on either side of the map of central Europe. He studied the familiar outline for some time. 'I do not know what is legal, what is not,' he said slowly. 'Look at it, my friend! Not a frontier that has not been violated, not a code of law that has not been ignored. There is nothing in Europe but for a savage anarchy and the graves of the unfortunate.'

Armstrong said quietly, 'But we have fought to re-establish the law. You — I. That has been our purpose from the beginning.'

The Prince lifted his eyes from the map and looked at Armstrong with something like sympathy. 'Forgive me if I correct you. I do not mean to cause you pain. Last night your squadrons attacked Neustrelitz from above the clouds in a blind assault that cannot have been accurate. In similar manner they have obliterated every city in Germany. I do not know how such a thing accords with the rules of war or how the British can count themselves free from offence. I ask your pardon for speaking so.'

This morning Armstrong had no mind for the dialectics of warfare and could think only of the officers who had died. He said, 'I — I cannot deal with that question now. I am concerned simply with my own command and the safety of my own people, and there is a feature of last night's operation that distresses me. When Wing Commander Chance sent this message, his aircraft was already in difficulty. It may be — I cannot say — that by using his transmitter he disclosed his position to the enemy and invited his own destruction. As you know, he has not returned. Can you tell me, Prince Karol, that you feel no responsibility for the loss of that aircraft?'

The Prince was visibly moved; he closed his eyes the better to see the truth. 'I did not know — I had not heard ——'

'A fine commander, in the fullness of his life —— '

'Ah, so! No, I cannot acquit myself of blame. I am at fault, even though I do not intend such an outcome.'

'There is always hazard in disobedience.'

'Do not torment me! I am humbled.'

'There were — others with him,' the Station Commander continued. 'One was a member of my own crew.'

The Prince turned his dark eyes upon Armstrong and there was no doubting the quality of his compassion. 'This they tell me! A young man of distinction, of superior birth, who was your special friend.'

'I have no special friends amongst my officers,' Armstrong said curtly. 'They are equally valuable. But sometimes bonds are formed within an aircrew that would not otherwise develop. We had survived together for many months and his loss has distressed me.'

'I have no words,' the Prince said.

Armstrong took the signal back into his hands, folded it and put it into his pocket. He held his voice steady. 'This message describes an act of criminal folly which, so far as I am aware, has no equal in war. You have given me no reason why I should spare you by keeping it to myself. I feel obliged to take it to the Air Officer Commanding with an account of our conversation. Until the matter is decided, you will of course reveal to no one the nature of the complaint against you, as disclosure could lead to an international scandal. Count Zulka will relieve you as Squadron Commander for the time being.'

He turned to go; there was nothing further to keep him.

'Wait, friend! One minute!' The Prince laid a hand on his arm. 'There are things you do not know, secrets we have not told you.'

'I do not see how they can affect the issue.'

'Yet they do! In justice to the Poles, you must hear them.'

'There can be no excuse for turning your weapons against a friend.'

'Even when that friend is distended with the corpses of men?'

'Even then. I shall go to Garfield Manor in the morning.'

He freed himself from the Prince's hand and went out.

They were beating on his door, those companions of his dreams. Never could he see them clearly. They came often enough to disturb his sleep, and though they struck a chord in his memory he could not give them names. They were faceless young men who did not speak but who showed much liveliness of spirit. Only recently had he guessed who they were, and then he had dismissed them as the illusions of a tired mind.

Tonight the tapping continued, waking him and bringing him to the door. It opened upon the moonlit grass where three figures were standing. Without affording him a moment's fear, it passed through his mind that the Poles had come to erase the

135

only evidence of their mischief; but then he saw that these men wore their best uniform and were standing at attention. Slowly, with a reverent emphasis, they came to the salute.

Prince Karol was plain to see. Although his figure was short he always commanded one's first attention; he brought total commitment to every movement and Armstrong did not doubt that his salute was offered in genuine respect. The bulky figure of Count Zulka was a pace to the rear of his commander. The third figure Armstrong did not at once recognize — a slight man, the whiteness of whose brow and cheek the moonlight could not disguise.

Armstrong said, 'Well, gentlemen, it is the middle of the night. I cannot think what business you have with me at this hour.'

'We come to tell you a story,' the Prince said.

'It is not the time. I have already told you, Prince Karol, that further evidence will not alter my opinion.'

'Sir, you must listen, you must hear us. We insist upon your attention.'

The two officers accompanying the Prince stepped forward silently, not so much in menace as in firm persuasion. The man he had not recognized now revealed a long whitened scar between the ear and the cheek and Armstrong recalled their last meeting on Christmas night; he remembered, too, what the Prince had said of him: *Captain Wolkow comes to us with news. He tells us where our comrades are.*

'I beg you, sir — do not oblige these officers to use their strength,' the Prince continued, his voice vibrant with guarded excitement. 'I break many laws, but never do I raise my hand to my commanding officer.'

'You cannot expect me to submit to force,' Armstrong said.

'I offer none. Only the urging of a desperate heart. It is necessary that we tell you the truth.'

'But I already know the truth.'

'With respect, it is not so! You must hear what happened at Kozlinaya Gora. You must hear Captain Wolkow's story.'

Had he been an English officer, Armstrong would have resisted his argument and sent him away, but the Poles had lived in a dimension of suffering that allowed a different treatment. He stepped back from the door and invited his three visitors into the small sitting room. He lighted the table lamp, gave them chairs and told them he would hear their story. As Wolkow spoke no English, Prince Karol undertook to translate his account sentence by sentence, and Armstrong — aware that a deposition would be required by the court martial — prepared to write down a record of his narrative.

He said, 'Gentlemen, as a courtesy to Prince Karol, I will hear what Captain Wolkow has to say, but only on the understanding that I may record his words in English and that he will later put his signature to the statement with Count Zulka as a witness. You must also understand that, in hearing him, I am doing nothing to prejudice my further action in respect of last night's operation and that I shall have freedom to use his statement in whichever way seems to me best. That is agreed? Very well: what has Captain Wolkow to tell me?'

The Captain, the worser side of whose face was now in shadow, did not speak immediately, as though he were reluctant to retrace the steps he had now to follow. At length he looked squarely at Armstrong with eyes that, despite his youth, were sapped of all freshness and gave his name, rank and service. Then, after Armstrong had written them down, he began his story.

TWELVE

Statement by Captain Wolkow of the Polish Army, recorded by Group Captain D. V. Armstrong between 0135 hours and 0415 hours on 29th April 1945 and twenty-nine years later, on 10th January 1974, handed by him to the Officer Commanding RAF Uxbridge.

My name is Wladyslaw Wolkow. I am twenty-six years old, though I may appear to be older, and I am a Christian. Before the war I was a student at the University of Lublin where I studied law and was a member of the Kosciuszko Society. This was a patriotic group dedicated to the creation of a democratic Poland free from foreign influence and to the encouragement of the liberal arts. At that time Lublin was a free city with a very political spirit; it was from Lublin that a group of workers and peasants had declared Poland's independence in 1918 and we in the Society aimed to preserve her sovereignty and to create workable institutions. But I did not believe that Poland could be defended by words alone and in January 1939 I joined the local battalion of the Reserve Army of the Republic and received the rank of lieutenant. The battalion was mobilized in July and sent to the Polish Ukraine, where we were encamped on the Dniester until the Russian invasion of 17th September. Many of our officers wished to engage the Red Army, but the Republic had collapsed and on 20th September I and my fellow officers were taken prisoner by the Soviet Union.

We spent one or two weeks at Khodorov — I do not remember how long it was — and at this time the officers were separated from the soldiers and the soldiers were sent back to Lwow, from where I believe they were handed over to the Germans for

138

forced labour. Under the Geneva Convention officers cannot be so treated, and early in October the officers were taken by train to Kiev, from there to Bryansk, and finally to the prisoner camp at Kozielsk.

I suppose there were five thousand Polish officers at Kozielsk. Not a pleasant place, but I had friends there. I met many officers, reservists like myself, who were eminent in different fields: there were scientists, artists, leaders of industry and commerce. There were also many members of the regular army who were distinguishable from the others by the stiffness of their carriage and their anger in defeat. One of these was friendly to me and after a time told me his name: he was Prince Karolajczyk of Radom-Striewicz and he had been taken prisoner at Bialystok. From him I learnt of the other prison camps at Starobielsk and Ostashkov where a further ten thousand officers were interned. I believe that at that time the Russians had a total of about fifteen thousand Polish officers in their keeping.

That winter we did not move outside the camp at Kozielsk. The snow fell heavily and in the walled compounds it was beaten an iron grey. It was a time of much anguish [*Marginal note. When the statement was read over to him in Polish, Captain Wolkow changed this word to 'introspection' — D.V.A.*] We had tasted humiliation on two fronts and our spirits were reduced still further by our meagre rations and by the great cold of the Russian winter. We had no news from Poland, but there were rumours of deportations from the eastern regions where many of us came from and of the privations of those still at home. To me it seemed as if Poland had ceased to exist and that we were a people with no country, but Prince Karol reminded me that in the one hundred and twenty years before 1918, when Poland had not featured on the map of Europe, the Polish people had nevertheless retained their language and their spirit and had finally reasserted their independence. Twice in those years they had risen against the Russian oppressor.

It became obvious to me that once again the Russians were trying to absorb or obliterate the Polish people. At Kozielsk we were obliged to attend classes at which we were told of the superiority of the Marxist-Leninist principles and the inevitable triumph of the proletariat. As a former member of the Kosciuszko Society I could not accept these views which indeed had little meaning to one who had lost his country and his right to live to the people who practised them. After the process of re-education, we were interrogated by intelligence officers, sometimes brutally and always within the framework of an incontestable doctrine. I made no secret of my association with the Kosciuszko Society, the opinions of which were described to me as 'incorrect and unrelated to the building of international socialism'. Some of the regular officers did not co-operate under interrogation and instead sang patriotic songs and told the intelligence officers to foul themselves. They were beaten, I believe, but not otherwise harmed. I do not know what these interrogations achieved. I had the impression they were required by regulation but that those taking part had no belief in them and were simply fulfilling a schedule of work; but we noticed that those officers who were less hostile to the Soviet regime were afterwards taken from the main body of prisoners and held in a separate enclosure. They were not many and they were ridiculed by the regular officers who called them *les petit volants* [*ie*, *'the little shuttlecocks': as spoken* — *D.V.A.*] None was from my battalion.

At this time I derived much encouragement from the resolute opinions of Prince Karol, as did many others that I knew. His name had been familiar in the district I came from where he had great estates and his family had been resident for many years. For me and my fellow captives he provided a link with the old Kingdom of Poland as he was descended from the Jagellon dynasty and could count Zygmunt an ancestor. The Prince would not allow that we had been defeated and he urged the utmost resistance to our Russian captors. Through that cold winter he gave the only warmth. In secret, and attested with an oath, he founded *The Society of White Irreconcilables* which took the lily as an emblem and which was dedicated to the liberation of Poland from Russian domination. He did not count the German occupation of western Poland as other than a temporary incursion, because Germany had lapsed into madness and would be beaten by Britain and France and, in time, by America. Hitler was insane and when he was destroyed the German people would recover their sanity. On the other hand the conflict with Russia was age-old and of mortal danger to the Polish people.

Spring came late to the Kozielsk region in 1940. I remember

how the snow rotted in the compound and ran away in rivulets of urine-coloured water and how the grey woodlands became marked with green. In March there was a new rumour in the camp; we were to be released. I did not know where the rumour came from but it was not contradicted by the guards, one of whom said, 'Yes, you are going away from here!' The officers became very excited as they supposed they were going back to Poland, but Prince Karol told them they might find themselves in some further state of captivity, perhaps cutting timber on the Peczora River or in the frozen forests of Karelia. The re-education had ceased, perhaps because it no longer had a purpose in whatever destiny was intended for us.

Finally, in the last week of March, a party of fifty officers was prepared for trans-shipment elsewhere. Their particulars were checked and rechecked, their finger prints were taken and they were inoculated. They were given rations of bread and salt herring sufficient for a short journey. They were very cheerful and we looked upon them with much envy, for no matter what happened to them they were going to be released from the boredom of Kozielsk. After six months of captivity we felt that a movement in any direction was to be preferred to continued confinement. Our comrades were marked for a change of scene. They were marched to the railway station, and I was told that they waved from the trucks as the train moved away. We did not hear from them again.

Throughout April and May further parties were assembled at Kozielsk and taken away by rail. Sometimes there were as few as forty in a party, sometimes as many as three hundred and fifty. At no time did we receive a message from those who had left although most had promised, by some means, to let us know where they were sent. The guards would not tell us and I think most did not know. One I spoke to said only, 'You must not ask me! I do not know where your friends have gone.' By the end of April the number in the camp had been much reduced, but Prince Karol and I remained. Now there were only seven in the room I occupied where formerly there had been eighty-six. Outside in the compound the remaining captives filled only a small corner, though in the hard ground you could still see the footprints of the much greater number who had once been there.

On the first day of May we were given a double ration of skilly and a slice of cake made with fat because it was the festival of the International Labour Movement.

I think it was on the following day that Prince Karol called me outside after it was dark and told me he had been listed for further detention at a place called Pavlishchev Bor. He did not know what would happen to him there or why he was being treated differently from the other officers, but he thought that his connections with the government of Pilsudski might have persuaded the Russians to subject him to further interrogation. At any rate he was to be transferred in the morning and he wanted to leave some record of his movement, so he asked me, if I should be released, to send word of him to the Polish government at that time in exile in Paris. I was to tell them that he had not joined the shuttlecocks. On his side, he undertook to give news of me to my family if he should be more fortunate than I and they were still living. We agreed jointly that, should we survive captivity, we would meet together in the future and uphold the principles represented by the white lily.

Before parting, I asked Prince Karol what he thought had happened to those of our comrades who had already left Kozielsk. He told me he did not know. I pressed him because I felt he did know or had a strong suspicion but he would not tell me. He said only that they, and the officers at Starobielsk and Ostashkov, were a significant part of the Polish ruling class, and I should draw what conclusion best fitted the evidence. He said also — which I did not understand at the time — that they might have been taken to Kozlinaya Gora, an ill-favoured place, where there was a government rest house.

I did not see the Prince again after that night and the guards told me he had been taken to Pavlishchev Bor the next morning. And at about this time those officers who had shown themselves receptive to re-education were also removed from the camp and only about two hundred of us were left. There was nothing we could do but wait until the Russian design for us was fulfilled. It was not an easy time.

Perhaps it was three days later that we were documented in our turn and given a small ration that would not take us far. I no longer believed that we would be released, but I had not let my imagination dwell upon the alternative: I had closed my mind to what might happen to us the next day, the next hour, and simply followed the others to the train, where we occupied carriages without seats. One of the intelligence officers who had conducted my interrogation was beside the track and to him I put the question that everyone was asking: 'Where are we going?'

'To the Hill of Goats,' he replied in Polish, 'which is not a long way. There you will find your friends.'

I do not know how long we were on the train but certainly a night passed and perhaps half of the next day. When I could I sat on the floor and supported my head in my hands because there was no other means of rest. I do not know what brought the words into my mind, but at some moment I recalled how Prince Karol had told me that our comrades might have gone to the rest house at Kozlinaya Gora, and now I remembered that in Russian the name meant 'hill of goats'. I cannot say why the name should have frightened me but I was shaking even above the shaking of the train. I think my companions had also become aware that our destination was one of ill omen; they did not speak of it, but their faces had lost their individual character and become alike in their fear. Some words in Polish were written on the side of the truck at the level of my eyes. I had watched them for more than an hour before I understood their meaning. As far as I can now remember they said, *We are leaving the train at Gniazdowo. We do not know where we are going but we have little hope.* Then followed some names and regiments that were familiar to me. These few words were I believe the only message that ever came back from the thousands who had preceded us.

In the afternoon we came ourselves to Gniazdowo. It was not much of a place, just a siding without a raised platform at the edge of the Katyn forest. The only buildings I saw were some sheds, a plate-layers' hut and a tank for the watering of locomotives. Here we alighted into a square formed by soldiers in the uniform of the NKVD who had their bayonets fixed. It was cold for the season and I was grateful we wore greatcoats and gloves. The first to alight were put straight into lorries and driven away under guard, and we watched them until the lorries became obscured by the trees. Those of us who were left had a long time to wait; we sat upon the ground while the afternoon advanced, not speaking, because no one wished to give words to the single thought that was in our minds. You may ask why so many officers trained in assertive action made no attempt to overpower the guards and run away; I can only suggest that we had learned the fatalism of prisoners, or that we still had hope. One officer asked the guard if he could eat his ration now and he was told that he might as well.

It must have been late when the lorries returned, for the shadows had grown in length and the air had the taste of evening. We boarded the trucks and four guards swung up on to the back of each and cleared a space for themselves with their bayonets. They were not brutal that I saw; they simply moved the men forward, like peasants stacking hay, because otherwise there would have been no place for them to stand. We were driven some distance through the woods of spruce and larch — how far I do not know, but it must have been well beyond earshot of the station — to a place where there was a wooden house amongst the trees. Certainly this was the rest house at Kozlinaya Gora. Here we were discharged from the lorries into a barbed-wire cage surrounded by guards and I believed our destination to be only a few yards away. There was nothing exceptional about the place but for the silence.

In the succeeding hour, the officers were taken from the cage and escorted through the trees to the rest house, and then to somewhere beyond our sight. The first to go — a man whose name I have forgotten — was a tall, regular soldier from a fashionable regiment who ridiculed the guards and walked with a proud, contemptuous step. His pace was faster than that of the escorting soldiers and they broke into a run to keep up with him. It seemed a long time before the shot sounded from inside the wood and then it was the snap of a pistol and not the more solid report of a rifle. It seemed a tiny thing, like a twig breaking; we might have missed it had we not been listening. He was followed by an older man called Badzynski, a reservist academic from the University of Poznan; his face was liquid with fear and the guards used their bayonets to keep him moving forward and once to raise him from the ground. Thereafter the prisoners were dealt with more quickly and usually there were two or three under escort at the same time, and the shots sounded in groups and not singly. The need for haste was obvious as the light was failing and there was still a large number of officers in the cage. For myself, I resolved simply to walk like the regular soldiers and not to fall down; I saw no point in struggling, or in abusing the guards, as some of the young men did, for they were pricked into obedience by the bayonets and it made no difference in the end.

Indeed, from their faces, which were dull and empty, the guards seemed hardly more alive than we were. The division between captor and captive was difficult to draw when both were involved in the same mischance, and often when they walked into the deep shadow under the trees you could not tell which of the uniformed figures was the prisoner. It was growing dark and the cage was nearly empty. I could see just the white faces of those of my companions who were left. I felt as if we were already dead — as if we were a company of ghosts still in the vicinity of Kozlinaya Gora but seeking the new direction. When the hands of the guard were laid upon my arm and I was taken out of the enclosure, I felt no increase of fear; I was already beyond this place and the garment of pain I had worn in the last hours; I was the one free man in the company of menials and I even felt a slight pity for the two shambling creatures who conducted me away from my companions and towards the rest house in the trees.

There was still frost in the ground, but I could see how a path had been worn through the thin grass by those who had preceded me. When we came under the first trees the shadows added to the darkness and one of the guards stumbled. We reached the rest house where uniformed figures stood inside the door. These men were in the uniform of the People's Commissariat for Internal Affairs and like the guards they were slack in their bearing as though they were tired. They did not speak. They pulled my hands behind my back and tied them with cord, and they turned up the wide collar of my greatcoat until it covered nearly the whole of my head. Now I had only a narrow sight between the lapels of my collar. I was led through the rest house and across a verandah where the boards sounded hollow under my feet. From there a path sloped downward into a clearing where figures moved in some exhausting labour. I was led forward — no, I was pushed by the shoulders — until we reached the clearing and came close to a trench which now was filled with shadow.

I was arrested by firm hands perhaps six yards from the edge, and for the first time I realized that my guards had been changed; these were not the low-ranking soldiers of the NKVD but men skilled in their work and performing it with a certain wearied detachment. We could not move forward; there was someone ahead of me, someone whom the attendants kicked behind the knees as they obliged him to kneel and whom they held by the shoulders to keep his body steady. Of the man with the pistol, who came from my left side, I could see little but for his back and that told me nothing but that he was built squarely in the Russian mould and that he was very tired. I saw him extend the pistol until it was touching the upturned collar and feel for the occiput with the muzzle. I do not think that I heard the shot, for the power of dream had dulled every sense except for my sight; but I saw the prisoner start abruptly forward as though touched by a hot iron and then fall loosely on to the ground.

The guards stooped, showing their fatigue, and dragged the prisoner to the lip of the trench, where now that my eyes had grown accustomed to the dusk I could see that other men were working. They, too, were forcing back the onset of sleep as they carried their burdens to a part of the trench not yet filled. The method of their work was plain: at the edges of the trench, where there was a need for tidiness, they had laid the officers head to toe as if they were building a wall and already the wall was about eight bricks deep. In the centre they had worked with less precision. I had seen such methods used in those parts of the country where walls are built out of dry stones and there is no need to keep them narrow.

A lassitude marked every movement in the clearing. Using the weapon as he might have used his hand, the man with the pistol motioned to the guards that I was to be brought forward; so might the lazy dominie have beckoned in the last boy from the school yard. I caught sight of his face as I was taken forward — Russian in outline, not brutal that I could judge, just brought to indifference by an exacting routine that had continued all day. I knew he was exhausted; I knew he was caught in the same remorseless dream as I was. The guards compelled me forward and made me kneel some yards short of the trench's nearer edge. One of them — I could not have said if he was to the left or to the right — increased his pressure on my shoulder in what may have been an affectionate gesture; and then I knew nothing more but for a sensation of violent insult and for the occluding of the mind.

[*Captain Wolkow's statement was suspended at this point to be resumed ten minutes later with the same interpreter and witness.*]

I cannot give you an account of the ensuing hours, nor can I explain exactly how it was that the Soviet machine, which had so far performed with such efficiency, should now have missed a stroke. I do not know what weakness in the mechanism allowed such a thing to happen. I can only infer that, where the chances of survival are a million to one, the millionth prisoner will be spared by mathematical probability. It had to be someone; in this case it was me. I know the executioner to have been tired almost to insensibility and perhaps infirm of purposes after a full day at this work: what is certain is that he missed his mark and only scored the side of my face with his bullet.

Thereafter I remember a slow recovery of sensation in which pain was the mastering element. I opened my eyes to a posthumous twilight that showed me nothing. Yet I knew were I was, and in such a company I had to believe myself dead too and these stirrings of thought the first moments of a long, dull immortality. I could not see the face of the man beside me, but I knew his name and drew some comfort from his companionship. There was no sound but for a tiny hiss that after a while I knew to arise from my own lips. I do not know how long it took me to realize that the drawing of breath was inconsistent with the state of death, but I think it must have been an hour or more and that meanwhile full night had come to the clearing. Of course, the perception that I was alive reawakened the emotion of fear and I began to tremble. In no way did I welcome the gift of life with its continuing pain; I would have preferred to be at one with my companions, a part of a lost dynasty already receding in time and memory; I did not want to lose my membership of this splendid company and face again the cruelty of Katyn forest — alone. But those who are alive cannot escape the responsibility that life entails, and I knew I must relinquish their company and take myself away from this place and back into the fullness of existence. At that moment I had no thought that I might tell the story of Katyn; I had no memory of the white lily and the duty it implied; I was simply moved by a primitive force

147

to get up from the pit and leave the clearing behind me.

There were no guards in Katyn forest; there was no need for them. Nothing moved in the clearing but for my startled heart.

I cannot rely too closely upon my recollection of the next minutes. That I was assisted in leaving the forest I am unable to deny, but from what quarter that assistance came I cannot be certain: let me say only that a hand was laid upon me, much as it had been when I was taken to the lip of the trench, and that it guided me through the trees and on to a path of escape. I have often wondered if this hand was the same that pressed my shoulder at the moment I should have died. It does not seem unlikely. Later I was to hear rumours of what happened to the guards when their job was complete, and it may be my helper already suspected how his silence was to be assured and perhaps desired the news of Katyn to escape. But I may be wrong. It may be that my escape was part of a larger design by the power — I give it no name — that does not allow the truth ever to be wholly suppressed, and that the hand that guided me had no substance other than in my mind.

At daybreak — and of this there is no doubt — I was aided by some countrymen from a Christian community who found me and dressed my wound. They asked me no questions, for plainly they knew the purpose of Katyn forest. Indeed I learned afterwards that the forest had been used as a place of execution since the first days of the Revolution. Czarist officers had been shot here in 1919, Ukrainian dissidents in the late thirties. And I believe those who befriended me may themselves have been taken into the forest later on, when all traces of the massacre were erased and young spruce trees were planted over the graves.

What happened to me after that is not important. There is a wide fellowship of Christian people inside the Soviet Union and with them I lived and worked until Germany invaded Russia a year later, when I became a refugee before the German army. At that time the Polish prisoners still living were released to join the Polish forces, and ultimately I was able to return to the army myself. Of the prisoners released only about four hundred were officers; the rest of those in Soviet custody, numbering nearly fifteen thousand, were never to reappear. I have told you what became of those from Kozielsk, but I cannot say where the rest are lying. I have heard that those from Starobielsk were buried near Kharkov, and that those from Ostashkov were drowned in the White Sea, but as there were no witnesses I cannot say for certain.

In August 1942 I left the Soviet Union and served with the Polish army in the Near East and Italy. I reached England on the 24th December 1944, and the following day I was able to fulfil my undertaking to Prince Karol and the principles of the white lily, given four years earlier at Kozielsk, when I reported to the Prince at Moreton Valence.

Wladyslaw Wolkow
Captain

Translated from the Polish by Prince Karolajczyk of Radom-Striewicz and witnessed by Count Tadeusz Zulka, both officers of the Polish Air Force.

THIRTEEN

The office into which Armstrong was shown had none of the elegance he had expected. The furniture was undistinguished and the paint had not been renewed for a generation. A surplus of books had spilled out of the shelves and on to the floor where part of the filing system was also accommodated. From a small window the daylight made a weak intrusion, and this was supported by naked electric bulbs kept permanently alight. It was not a place where Armstrong himself could have worked with any comfort, but Mr Shane-Gould seemed to find nothing wrong with it.

He lifted his rump one inch from the chair in a gesture of salutation and invited Armstrong to be seated. Armstrong removed a cat, a raincoat and a faggot of newspapers from the visitor's chair and composed himself as well as he could. He felt some lack of confidence in dealing with a civilian whose rank and area of work were by no means clear to him.

He said, 'I have sought Air Ministry approval to visit you in London, as I feel the need for your advice. You will recall our last meeting at Garfield Manor following the attempt by Count Pakorski to carry supplies to Warsaw. I have a further complaint against the Poles — no, not really a similar complaint — with which you can help me.'

Shane-Gould, having spent the whole of his energy in greeting Armstrong, had collapsed into his chair like discarded clothing, but he managed to open one eye and to reveal the hard intelligence that dwelt there. 'Well, what have the Poles been up to?' he asked.

'I would prefer not to say at present. I do not wish to embarrass your department. So far I have kept the matter to myself, not even telling my AOC; I have done this because I am not yet certain what action I should take. If I decide not to prefer charges. I should not have disclosed the offence.'

The sour eye of Mr Shane-Gould did not respond to this sophistry of the military mind. 'As you wish,' was the whole of his reply.

'I confess to some conflict of duty. I have always believed that an act of disobedience, no matter that it may seem justified by circumstances, can never be excused because the act itself is intolerable. No good will come of it that can possibly make up for the harm that has been done. That remains my opinion; but it may be there are cases where the service convention cannot be applied without risk of injustice — where, if I may put it so, the mitigating factors are strong enough for the offence to be overlooked.'

Shane-Gould offered no help and Armstrong realized he had done nothing but put his mind in order.

He continued rapidly, almost desperately, 'You understand me — I have always supposed that one offence could not be used to justify another, and that the duty of the serviceman was absolutely to resist provocation. But the factors involved are so appalling I might have to change this opinion.'

The tumbled frame of Mr Shane-Gould came to minimum life when he realized that Armstrong had finished speaking. 'How much does it matter?' he asked. 'An armistice in Europe will be proclaimed next week and after that a large measure of demobilization will take place. With respect, I cannot see how a failure to press charges can make much difference at present.'

'I believe any departure from discipline to be of consequence, sir. However, as the local commander, it is for me to decide what further action is to be taken, but before I can do that I need you to confirm what the Poles have told me.'

'Very well; what is their story?'

'A terrible story. I find it hard to believe, and yet it was told to me in sincerity.'

Shane-Gould separated his hands, to indicate that these days frightfulness came in every dimension.

Armstrong said, 'I am asked to accept that in 1940 the Russians murdered the whole of the Polish officer corps then in their hands.'

He could not tell if Shane-Gould was surprised. His lower lip, attached only loosely to his jaw, swung back and forth under some meagre stimulation, but in no other way was his composure broken. Then he sat up and engaged Armstrong with a weak smile.

'Of course, the charge is not a new one,' he said.

'It is not?'

'My dear chap, Doctor Goebbels made great play of it two years ago, when the German army disinterred some graves near Smolensk.'

'I did not know. I had not heard.'

'It was reported in the press at the time, not prominently, because we saw no need to repeat German propaganda.'

'But the story was true?'

'I have not said so. The Russians of course claimed that the Germans were guilty and last year assembled a commission to prove it.'

'Then what is your opinion, sir?'

Shane-Gould closed his eyes, as if the answer to this question could be perceived more readily in the dark. 'His Majesty's Government has not conceded that the Soviet Union is guilty,' he said.

Armstrong's heart sank; he had hoped for clear guidance; but none the less he pressed his point. 'Look, sir: I know nothing about political necessities. I don't even read the newspapers very much. But can I assume, if the Government takes that view, that the Russians are innocent?'

'It would be as well to do so.'

'I can see the advantage of siding with an Ally in a dispute of this sort, but when we are talking about the murder of fifteen thousand servicemen we would, I take it, speak only the truth.'

The official opened his eyes again, just a trifle more widely than hitherto, as if he looked upon a new prospect. 'I have said, Group Captain, that the British Government has not accused the Russians of this crime, and certainly they do not wish to give further circulation to Nazi propaganda. If it is of help to you, I will point to certain factors that attest to German guilt. In the first place, the Smolensk area and the prison camp concerned had been in German hands for eighteen months before the good Doctor Goebbels discovered the graves in Katyn forest — that is to say, plenty of time for them to have shot the prisoners and rigged the evidence to incriminate the Soviet Union. It has been the aim of German foreign policy to divide the Allies wherever possible, and the fabrication of a Russian atrocity against the Poles would serve this purpose very well. You cannot tell me the Nazis were not capable of executing a handful of prisoners: the incident has their style, and it matches their behaviour in Poland as a whole. There is a further point that you, as a military man, will find convincing.'

'What is that?' Armstrong asked. Any guidance in this dark forest would be welcome to him.

'It has been established that the prisoners were shot by seven-point-six-five-calibre bullets.'

'And that is significant?'

'It is, when you recall that this ammunition was only made at the Genshow factory near Karlsruhe.'

'I see.' Armstrong sighed; there was no easy solution to his dilemma. 'You told me last year that the Russian failure to take Warsaw was designed to eliminate the resistance. I had thought the murder of the officers might be part of the same policy — that of destroying the Polish leadership.'

'I suggest that you have taken too simple a view of Eastern European politics.'

'You may be correct. I have said that I do not understand these things.' Sadly, he rose to leave. 'There is one point that still troubles me —— '

Shane-Gould looked at him with eyes that, behind their opacity, might have been amused. 'Which is?'

'Why should the Poles have so fierce a dislike for the Soviet Union?'

'My dear chap, they've always hated the Russians, ever since the annexations under the Czars. This has been an obsession with Poles of the ruling class.'

'If they could produce a witness to the massacre —— '

'He would be an imposter. There were no witnesses.'

'A survivor, perhaps?'

'Could anyone have survived?'

Armstrong took up his hat and gloves, aware that his problem had not been removed.

'Sorry to have destroyed your theory,' Shane-Gould said

good-humouredly, while his hand sought in the tray for his next employment. 'If I were you, I shouldn't become involved with the Polish neurosis; they're given to fantasies of the most fearsome sort. Many Poles sincerely believe that the Bear will devour them and they can see nothing but menaces in Soviet attitudes. It's a national delusion best overlooked. Needless to say, we do not wish to impugn the Soviet Union.'

'I understand,' Armstrong said, taking his leave. 'Of course, your evidence does not help me in disposing of the case against the Poles.'

'Padre,' he said, 'a word with you, if you please. I will not keep you long.'

The defaulters had kept the tiny station church in a high state of polish, as if for inspection. The altar linen was clean and well starched and by the door the prayer books had been mustered in a precise formation.

'It is possible you can help me. I am troubled.'

Padre Shenstone ushered the Station Commander into his office, where the same good order ruled. Armstrong took a seat facing the Chaplain. He saw the broad shoulders, to which the service boxing ring had given a forward inclination; he saw how the nose had been broken in some fierce combat of long ago.

He said, 'I have a difficult duty, one I must find strength enough to perform. An officer within my command has committed a most serious offence, and he has produced evidence in mitigation that may or may not be true. If it is true, I might have to forgive him. If it isn't, then he has made a deliberate attempt to deceive me and to secure my silence and is, of course, the more guilty. I cannot see my way ahead.'

The Padre hammered his fist into the palm of his left hand with force enough to discourage any moral backsliding. But it was more a statement of faith than a solution of Armstrong's problem. He scratched his chin, seeking inspiration. 'You have said that the evidence, if true, would mitigate the offence. It would not, I presume, remove it.'

'It would not.'

'Then you must ask yourself if the offence, even when all the circumstances are taken into account, does not itself remain worthy of punishment.'

Armstrong didn't reply at once; he was looking deeply into his heart. 'I believe it does. I believe it to have been unforgivable by the standards of conduct I was taught to respect. But I am no longer young and I may be too rigid in my sympathies.'

Catching sight of a familiar feature, the Padre said, 'Sir, you can only act within your conception of guilty conduct. You were appointed to this command to apply your judgement: therefore you must use it fearlessly.'

'Perhaps ... perhaps.' Armstrong did not feel the Chaplain's certainty. 'It seemed a simple matter at first, but on reflection I foresee terrible consequences. I believe my country will be embarrassed at the moment of victory and that other officers, whose only fault was to obey their superior, will have to stand trial.'

Shenstone raised his great shoulders. Not a reflective man, he was prepared to let the consequences fall where they might, like crows alighting in upper branches. 'I don't think you should concern yourself with every possibility. Your job is to define whether or not there are charges to answer. Your conscience tells you that an officer is in default and deserving of punishment. Very well — call him before you. If you attempt a compromise you will damage your own moral nature.'

Armstrong stayed silent, looking at the polished linoleum. He said, 'There is the officer himself. Not, I am sure, a wicked man, and undoubtedly one who has suffered. A man with courage and a certain dark patriotism. A man I can even like in a strange way. I do not know what will happen to him if he goes on trial.'

'He will have only himself to thank for the penalty.'

There was comfort in this simplicity; it was like an old familiar cloak that Armstrong could gather about him in thankfulness. He remained silent a long time. Then he said, 'I think you are right. I don't see how I can fail to bring charges. In my heart I don't believe that revenge for injury is ever an excuse for a crime of your own. In war we must bear terrible pains and stick to our duty. The officer must account to a court martial.'

He considered the point again, nodded briefly, and stood up.

'Thank you, Padre. You have helped me a great deal.'

He kept his voice low, so that it should not carry to the outer office; he had still to keep the closest guard upon the nature of the Polish offence. He was also speaking with extreme difficulty.

'You will understand, Wing Commander, that I have only reached my decision after long and painful reflection, but I am convinced that an attack upon an Ally in time of war—no matter what the underlying circumstances — can never be tolerated. It abuses the sacred trust the head of state has vested in the individual when appointing him to a commission. It is an affront to all those who have obeyed their orders and done their duty. In the circumstances I can only inform the Polish Air Force that I intend to order a summary of evidence with a view to the formulation of charges.'

He had not invited the Prince to be seated; the matter was too grave for that. The Prince stood before Armstrong's desk, his hands at his sides, his lips in small movement as if he were attempting a smile.

He said stoutly, 'Very well! Do as you must. I am at fault.'

'You will recognize the danger of your position.'

'Mon Dieu, I have lived with peril since the day I was born.'

'I have yet to see the evidence written down,' Armstrong pursued, 'but I do not see how the charges can be other than most serious. In attacking the forces of an Ally, you were without doubt giving aid to the King's enemies, and that would seem to require a charge of treason. Under the Treachery Act of 1940 you do not have to owe allegiance to the British Crown to be convicted of this offence. The penalty, I think, is known to you.'

'So it is! Take him out, bind his hands, bang! An end to wickedness.'

'I must tell you I am not joking.'

'Dear friend, I can see from your eyes that you are not joking. You are dismayed. I have used you cruelly.'

'I admit that my decision has caused me some distress.'

'Then I am grieved,' Prince Karol said, a claim that strangely Armstrong found himself ready to concede. 'None of my actions do I regret but that I have made my commanding officer suffer.'

'I was obliged to take into account that, probably as a result of your disobedience, an RAF aircraft was lost.'

'I carry their names in my heart.'

'I cannot be certain that political considerations will not prevent a trial from taking place; the whole matter may be suppressed before charges are raised; but I feel compelled to take some action in what I believe to be a guilty venture.'

He wished that Prince Karol would show some concern for the danger in which he stood. The signal from Hayden Chance, transmitted in the hour of his death, and the Prince's own admission to his commanding officer, would together be more than enough to convince a court martial that he was guilty of the most terrible of all crimes — an act of treachery. There might also be charges against the aircraft captains who accompanied him. Furthermore, if the Soviet government got wind of the proceedings they would press for exemplary punishment for this exponent of the counter-revolution and doubtless for the officers who supported him. The Stettin raid could become one of the most notorious military adventures in history.

The Prince fastened his eyes upon Armstrong, not in estrangement but in affection. 'From the beginning I know that you will charge me. You are a man of good faith who can do no less. Indeed, I do not wish you to blunt your honour on account of the madcap Poles whose memories you do not share. I desire only that you know why we act so. A trial, of course, will illuminate our cause.'

'A trial, Prince Karol, would plainly be held in camera. An attempt would be made to limit publicity, to conceal any evidence that might embarrass this country in its dealings with the Soviet Union.'

'You will excuse me, but it cannot be so. If I am tried there will be questions from influential Poles. At present they do not know of my transgressions, but they will learn. The matter will be raised in the British House of Commons by those Members of Parliament who wish to darken the name of Russia. The story of Katyn will be revived, so will the martyrdom of the Warsaw patriots. The Soviet *apparat* will be seen for the bloodthirsty tyranny it is.'

Armstrong could not let his mind venture into the larger world of political consequences. He folded his hands. 'That may be so. I cannot judge all the issues; I can only apply what I believe to be the correct procedure in a case of disobedience.'

'Aye, so! I am disobedient; I do not deny it.'

'You will of course be entitled to produce what evidence you please in mitigation of sentence. If the relief of Warsaw is raised, I will be prepared to say what I know of Count Pakorski's flight and the forces bearing upon him. The statement made to me by Captain Wolkow will be available to the court and they may place on it what credence they please.'

Now the Prince turned a wondering gaze upon Armstrong, the look of a man who for the first time appreciates a danger. He said softly, 'Then you have not believed me. Ah — so!'

'Where Wolkow's story is concerned, I cannot express an opinion. That will be a matter for the court —— '

'You think I bring Wolkow to you, simply to tell you lies? You think I come by night to deceive you?'

'You do not have to convince me one way or the other, Prince Karol. In any case, even the sharpest provocation would not justify a private war against an Ally of this country.'

'My friend, you lacerate my heart. I do not care that you have me shot for the Stettin raid; I have been a dead man from the beginning. But do not tell me I have come to you with a falsehood.'

'I cannot judge.'

'Never have I lied to my commanding officer!'

'It is not, at this time, a matter of consequence. I would be able to tell the court that Wolkow made his statement to me in apparent sincerity, and you would be able to call him as a witness in a plea before sentence.'

'Such things are trifles if, in your heart, you think me guilty of deception. I belong to the old order in Poland and I do not offer a fallacious story to the officer set over me and whom I revere. Tell me you have not doubted my word!'

At this moment, with the Prince facing court martial on a capital charge, Armstrong wished he could extend this comfort to him, but the advice of Shane-Gould was still a powerful influence in his mind. He said, 'I do not want to disbelieve you, but there is a difference of opinion over Katyn. The British government does not take the view that the Russians were responsible.'

'No! They take the part of the Soviet Union, they say it was the Germans. It is political knavery —— '

'I do not think I should express an opinion,' Armstrong said.

No doubt that the Prince was troubled; his eyes sought in Armstrong's face for evidence of a restored trust. 'Do not think that I lied,' he implored softly. 'You and I, we care nothing for the men of politics. Their world is an ugly place where they practise the black art of expediency. They will be damned when the reckoning is made — them and their vile servants together. But we are military men with an ancient code of which fidelity is the principal part. Wolkow told you the truth. So have I. We could do no less.'

These words, which found an answering harmony in Armstrong's mind, might have convinced him of Wolkow's good faith were it not for his opinion that no official of the Foreign Office would convey an absolute untruth. He wanted to believe the Prince, the warmth of whose friendship might have filled the hollow places of his heart, but he did not see how this was possible against such important testimony.

'Listen!' Prince Karol laid a hand upon Armstrong's own, which did not seem an impertinent gesture then. 'I will give you proof. There is a man who knows the truth of these things. A Doctor Skatowicz. Not a man you will care for — a renegade Pole, a man who before the war followed both the Left and the Right and who ended in bitterness. It is possible we can reach him now that western Germany has been occupied. Members of the exiled government have been looking for him, and maybe they have found him; they will need his testimony for the trial of war criminals that must follow the end of the war. I will take you to that man and you will hear from him what happened in Katyn forest.'

The interview had left Armstrong without strength. He did not wish his decision to be deferred still longer, but he could not deny a brother officer the chance to redeem his good name on a point that mattered to him. With exhausted patience, he said, 'I cannot see that the truth or falsehood of the Katyn story should alter my attitude to the Stettin raid. One offence does not justify another. But if my faith in your honesty of purpose is of concern to you, I will listen to what further evidence there is.'

He could grant that much to a man facing death and one whom he could have liked if things had been different. He stood up, declaring the interview at an end.

The Prince was relieved of his disquiet. 'You are kind, sir. I do not care what penalty I suffer so long as you believe me. I will make all arrangements for a meeting with Doctor Skatowicz, when you will be a guest of the Poles.'

On 4th May, the Commander-in-Chief declared that operations in Europe were suspended while an armistice was arranged. At Moreton Valence they pulled tarpaulins over the aircraft engines and removed the ammunition belts from the gun turrets. But elsewhere the squadrons had turned to other work. British personnel were pouring into the occupied areas of Germany, bringing a new administration to the ruined cities: they were carried by the bombers that now put in to German airfields hastily repaired for the task. Airmen walked in the towns that hitherto they had seen only from a great height. Operation Exodus, the recovery of prisoners of war from Germany, had been in progress for more than a week, and a Polish squadron forty miles away at Faldingworth was committed to this task. It was in a Lancaster of this, the Masovian Squadron, that Armstrong and Prince Karol flew to Germany on 6th May. Armstrong didn't know from what sources the Prince derived his information, but clearly Polish agents had been active in seeking out witnesses to atrocity and had traced Doctor Skatowicz to Cologne. It was believed they would find him there, and Armstrong felt obliged to grant Prince Karol this indulgence; the Polish Air Force had made the other arrangements, with courtesy but with a lack of interest that made it plain they knew nothing of Prince Karol's offence.

The sun blazed in the Channel and the cockpit was filled with light. They flew towards a continent redeemed, the guns manned against a final enemy initiative but with little fear of interception. From the cockpit windows Armstrong saw the outline of the Schelde which he remembered as if from an ugly dream. Now the armies of the east and west had joined, Berlin had fallen, the malevolent creature who had abused Europe for twelve years was dead and his body had been destroyed. The sun played upon the fields of Westphalia as if to dissolve all memory of the sinister forces that had been in occupation there; but as the Lancaster lost height into the airfield at Wahn, Armstrong saw that the ground was broken by craters and that half the houses were burned.

From Wahn they were conducted by a silent courier — Armstrong did not learn his name, and he wore plain clothes — to an undamaged house on the outskirts of Cologne where Armstrong was introduced to Doctor Skatowicz.

Not a big man; indeed, the flesh covered his frame only poorly and the clothes he wore seemed to have been built for someone larger, happier. The long head, where the lines of the skull were easily traced, was in constant but irregular movement, as if he were trying to escape from restraining hands; the eyes retained their sharp intelligence, but the lower face, the fallen cheeks, the supple mouth, were marked with a fatalism which now and again hardened into disgust. Here then was Europe in defeat. The courier had spoken in German, but Prince Karol addressed the witness in English, the language of the victors.

'You understand me, Doctor? I believe you are fluent in several languages.'

With a dismissive shrug, Doctor Skatowicz said, 'I speak seven European languages. I am a doctor of philosophy, of medicine and of other things besides. I suspect I will understand you.'

For Armstrong's benefit, the Prince then gave an account of the doctor's credentials. He was a Silesian Pole formerly of the faculty of the University of Breslau; he had been domiciled variously in Poland, France and Germany, and it was now his wish to become an American citizen. Before the war he had adhered to the far Left, but with the German-Soviet alliance of 1939 his sympathies had lurched rightward: today he had no politics but for an angry disbelief in everyone's intentions. In April 1943 he had joined the Polish Red Cross Commission appointed under German auspices to examine the newly discovered graves at Katyn.

'I had no love for the Germans,' Skatowicz said, and it was clear from his voice that he did not care if they believed him or not, 'neither had the other members of the Commission. Poland had endured three years of their occupation. Only a week before our arrival in Katyn the Germans had started the systematic murder of Polish Jews in the Warsaw ghetto. We were suspicious; we were looking for any evidence that might support the Russian claim that the Germans themselves were guilty. But it is the truth that we were not hampered in our investigations or coerced in our findings.'

In consideration for Prince Karol, Armstrong turned his mind to the dark forest far inside Russia where two years earlier Skatowicz had stood at the graveside as the Polish officers were exhumed. He heard how the officers were lying face downward, their hands tied behind them and pulled up towards the neck, where there was a second knot. The weight of the dead and the acid of their decomposition had caused the bodies to fuse together and pickaxes had been applied to separate them. The glade had filled with the terrible stench of putrefaction. When the bodies had been torn apart, they were examined by the Polish Red Cross and by the members of an international commission which had also been brought to the forest. In every case the bullet had entered at the rear of the skull and followed an upward course to exit from the forehead. They slit the pockets and looked at the papers concealed there, learning the names and the intimate secrets of the dead. They examined the rope, the ammunition, the young spruce trees planted over the graves. They were not hindered by the Germans, only by a cloud of flies that had gathered in the glade as soon as the grave was opened ... Armstrong listened with the care he always gave to spoken testimony, knowing that his instinct for falsehood would warn him if the evidence was untrue; but this sour witness, who spoke without commitment, with just the lassitude of disillusion, did not seem to be lying.

'I think I wanted the Germans to be guilty,' Skatowicz said. 'Their crimes were so great it would have been simpler to add this to the indictment against them. It is comforting to contain villainy within one nation. I had been a man of the Left and had still some belief in the Marxist solution. And certainly the Germans had the stomach for this thing. But we were scientists trained to examine the evidence and to base our finding upon what we saw, and there could be only one conclusion.'

The Prince was looking, not at the doctor but at his commanding officer; he wanted to know if the doctor's next words would restore Armstrong's faith in his truthfulness. It was strange to see anxiety in such a proud man and Armstrong was moved more than he cared to be then.

Skatowicz said, 'One factor alone would decide which hand had killed them — the length of time they had lain in the ground. Katyn forest was not taken by the Germans until the autumn of 1941; it followed, by a logic so simple that even the Nazis could understand it, that if the bodies were more than eighteen months old only the Russians could have killed them.' He paused, the ghost of a smile moving his lips, as if he were asking how much it mattered who killed them when in Europe the graves lay thickly together and outside these windows Cologne still smouldered.

'Well?' said the Prince.

'They had been in the ground at least three years. We were doctors; we could not have been mistaken. The decalcification of the skulls and the degeneration of tissue pointed to execution in the spring of 1940. If you find that evidence obtuse, then consider this.' He made his next points with the unconcern of a scientist assembling data. 'The rope was Russian made. Many of the younger men had bayonet wounds made just before death, and they were square, matching the Russian bayonet. The manner of shooting was that traditionally adopted by the NKVD in their execution of political opponents. The Commission had found no documents on the men dated later than May 1940, and the trees planted over the graves had three years of growth. If it matters to anyone,' Skatowicz concluded, and his voice implied that it did not, 'every authority present at Katyn in the spring of 1943 agreed that Polish officers were murdered by the NKVD in 1940, soon after they were known to have been taken from the prison camp at Kozielsk.'

Armstrong nodded. He wanted to believe this witness; he wanted to reaffirm his trust in Prince Karol even though he could not suppress the charge of treason. But one point remained in his mind from his interview with Mr Shane-Gould in London. He said awkwardly, 'There is the question of the ammunition used to execute these men. I had understood it was of German make.'

Skatowicz lifted his head, stirred by a memory. 'It *was*. It was Genshow ammunition.'

'Would that not suggest the Germans were responsible?'

'It might, if that were the only factor considered. But the Commission examined the records of the German ordinance and established that ammunition of this type had been exported to Poland, the Baltic states and the Soviet Union in the years before the war.'

'Very well; the point is not valid.' Armstrong let it pass from his mind to join the cloud of fabrication and false witness that was accumulating over the incident, even as the flies had been drawn to that distant clearing. 'I am satisfied with the evidence I have heard,' he said. 'I see no need for elaboration.'

Skatowicz said abruptly, and for the first time his voice was hardened by indignation, 'It is the truth, but it will not survive. No, not for a minute! The victors will suppress Russian guilt and the Poles will get no hearing.'

'The truth will come out after the war,' Armstrong assured him.

'Friend, you have a faith in Allied motives I cannot share. When the war criminals are put on trial, the Russians will include the Katyn massacre in their indictment of the German leadership. The guilty will play the part of prosecutor. When they find they cannot prove it, the charge will be dropped for want of evidence and the Germans will continue to be blamed.' He laughed; it might have been the last laughter in Europe.

'I hope that is untrue,' Armstrong said. 'We have fought to re-establish justice.'

Skatowicz did not argue but looked through the window, smiling faintly, to where the ruin of a neighbouring house offered some sort of contradiction. 'I will not destroy your illusion, friend.'

'Prince Karol, I see no need for us to remain here. I am grateful to the Doctor for his evidence.' Armstrong had resumed the role of Station Commander, from whom authority must flow. He went outside the house, leaving Skatowicz to his bitter reverie. He drew the Prince to one side where the courier could not hear him.

At first he could not find the words he needed. 'I had not wanted to disbelieve you,' he said after a while. 'It was simply that I was given a different story by those I had supposed incapable of falsehood. I now accept that they lied as a matter of expediency and that the Russians have made a deliberate attempt to destroy the Polish leadership.'

The Prince was a shorter man than Armstrong, but he drew himself to his full height as if fortified by this renewed trust. He gave a stiff little bow, saying nothing.

'You understand, I can only reaffirm my confidence in your good faith; I cannot condone the Stettin raid.'

'I ask nothing more. Of the Stettin raid I am guilty.'

'However, as it plainly matters to you, I now accept the truth of Wolkow's statement and concede without reservation that you have never attempted to mislead me.'

'Then I am restored to your heart!'

Armstrong moved his feet in embarrassment. 'If you wish to put it like that — yes. I assure you of my continued fellowship and affection.'

A strange thing to say to a man facing trial for his life but here in the sunlight of a ruined city he knew it to be true.

The car was starting towards Wahn when Armstrong said upon impulse, 'I would like to drive into Cologne.'

The courier, who had not spoken before, now looked over his shoulder from the driver's seat. 'I cannot believe that Herr Oberst wishes to visit Cologne,' he said.

'I would not have asked if I did not wish it.'

'Markovski, please do as you are bidden,' the Prince said.

'But in Cologne there are things that should not be seen ——'

'Even so, we must go there. Kindly turn the car.'

The courier did as the Prince told him and ten minutes later they were approaching the ruins of Colgone.

Armstrong, like every airman in Bomber Command, knew the shape of the old city on the Rhine which had been at the centre of the air war since the bombers found their strength; he had seen it from a high vertical point of vision, like a lifeless map, and he remembered the configuration of the railways, the placing of the Rhine bridges and the position of the great Gothic cathedral that had always caught his eye. That pile of red stone had never gone down but had remained throughout the onslaught to mark the centre of the town — to affirm, as well, a continuing life on the tormented ground: the twin spires of fretted masonry had risen above the ruins for three whole years of war. Armstrong had not wanted to see Cologne without the intervening distance, but he had been moved by a sudden sense of obligation to visit the city he had helped to destroy.

The road they followed had been cleared of debris leaving a narrow space where a vehicle could move slowly. At first he could not see over the banks of rubble that rose on either side, but he could smell the fire and taste the pungent smoke. Markovski told him they were on the old Frankfurterstrasse that led into the city from the south-west, but he would not have known. Once, twice, they were halted by heavy vehicles coming towards them, bearing away loads of fallen brick. Although Cologne had surrendered to the American First Army a month before, ambulances were still in movement where access to the ruins could be gained; they were lifting the dead as they were uncovered and taking them outside the city. Their view widened at what had been the junction with Kalkerstrasse and Armstrong could see how the devastation continued in level planes to the river. The bombs had brought an anonymity to these streets which were alike in their ruin: only a church, a school, an arcade of shops retained a semblance of their former shape. They continued to the bank of the Rhine where the old road bridge was breached at the centre span and they could go no further.

Armstrong got out of the car and walked on to the first arch of the bridge from where he could see the greater part of Cologne. He stood quite still, as though in the presence of an august authority. Beyond the river, like a desolate ocean, lay the ruins of the old city; he saw succeeding waves of rubble reaching away until dissolved in the haze. There was no movement but for the tiny endeavours of the searching parties. Here and there the smoke drifted from buried fires. Northward, two spans of the railway bridge lay in the current, while to the south there were barges and sea-going craft sunk at their moorings. Only the great cathedral had substance in this terrible place, but even that glowed rose-red in the sunlight as if it still contained some part of the fire.

After a while Armstrong turned to Prince Karol, saying, 'I had not known. I had only seen it from the air.'

'Come, you must not distress yourself,' the Prince said, taking his arm to guide him back to the car. 'It was all in settlement. The Germans were guilty beyond forgiveness.'

Armstrong freed his arm and spoke to Markovski. 'Can you tell me, if you please, how many people died here?'

'I can, mein Herr, but I suggest the matter is better disregarded.'

'I wish to know.'

'I understand that so far twenty thousand bodies have been recovered in Cologne and the suburbs.'

'I see. That is a large number.'

'There were more than two hundred and sixty raids upon the city,' Markovski said.

The Prince said strongly, 'They were guilty. They devastated Europe. They deserved no pity.'

'I suppose not,' Armstrong replied.

He walked slowly off the bridge to where the car was waiting. Some bystanders looked strangely at the RAF uniform, but their faces were dulled by the tedium of disaster and they did not speak.

When Armstrong was again seated, he said, 'I had not known. I had expected great damage, but this I had not imagined.'

He sat in silence while Markovski drove them through the broken suburbs towards Wahn.

After a time, as if rising from the bottom of the sea, the Prince said, 'So, justice was done! We came by night and blew the Boche to pieces. Recall, my friend, the people they had killed.'

'I had not forgotten them.'

'It was a majestic reckoning.'

'Prince Karol, I did what my duty required. I made ninety-six operations, of which seven at least were against this city. I believed it necessary to destroy German industry and that the means were justified in the context of a ruthless war. But I have to confess that the sight of Cologne has distressed me. Why, quite, I do not know.'

'It has been a long war. There are thirty million dead in Europe and Asia. We will not let the sight of one ruined city disturb our judgement.'

But at that moment Armstrong could not employ his judgement at all; his mind showed him only the ravaged stones. He said, without knowing why, 'You told me the number of Polish officers murdered by the Russians. I have forgotten it.'

'We believe there were fifteen thousand,' Markovski said.

'In other words, fewer than have died here.'

At his side, the Prince stirred in disquiet. 'Sir, you are tired —
you have seen things that perhaps you should not have seen.
You cannot compare prisoners murdered by the secret police
with those who die as a result of their own transgression.'

'Perhaps not,' Armstrong said, feeling his ignorance. 'I am not
a philosopher — I am just a regular officer. It is simply that I
find it difficult to choose between one dead body and another.'

On his return to Moreton Valence the following afternoon, Armstrong sought the seclusion of his rooms. It was not his custom
to reflect; usually he made his decisions swiftly and thought no
more about them. Through the perilous days of the bomber
offensive he had exercised command with detachment and with
no break in his composure. It was not so now. Once he took up
the telephone and placed a call to the Air Officer Commanding,
but a minute later he cancelled it with equal decision.

As the empty rooms gave him no help, he took his car and
drove at a steady pace round the perimeter road. At a place
between one dispersal and the next, where no one was in sight,
he walked in the long grass near the boundary fence. Eyebright
and pimpernel were growing under the wire. The airfield was
quiet; likewise the sun-suffused sky where there was no intrusion
but for some ribs of cirrus far above him. A minute passed,
another followed. He watched the shadows extend as the afternoon advanced. But the answer was not here either, and Armstrong returned to his car, rebuking himself for this waste of
time.

At the car door he stopped. Where the brow of the airfield cut
across the lower sky, coloured balls of fire were rising and falling, leaving trails of smoke. The tower was firing Verey lights.
He drove at a brisk pace to the other side of the airfield and
parked under the tower.

The Air Traffic Control Officer, Squadron Leader Cooper,
was on the balcony above him.

'What is it, Cooper?' Armstrong called.

'The end, sir. The German armies have surrendered.'

Armstrong felt nothing: in his mind the resonance of war still
continued.

'When is the victory to be celebrated?'

168

'Tomorrow.'

'Very well. You may stand-down the aircrews. I will announce details of a commemorative parade within one hour.'

He went into his office and summoned the Adjutant and the SWO, and together they drafted an order for a parade at nine o'clock the next morning. Then he sent them away with no acknowledgement of the war's end.

He remained at his desk, motionless. Once he heard raucous voices at a distance as elsewhere the victory was marked, but mostly the station was wrapped in the silence of peace. So, it was over. He had not meant to beckon the past, but now he remembered the outrageous nights when they had ridden in the folds of darkness while on the ground the fires were spreading with the wind. Hamburg, Dresden, Cologne — these names had been festivals in the calendar of Bomber Command; but the towns themselves had lain beyond comprehension, like objects at the bottom of the sea, and he had not known how completely they had been destroyed.

Cologne . . .

Half an hour later, his movements as spruce as ever, he took up his cap and gloves and went out to his car. From the domestic site a mile away he could hear the beginnings of celebration. He drove right-handed round the airfield until he came to the Polish site where he stopped outside the squadron headquarters. Salutes were flung at him from left and right; so plainly the Poles had not relaxed their discipline at the moment of victory and were keeping their muscle firm. He entered the headquarters and knocked at the commander's door.

Armstrong could tell that Prince Karol was glad to see him. His face gathered warmth as he rose from his chair, but there was wonder in his eyes as well, as if he had already divined the purpose of Armstrong's visit.

'I will not sit,' the Station Commander said. 'I will be brief.'

The walls of the office were hung with swords, flags and trophies — symbols of a tradition Armstrong did not share.

He said, 'The war is over and we have won.'

The Prince shook his head. 'Forgive me — the Poles have not won. The Red Army is in occupation of our country.'

'Nevertheless operations are ceasing in Europe and tomorrow is the first day of peace. I must try to see things plainly.'

He walked the floor to set his mind in movement. He came face to face with the head of a wild boar mounted upon a shield and backed by crossed lances.

'I know nothing of your country,' he said then, with the vehemence of embarrassment. 'I do not know what it is like when your homeland is invaded and your houses burnt. More particularly, I do not know what you feel when your fellow officers are shamefully murdered and hidden in an unmarked grave.'

The Prince raised his head in proud remembrance of that excellent company. 'You are blessed,' was all he said.

'But I have played a part in war and I have seen a town I helped to destroy. The dead are the dead, no matter how they died. I really cannot judge your action at Stettin.'

The Prince didn't seem relieved; he simply looked away from Armstrong at some dark future of his own devising. 'You are kind —— '

'Kindness has nothing to do with it. In my opinion you are guilty, as the raid was inexcusable. By the rules of war you should face court martial and suffer the consequences. But I concede that the provocation was very great and that — in a sense — we have ourselves added to the horror of these years. I have nothing more to say.'

As though still in a sombre dream, the Prince rose from his desk and stood facing Armstrong. 'I have placed you in great difficulty. It has hurt me to use you so, but I could not help it. It will be better for you to arrest me —— '

'I have given you my decision.'

'Come, my friend!' The Prince held out his wrists, inviting Armstrong to bind them. 'Put the manacles on my hands. Throw me in some darkened place. Do not deny your conscience on account of me.'

'I haven't done so. My conscience tells me nothing.'

'But the war is not yet over for the Poles, and I may still offend you!'

Gently, Armstrong moved away from the Prince, declining to make him captive, speaking softly now. 'There is nothing more you can do. Your squadron is disengaged, and all other units are being brought to a standstill.'

'I cannot acquiesce in the injury done to the Poles.'

Armstrong could feel only sorry for these grief-driven people and he tried to find words of comfort. 'Your struggle must take a different form. I'm sure the guilty will be punished, no matter on which side they served. There will be a reckoning —— '

'Aye, the guilty will be punished — they will be derided and hanged. But only those who were defeated.'

'You must cool your temper. Everyone has something to forgive.'

'Forgive? I do not understand the word. You cannot forgive when your belly is liquid with bitterness.'

He could not soften the Polish anger and had been foolish to try, but he was repelled by the idea that the war didn't end with the surrender of the enemy. He realized they were no longer alone, that the taciturn figure of Count Zulka was behind him, leaning against the door as if he were holding Armstrong prisoner.

The Station Commander changed his position, feeling himself threatened, feeling the need to keep their voices fluent. He said, 'Come gentlemen, we will celebrate the victory. You will accompany me to the mess where I am sure the officers are already gathered. We will take my car —— '

Making not the smallest concession to good fellowship, Zulka said, 'The Squadron Commander is otherwise engaged.'

'Really, there can be nothing further for him to do.'

'He has a duty.'

'Zulka is right,' the Prince agreed, 'I cannot come. We would join you in thanksgiving but there are too many of our comrades absent.'

It seemed a dismal way to commemorate a victory, the moment when Europe emerged into sunlight, and Armstrong was disturbed.

'A pity,' he said. 'I am sure the party will be a good one.'

Quietly, so as not to dull their spirit, Armstrong stole into the hall of the officers' mess and placed his cap on the peg reserved for the commanding officer. The unplanned victory party was in strenuous life in the rooms beyond. He hoped they would pay him no attention, but when he entered the ante-room the voices lost their stridency and then, surprising him, burst out in renewed enthusiasm. When the Old Man joined them, the party was no longer a shapeless jubilation but had acquired the rudiment of ceremony. He was lifted shoulder high and carried the length of the room while the officers applauded. He was made to stand on a table under the Sovereign's portrait. 'Speech,' they called. He had not prepared himself for this. He did not speak well without notes. He could not free his mind from the vibrance of war. But he said, letting their spirit guide him:

'Well, it is over. It is over thanks to you and to those who were here before you. The squadrons are standing down and you will not be required to risk your lives again. I thank God for that! It has been no pleasure to see young men killed. I remember them all — men whose names I may have forgotten but whose faces are still familiar to me. There have been times when I thought the war would never end — when we seemed to relish the war for its own sake — but those days are in the past and we must turn our minds to something new. It's not going to be easy. Somehow we will have to get the war out of our systems. It's simpler to die than to survive; but we have survived, and now we must lead the lives we did not expect. I don't quite know what I shall do myself . . . ' They would cheer him no matter what he said. He sought in his mind for the things he really meant, but he could see only the faces of the lost airmen. Then he told them of the days before the war when they flew in canvas and plywood and the cold air penetrated the seams like a knife. Many had died then, finding the way. He recalled the first raids when they attacked the enemy with nothing but a compass and sextant to guide them. He told them of the heroes who had preceded them across the enemy coast into defended territory — of Hanna and Nettleton, of Garland and Gray.

Finally he paused, knowing that something was unsaid, while the more impetuous members called 'More, more!'

'Very well — I will say one thing more. It has been my job to command this station for eighteen months, through some of the worst days of the offensive. I know very well that you would have preferred a more colourful personality to lead you. Indeed, such an officer was with us until a few days ago, and he would perhaps have made a better station commander than I. It may be so. I know that I have been severe and remote and that my style of command has been a plain one. Even had I wished it, I could not have made it different, because that is the way I was made. I am an old regular officer accustomed to the disciplines of a former age. But I have been touched by the loyalty you have given me no matter that I may have disappointed you, and I offer you my thanks.'

There were no other words in his head. He jumped down from the table to enraptured applause. The officers pressed forward to touch his arm or slap his shoulder — to acknowledge their affection, to confirm his leadership; and Armstrong was surprised at the warmth they showed him.

At the bar, when at last he reached calmer water, he found Padre Shenstone and some of the older officers. A glass was pressed into his hand but he did not drink from it.

The Chaplain said, 'In fact, dear sir, you have been an excellent commander. Their cheers attest to your leadership.'

Armstrong did not find his voice at once. He restored his uniform to its proper shape and tidied his hair with his hands. Then he said cautiously, 'I have never seen myself as a popular commander. I was too straight-laced for that. But it may be they have not entirely disliked me.'

He had no appetite for the party that followed. Better to have gone away, but he knew that elsewhere there was nothing but the stillness of an exhausted continent which he wasn't yet ready to sustain. Now that it was over, the service would not long retain him, for he had nothing to give to the peace. His vision of the empty days frightened him. He had nowhere to go, no thread to follow. He listened to the roar of voices in the ante-room and knew that it marked the end of his life's purpose.

A figure at the end of the bar held his attention. A man alone, who drank as if he too had a need to extinguish the thought of victory — a man who should have died sometime in the last year when he let slip his option upon life. With that gesture made, some combination of dangers drawn into fatal accord should have carried him off, but in fact Peter Marek had survived, thrown back out of the darkness with a derisive flourish. They had even given him a medal for gallantry.

Armstrong approached him, aware of his dilemma. 'Well, Peter, the peace will be strange, but I expect we can learn to live with it.'

Marek turned his face slowly towards the Station Commander, his eyes hard, his lips supple with bitter amusement. 'Oh, sure. Like living on bread and water. Like living with an old whore who's forgotten what it's made for. I can live with the peace.'

'The readjustment will take some time, some effort. What will you do?'

'Hell, I'm not going back to barbering. Who wants to shave heads?'

'You will get used to it.'

Marek sank back into gloomy reflection. 'Want to bet?' was the whole of his reply.

'You have been of great assistance to me,' Armstrong continued, raising his voice to keep it audible, 'particularly in my dealings with the Poles. I could not have managed without your help.'

'Don't thank me, brother. I did you no favours.'

'On the contrary, I am grateful to you.'

The Polish-American looked at him sideways in gleeful reticence. 'See here. They've given me a medal but I'm not a hero. You tell me you're grateful but I did nothing to help you.'

'I was satisfied with your service, Peter.'

'Heck, I kept more to myself than I told you.'

Something lay in the centre of his mind — a sombre burden that troubled him.

'Say, let's get out of here,' he said suddenly, rising untidily from the bar. 'I'll tell you just how well I served you.'

Marek steered a weaving course out of the room, by a miracle avoiding an accident, and Armstrong followed at a distance. He came finally to rest in the officers' latrine, where he took hold of Armstrong's jacket and pulled him close in elaborate confidence.

'Look: I was a Polack, see? They put me straight as soon as they got here. They gave me a beating and told me to keep out of it. Oh, sure — I could teach them Group procedures and all that crap, but they didn't want me close, where I might see what they were doing. The Prince would have killed me if I'd crowded him.'

'Steady on,' Armstrong said, who didn't like exaggeration even at the moment of victory. He freed himself from Marek's grasp and waited patiently for him to continue.

'But I knew the Polish spirit. I was in Poland as a kid and I'd seen a nobleman use his whip against a churl. The Prince didn't tell me what he was doing. He didn't have to; I knew. He was belting his officers until they were ready to eat dirt. If they crossed him, he hammered them with the gloves or bloodied them with the sword and they didn't cross him again. If it wasn't the Prince, then it was his buddy Zulka.'

Marek slithered up to Armstrong with all of a drunkard's guile. 'I'll tell you something else. You knew about the Warsaw flight, didn't you? You knew the Prince had his officers in York stripping the drug stores of their swabs and plasters. You knew that he cut up Stefan Pakorski and sent him on a mission that sure as hell was going to kill him. You knew it, didn't you?'

Armstrong said calmly, 'I didn't know about it until afterwards. Had I known, I would have forbidden it.'

'And — boy, this one takes all prizes! — you knew the Prince and his captains overflew Neustrelitz and beat the hell out of the Russians at Stettin.'

'Again, if was only afterwards that I learned of it.'

Marek pulled himself upright in a parody of self-importance. 'But I'll tell you something you didn't know. I'll tell you a goddam secret. Sure I will.'

He made a wayward tour of the officers' latrine, looking beneath the cubicle doors to confirm their vacancy. He fell; he came back to where Armstrong stood.

'Listen to this. Once they killed a guy.'

'I beg your pardon?'

'No one that mattered. A punk, a gowk.'

'I think you'd better tell me what you mean.' But Armstrong had already scented the final truth: the place where he stood, with its foetid odours, had brought back the shape and character of a man he had known. 'Tell me, Marek.'

'There was this guy who crossed them when he pulled down their flag. A crap-handler. You wouldn't remember him.'

'Are you telling me the man who violated their emblem on Christmas night was Haines, the defaulter?'

'That's right. A little guy. No one to bother with.'

'I am concerned. I must know what happened.'

'Well, they caught him in the dining room when he threw over a table of glasses. They caught him with the emblem in his hands — a hand that was stained with excrement.'

So that was the truth: Armstrong had not known.

'Boy, were they sore! That emblem was sacred; it stood for their private war with the Soviet Union, and for their murdered friends, and the Prince could not see it fouled up. He took the little guy out into the fog. He didn't take a sword. No, that weapon could only be used upon a nobleman, not upon a slop-carrier who stank of the pit. I don't think he abused him or even spoke to him. He just took his neck into his hands and crushed it until the little guy was dead; then Zulka picked him up like a bundle of trash and took him away to the disposal pit — to the place where he came from — and dropped him into the filth.'

'You are telling me the truth?' Armstrong asked. 'I believed Haines to have deserted.'

'You bet it's the truth.'

The Station Commander contained his shock. He looked sharply at Marek to test the quality of his evidence; but in fact his inner mind had given an endorsement even as the story was told. In the shuttered imagination of Prince Karol this was not a murder but an execution. Armstrong could see his fog-softened outline as he stood over poor Haines and dismissed him into the outer reaches of that December night: it was a scene that, with a ring of certainty, took its place in the history of the White Squadron.

Armstrong took a deep breath as he tried to force his practical mind to serve him. He spoke severely, as he might have done to Haines himself. 'Why have you kept this information from me until now?'

Marek circled the small space between the basins and the urinal, like a dog broken by reproof. 'Hell, I wasn't going to tell you a thing about the Poles. They could fight whichever enemy they chose. They could avenge themselves on a crap-handler if they felt like it. Sure they could. I was a Pole, too — in my way.'

'But you have told me now.'

'Yes, I have told you now.'

'I don't understand your motives.'

'You will very soon.'

Armstrong could waste no more time with Marek. He went to the door and opened it. 'Please do not think I can overlook your suppression of this evidence, Peter. If it is true, you will have much to answer for.'

But Marek simply shrugged his shoulders. He was numbed by the victory he had not expected to see and threats of this sort could not reach him. Besides, he had urgent business at the urinal.

Daylight was vanishing off the face of the airfield as Armstrong drove round the perimeter as fast as the regulation allowed. A lifetime of armed service had taught him to suppress his anger, but his mind burned with indignation and his hands were shaking. One by one he passed the dispersed aircraft, shrouded now, their usefulness at an end, but he did not see them. He saw nothing but the broken body of an airman borne on Zulka's shoulder to the pit. This time there could be no excuse for Prince Karol, who must answer for his fault; no depth of provocation could justify the murder of an airman under Armstrong's command. Haines was a poor thing, unkempt, ill-disciplined, but in common with all other members of the station he had a right to Armstrong's protection. The Prince was not at the Polish mess and the staff there didn't know where he had gone.

Armstrong drove back on to the airfield, his anger unconsumed. Far down the perimeter, in fading light, he could see a group of figures near the Polish dispersals. They stood in a circle as if they listened to a prayer; likely enough they gave thanks for the victory at the place from which it was gained. Armstrong stopped his car and watched them as the dusk thickened. Then, alerting every pulse in his body, he heard a sound, familiar enough in this setting but one that did not accord with the newly found stillness of peace: the starting of an aircraft engine. At once he set the car in motion and covered the intervening distance at a brisk pace. When he drew level with the circle of men he saw them to be the Polish senior officers. They did not stir when he approached them on foot. Two were in flying kit, and he was quick to identify them as Prince Karol and Count Zulka. Behind them on the dispersal pan, with its engines turning, stood the *Snow Princess*.

He did not wait for the prayer to finish but addressed himself to the Prince, raising his voice above the idling engines, careless of the others who might hear him. 'Wing Commander, you have not my leave to fly. The aircraft is to be stopped at once and the hatches sealed. You are confined to the station while the service police investigate the disappearance of Aircraftman Haines.'

The Prince awoke slowly, as if from a profound reverie. 'Yes? You were speaking to me, sir?'

Armstrong repeated his message with no loss of indignation, and only then did the Prince incline his head in acknowledgement. 'Haines — I remember him well. An unfortunate man. He tore down our emblem on Christmas night, which was an insult we could not tolerate.'

'What does that mean?'

'That we had to demonstrate our anger.'

'Are you telling me that you killed him?'

The Prince smiled briefly as if Armstrong had just mastered a simple truth, and meanwhile the officers closed upon him, without menace, but bringing their strength within call should the Prince be threatened. Zulka alone had not moved.

Armstrong stood his ground, stiffened by his memory of the wretch who had died. 'That was nothing less than murder. There are no circumstances in which you would be justified in taking the life of a fellow airman. I have found it possible to excuse the Polish squadron for some strange actions, but this latest disclosure I utterly condemn.'

178

A voice spoke on his right hand and, without looking, he recognized the courtly accent of Pilot Officer Nikolski. 'He was a vile fellow, with crooked legs. He was sour to the nostrils.'

'He was an airman under my command.'

The Prince dropped his eyes, seeking to translate an alien terror into simple English. 'Friend, believe me there are times when the sky blackens and you cannot see — when there is little difference between the living and the dead and all you can hear is the howl of the insane. So it has been for years past in Poland. We raised a flag in the midst of this anguish. Aye, we did! We raised it at Kozielsk when we were captive and at the edge of the grave. Did you really think I could see that flag violated?'

But Armstrong would not yield. 'You were in a country where the law was still respected. Together we had the means to punish sacrilege. But instead you cruelly murder an airman of weak intelligence who had probably no conception of what he was doing.'

'In the darkness the guilty have all the same face.'

From his place at the back of the group, showing no interest in the vindication of murder, Zulka said, 'We have little time. The light is failing.'

'Have patience, Tadeusz! I do not wish to leave while my commanding officer is unsatisfied.'

'There are matters more urgent.'

'No, there is none.' The Prince took the arm of his superior and led him away from the group and the sound of the aircraft. They stopped on the grass short of the perimeter. 'Sir, if you cannot understand me, then grant me at least your forgiveness.'

'I can forgive you for your attack upon the Russians, not for the murder of an airman,' Armstrong said. 'For that you must stand trial.'

The Prince averted his eyes, but not before Armstrong had seen their disfigurement. 'I am dismayed —— ' he began.

'What is more, I forbid you or any of your officers to fly this aircraft. The war is over, the airfield is closed. I am placing you in arrest.'

'Dear comrade, do not have me add to my guilt! I cannot comply with your orders; I can only respond to the anger of the dead. If you attempt to arrest me, these officers will restrain you.'

Here at the edge of the airfield, with the light passing from the sky, Armstrong was bound to concede their greater strength. The fundamentals of good order had lurched into disharmony. He knew himself powerless, but none the less he said, 'If your officers lay their hands upon me — if they prevent me from arresting you — they will be guilty of mutiny.'

'Yes, mutiny; but each has volunteered his life.'

'You cannot lead your subordinates into something so disgraceful.'

'Sir, there has been nothing in Europe but the deepest disgrace for more than ten years. I can only take the least shameful path. Even so! If my officers must dissuade you, they will do so with respect and you will not be harmed.'

'It will be mutiny nevertheless.'

Armstrong looked about him for reinforcement. He saw nothing but the empty grass, the road bare of traffic, and a group of silent Poles standing beside an aircraft prepared for flight. It was his duty to prevent a mutiny from taking place, not simply to arrest the mutineers after their offence, but he had no means of enforcing his authority. His strength collapsed within him. He knew he could do no more. He felt even a dull relief that matters were decided and that he could bid the Prince farewell.

His eyes came to rest on the *Snow Princess*. He said, 'In particular, why must you fly this evening?'

'I cannot tell you, though it grieves me.'

'There is nothing further that you can do.'

'One flight. No more. I take only Zulka with me.'

'You cannot escape court martial by leaving the country. The whole of Europe is now in Allied hands.'

'I will escape nothing, my friend. Instead I deliver myself to judgement. Though I have not your leave to fly, I none the less ask for your blessing.' Painfully, the Prince searched in Armstrong's face for traces of a lost regard, but Armstrong could show him nothing but his inner desolation. 'Please, of your kindness . . . '

Armstrong said, spending the words with the utmost thrift, trying to express the guarded sympathy of his heart, 'I have never denied you my affection. Even now I count you my friend. But I do not understand your present disobedience.'

'My disobedience — it is nothing!' Prince Karol said with soft urgency. 'It matters not at all if I have your affection.'

Armstrong paused, looking into the gathering dusk. Despite his failure, he knew that an unfamiliar truth had loomed close to him, lighting his way, lifting him from dejection at the moment when his authority was finally broken.

'I dare say not,' he replied. It was the closest he could get to the truth. His hands, it seemed of their own accord, had meanwhile clasped those of the Prince, in friendship, in sadness. In the suppressed part of his mind he knew the Prince would offer his own amends for the murder of Haines, and that it was better so.

But Zulka was calling again from the aircraft entrance. 'Come, sir, before it is entirely dark!'

The Prince said nothing more, but hampered though he was by his flying clothing he took Armstrong into a firm embrace and held him there while the seconds passed. Nothing stirred in Armstrong's mind but for a sense of irredeemable loss.

A moment later Prince Karol started towards the *Snow Princess* and Armstrong accompanied him, making no attempt to restrain him; he just walked at his side as if he were bidding him farewell and the officers did not intervene.

When they came to the rear hatch they paused while the ground crew jumped down; then Zulka climbed into the fuselage. Armstrong did not assist the Prince to embark; he could not bring himself to abet a mutiny. But with his practical voice, he said, 'You cannot fly a Halifax with a crew of two. Take at least an engineer.'

'Nay, two is enough,' the Prince said. 'Good-bye, my dear friend.'

'Good-bye.'

The Prince entered the aircraft and closed the hatch from the inside. Armstrong joined the other Poles on the grass by the dispersal neck. They did not speak. They watched the aircraft as the idling engines increased their pace and the wing tips steadied in the greater flow of air. Then the heavy machine rolled off the pan towards the perimeter road. The Poles came to the salute as the aircraft passed, and Armstrong followed them, seeing no point in withholding his respect; and together they maintained the salute until the aircraft joined the road and taxied towards the downwind end of the airfield.

Five minutes later the *Snow Princess* took off, using the full runway and climbing slowly into the dusk. It vanished before

Armstrong could see what course was set.

'Nikolski, you must tell me where the aircraft is bound,' he said. 'It was obviously fully laden.'

But the Pole lifted his shoulders in ignorance. 'I do not know. The Prince told no one what flight he intended.'

What flight did he intend? Within minutes the *Snow Princess* would be over one coast or the other.

Armstrong burst into the empty operations room and switched on the light. The staff had covered the tables and drawn the curtains across the wall display before going off duty; they had supposed the war at an end. He took up the telephone and waited two minutes for the exchange to answer. When the girl replied, he rebuked her for the delay, placed an immediate call to Group and then rang the officers' mess. Again he waited while the bell rang. In the meantime the *Snow Princess* was increasing her distance from Moreton Valence, the darkness closing upon her. When the phone was lifted he heard the bellow of celebration and a voice that could not suppress its laughter. Yes, what did he want? Didn't he know the war was over?

Armstrong bit the speaker's head off and told him to send the Intelligence Officer to the operations room immediately.

Then he opened the wall display and stood looking at the map of Europe. The staff had removed the battle symbols and nothing remained of the conflict but for the pin holes in the paper. Where in that vast area of sea and land had the *Snow Princess* gone? The east of the continent was in total darkness; there was a fleeting twilight in the west but that would soon move into the Atlantic and vanish.

The phone rang and he was connected to a bibulous creature at Group operations whose speech was much hampered. Armstrong reported an unauthorized take-off from Moreton Valence, the aircraft passing out of sight and heading in an unknown direction.

'Nunorforize stake off,' said Group operations.

Armstrong said, 'Will you put someone on the phone who is not intoxicated. This is intolerable.'

A firmer voice spoke to him then, which he recognized as that of Wing Commander Dancy. He repeated his message. 'I will try to determine the load and endurance,' he continued. 'There may be more to this than simple high spirits.'

'More, sir? Can there be more? There has been widespread indiscipline in the Command. At Binbrook the Australians have smashed up a Lancaster.'

'I will report developments,' Armstrong said, and rang off.

He returned to the map and switched on the illumination. They had gone east; of that he was certain. They had flown into the ruined continent on some private errand and now the aircraft would be concealed in darkness. He could not say what defences were still in being because the armistice had yet to be ratified in Berlin, but it seemed unlikely the *Snow Princess* would meet resistance. In the north the British army was in Lübeck, and southward the Americans were far down the Elbe and into Bohemia; the *Snow Princess* could range widely over the disarmed territory to the limit of her fuel.

Squadron Leader Keeble, the Intelligence Officer, joined him in the deserted operations room after ten minutes, and mercifully the old scholar had kept himself sober.

Without turning from the map, Armstrong said, 'Prince Karol has taken off in the *Snow Princess*. I want you to determine her load. Check with the bulk fuel installation and the explosives compound. At once, if you please.'

It took Keeble twenty minutes of harassed endeavour to gather the information he required, and then more than half an hour had passed since the aircraft disappeared into the shadows.

'She had maximum fuel with fuselage overload,' he told Armstrong. 'And ... '

'And what, man?'

'Well, it may be an error. There may be a mistake in the explosives inventory. The record suggests he loaded eight thousand pounds of bombs.'

Armstrong did not speak.

'It must be an error,' Keeble continued with more assurance than usual. 'There would be no point in loading bombs.'

184

'I cannot be sure,' Armstrong replied.

His mind's eye showed him the aircraft, bomb-doors closed, rolling off the dispersal with the slow gait of an over-laden beast. Even then he had known she had something in her belly that depressed the suspension beyond the normal limit.

He paced the length of the operations room, ignoring Keeble. He tried to enter the darkened mind of Prince Karol on the last day of the war — in the final hours before the restraints of peace robbed him of strength. Where would he go? What would he do? Armstrong had no need to refer to the loading tables to assess the range of the *Snow Princess* in Europe; full tanks and eight thousand pounds would give her about sixteen hundred miles in still airs if he flew carefully.

Armstrong returned to the map. He took a tape and measured the equivalent of sixteen hundred miles against the calibrated scale. One end he fastened with a pin to Moreton Valence; with the other he inscribed an easterly radius marking the extreme range of the *Snow Princess* in Europe. The curve bisected the Soviet Union from Murmansk to Odessa — from the White Sea to the Black — passing just to the east of the Russian capital.

He stood still, his mind hardening upon a terrible possibility.

After a while he said, 'Keeble, get through to the Met Section. They are to assess the winds over northern Europe in the next eight hours.'

The Intelligence Officer hesitated. 'Can it matter, sir? I'm sure Prince Karol is still in the vicinity and will land very soon.'

'I believe it to matter profoundly. They are to give their reply with the utmost urgency.'

While Keeble fought with the telephone, Armstrong closed his eyes and let his mind follow the *Snow Princess* across the North Sea and towards the shrouded country he now believed to be her destination. Could it be done, with only two aboard to guide the heavy machine across featureless territory in darkness? Well — perhaps. Zulka would navigate and switch the fuel tanks. They would fly without radio and with only their own voices for company. They would follow the stars until the dawn pointed their direction. By taking off at dusk, the short summer night would cover them as they crossed the North Sea and the Baltic and passed through the outer defences of the Soviet Union. Morning would find them over the forests of Smolensk,

185

where perhaps they would dip their wings in remembrance of the proud company who lay there; and then beyond doubt they would point their aircraft at the one target that would satisfy their temper. At that hour they would see it clearly, as the towers and crenellations caught the first sunlight — that is, if they had endurance enough to get there.

Keeble was again speaking to him. 'Sir, do you hear me? The winds are easterly, with speeds of ten to fifteen knots at thirteen thousand feet, and rising.'

'Easterly? Very good. Thank you, Keeble.'

Armstrong fell into a chair and took his head into his hands. Friend, what have you done? he thought.

His mind cleared slowly. The Prince had planned his flight to fine limits. By reducing the bomb load he could have added some miles to the range and allowed for contrary winds, but this he hadn't done. He had carried the maximum load to the exact distance, the action of a man driven by anger and not by circumspection.

In the silence of his mind, Armstrong said, Friend, friend, the winds will defeat you. Better so, better so!

'Can you tell me where you think he has gone?' Keeble asked then.

'I believe he has gone into eastern Europe. I cannot be certain of his aim. I can only guess.'

'Of course, from that distance he will be unable to return.'

'I do not think he intends to return.'

Armstrong rose, forcing his mind into practical courses. 'Keeble, I will be grateful if you will keep this matter to yourself for the time being. The Prince may think better of it and come back. If he does not, we may never know what happened to him.' He paused, looking again at the map. 'You may go now. I shall stay here overnight.'

From Flamborough Head the Prince had laid a course directly to his objective no matter that it was a vast distance off. He saw no point in evasion; this was not a military operation but a trenchant gesture in the face of indifference. He saw the light pass from the leaden sea as he flew into the approaching darkness. In the cockpit the light lasted a minute or two longer; then it faded as well until he could see only the luminous instruments in the

186

panel before him. The aircraft laboured on between the night-hung clouds. Forward of him Zulka worked at the navigation table, concealed by the curtain, but elsewhere the crew positions were empty, the turrets locked in the after alignment, the lamps extinguished: the body of the aircraft followed him like a large familiar shadow with ghosts at the armament. The intercom was silent. Zulka would say nothing but the few words necessary for the guidance of the *Snow Princess* on her long passage eastward. As well that Zulka was the strongest of the Poles.

Prince Karol trimmed the aircraft for level flight in obedience to his training while his mind took a different course. They were quite alone, surrounded by empty sky, bound upon a mission known only to himself and the taciturn navigator who served him. Tomorrow at first light their purpose would be disclosed, and it would be seen as the great denouement of the war, a *coup de théâtre*. He searched for his anger, the anger that had lain within him since those frost-hardened days in Russia when he had guessed the fate of his companions; but it was difficult to carry anger into the upper air. He felt the lapping of the wind at his cheek, the rolling of the *Snow Princess* as she struggled under his hands — sensations that bound him to the fellowship of the living and not to a legion of shades. He must not forget the dead. He held them in the centre of his mind, a gallant company and the most gifted group of men to suffer massacre since the French Revolution. But they were faceless now; they raised their hands in soundless, distant salutation. They occupied a fog-bound wood where five seasons of growth and decay had lain a conciliatory hand. He turned up his collar to keep out the turbulent airs. Better when the *Snow Princess* had passed the Baltic coast and there could be no thought of return.

An hour later Zulka reported their position north of the Kiel Canal.

The summer clouds had vanished a hundred miles back and now the aircraft floated in moonlight, in a world softened and changed. Anger had no force in these gentle airs. He wanted to turn and follow the moon-touched path back to Moreton Valence. South of him was the now silent battlefield where the forces had all drawn to a halt. In the whole of Europe his was the only machine in movement. But he could not return; he carried his resolve like a black burden, one his body was accustomed to support, and try as he might he could not throw it off now.

Zulka grunted in satisfaction, his first comment of the flight. 'The Station Commander could do nothing against the Poles. Never have I seen a man so dispirited!'

Prince Karol wished he had not spoken so, recalling to his mind how Armstrong had stood helpless at the dispersal. He said wearily, 'He was an honest man, diligent and fair. It gave me no pleasure to disobey him.'

A letter to Armstrong was in Nikolski's keeping, for delivery in the morning when the mission would have ended. The few words, written early yesterday when the flight was mounted, were a wretched attempt to repair the damage done to his authority.

'We speak no more of the Station Commander,' Prince Karol said.

One hour more — or so it seemed; he hadn't looked at the clock — and Zulka came back to the astrodome to fix their position by the stars. They had no navigational aids; they were following a track where the bombers had never been and where they must grope forward using the old methods. Their position by dead reckoning would be a long way out by now, but the stars were clear enough, offering their guidance to the truant aircraft as if in complicity. Zulka made his star-shot and went back to the table where he laid off a position line.

When his voice spoke on the intercom it had a sombre colouring. 'The winds have risen. They are easterly and strong. We have lost ground speed.'

'What does that mean?'

'That we may fall short.'

'But that cannot be!' the Prince said violently. 'There is only one target.'

The mission was pointless if they did not hit the very seat of responsibility — the fortified citadel from where beyond doubt the destruction of the Polish leadership had been planned. The chance of failure strengthened his will to succeed, to overcome the headwinds that were holding them back in some contrary design; his anger returned when it seemed likely that no one would acknowledge the murdered officers and that they would be forgotten in the jubilance of peace. What mischief lay behind this change in the airs, what drive towards forgetfulness?

188

Now it didn't matter to Prince Karol that they were alone and their flight sanctioned only by the claims of the dead. He would hold the *Snow Princess* in the air until Zulka had the target in the bomb-sight. If the engines were then failing, he would use the aircraft as a missile, aiming for the centre of the great walled enclosure, diving with their load between the towers. Whatever happened, they could not escape themselves.

When a while later Zulka told him they were north of Danzig and beyond the point of no return, Prince Karol felt a surge of the spirit. 'So, come what may, we go forward!' he exclaimed. 'Forward!'

He held his course across the Baltic, steering for a landfall north of Memel, no matter that the winds were against him and the stars had trembled into disfavour.

Armstrong kept a single light burning in the operations room. He had just the gloom to keep him company. After the first hour he had ceased to expect any report of the *Snow Princess*; she would be travelling in remote areas, beyond normal surveillance, and word of her would depend upon the outcome of her mission. He did not know if the air defences of eastern Europe were effective, but on the last night of the war there was a chance that all the combatants had dropped their guard and that the *Snow Princess* would escape detection. Once through the defences, there was a slim possibility she would outmanoeuvre the winds and reach her target. If that were the case, then Prince Karol's mission was likely to become the best-remembered operation of the war with terrible consequences for Allied accord. Had there been the means, the aircraft should have been shot down before she slipped into the dark, but once she had gone beyond range there was nothing he could do but hope she would fall short or succumb to some other hazard. More than once Armstrong had thought of calling the Commander-in-Chief at High Wycombe and suggesting that he warn the Soviet Union of the errant aircraft and its possible destination. But no, he was not sure of his facts, and even if he were, a warning would be unlikely to lead to effective interception; a message would raise the whole subject of Polish antagonism, and they would need to explain how a British aircraft had been allowed to fly fully armed against an Ally. The most suspicious nation on earth would scent collusion. He had reported the take-off to his controlling formation. Better to say nothing more, to wait until the *Snow Princess* had flown to her limit, when perhaps she would fall in rough country and become simply a part of the war's litter.

As best he could, he put from his mind the consequences to himself of the scandal that would surely arise if Prince Karol were successful. Such dangers lay outside the circle of light in which he waited. He had concealed his knowledge of the Stettin raid. He had declined until too late to put Prince Karol into any form of restraint. And the behaviour of the Poles should have warned him of the more flamboyant gesture to come. He knew well enough that a court of enquiry would censure him severely and that the Air Council would require at least his resignation: they would be obliged to offer that small satisfaction to an outraged ally. Of course, the Prince himself would be beyond punishment, his action left to the discretion of history.

At three-thirty in the morning, while it was still dark, the telephone rang and the duty officer called him urgently to the officers' quarters. He went at once, glad of alternative employment; he went on foot through the moonlight and past the familiar buildings. The station was quiet now, the party was over. He found the Adjutant, the SWO and the Medical Officer waiting for him in the officers' lines.

'Well, gentlemen, why have you called me?' he asked.

Flight Lieutenant Jarvis said, 'You'd better come inside, sir.' He conducted Armstrong into one of the wooden huts.

They entered a narrow room where the light had been left burning. There was nothing remarkable about it; Armstrong had spent his life in such bare quarters as these. Peter Marek lay close to the bedside, his body face downward; he had fallen untidily as if the strength had suddenly gone out of his limbs. Armstrong felt no surprise at this added consequence of the victory. He picked up the weapon which had dropped independently and opened the breech. One chamber discharged; well, it would take no more than that.

'Why did he do it?' Jarvis asked. Despite his years in the service he was shaken by violence. 'After all, this was a night for celebration.'

Armstrong didn't bother to explain. 'Jarvis, I will be grateful if you will prepare a casualty signal and get it away promptly. Doctor, we shall in due course require your statement. Mr Thorpe —— '

Instinctively the SWO came to attention. 'Sir.'

'When the Medical Officer has finished, you may take the body to the mortuary and secure the room.'

He went out into the fresh morning air, the SWO following him.

'A wretched thing, Mr Thorpe. He had survived some of the worst operations of the war.'

The SWO took a deep breath to smother the scent of that inner room; in thirty years of barrack life he had become used to paradox. 'I suppose it was anti-climax,' he said.

'Something like that,' Armstrong replied. 'None the less I shall accord him military honours.'

With a brisk step, he walked back up the path towards the operational site, knowing he must not lapse into slovenliness as Marek had done. Poor fellow, by the perversity of chance he had lived through to the end, and then he had repaired the war's omission with a scornful hand. With a mind enlarged by tragedy, Armstrong felt the sour spirit of Marek still close to him, as if he had still an hour of sojourn before the first light sent him on his way.

'Well, you told me what you knew,' Armstrong said to Marek's shadow, and with a touch of a station commander's asperity. 'But had you wished to do justice to Aircraftman Haines, you should have told me earlier.'

He re-entered the operations room and resumed his lonely vigil. He rang Group, but they had no news of the scapegrace aircraft. He had simply to wait until the *Snow Princess* had either broken into the world's startled vision or perished in obscurity. Either way, the Prince and Zulka would offer the only possible recompense for their destruction of Haines.

Outside the open door the light was growing, giving substance to the airfield and the unlovely buildings that served it. He heard the first birdsong from the nearby woodland, the starting of the vehicle in the MT yard. The *Snow Princess* had now been airborne for eight hours and must be near the end of her endurance. He estimated the distance she had flown, making an allowance for the headwind, and laid it off against the wall map: by this reckoning the Prince was still two hundred miles short of his destination and over empty terrain.

I don't think he'll make it, Armstrong said in his private mind, any more than Pakorski did. The winds are too great.

SEVENTEEN

More than fourteen hundred miles to the east of Moreton Valence the light was already well established, giving form to the ground below him and to some fragments of cloud high above the cockpit canopy. So far there was no colour, just the black of the forest and the white of the mist that here lay along every valley until, at the horizon, it joined with the lower sky. A landscape without end, crossed by tortuous rivers. Prince Karol had seen nothing in the sky since first light; he had broken into the great eastern stronghold without alerting any system of defence, and now he was approaching the heartland across empty country, holding a course a little to the south of due east.

Half an hour earlier, when it was still necessary to use the lamps, Zulka had come back to the engineer's panel to read the fuel gauges, after which he had continued to the rest position to connect the last of the overload. He had not spoken; he had not told the Prince how long the *Snow Princess* could remain in the air, but on his return to the nose he had placed his hand briefly on the captain's shoulder.

Prince Karol was tired, and he no longer cared so deeply for success. He had made the effort, launched the avenging mission, and the matter now rested with the arbitration of the winds. He was carried forward by the anger that had possessed him for five years but which had now faded almost to a memory. He would do the job and accept the penalty in obedience to the dead, but without relish. He could not believe there would be much difference in his mind's colouring once the *Snow Princess* had ended her flight; for long enough he had followed a lightless corridor with only phantoms for company, and then as now his companions had been the nameless, voiceless dead. He was not frightened, any more than Zulka was; he had simply to step from one shadow to another in a light-footed movement, a volunteer for the dark, the last of the wartime multitude.

Zulka asked for an alteration of course four degrees to the south, and Prince Karol applied starboard rudder until the new course showed in the direction indicator. They were still flying towards the target, still keeping to the belief that they might reach it. In these minutes the engines continued their beat and all the aircraft systems were alive, but for as far as the Prince could see there was no break in the forest. He searched the horizon for traces of the city that lay on this heading, and once or twice he imagined he saw domes and towers piercing the haze at a point ahead of him, but Zulka — harsh, honest Zulka — told him that these were dreams.

South of them, little more than a hundred miles off the starboard wing tip, in the valley of the Dnieper, the Katyn martyrs lay buried. The Prince turned his head in their direction and kissed the tips of his fingers. Rest, rest, he told them. Have patience, there in the ground! Your injury will be avenged.

That is, if the *Snow Princess* had life enough to cover the last miles . . .

Armstrong did not know if he had slept but he had the impression that time had passed. In the doorway the light dazzled his eyes. His long vigil had left him tired and with a slackness of spirit in which his fears kept their menacing shape. He looked at the clock: at about this time the *Snow Princess* would have spent the last of her fuel and the heavy machine would tilt into a steep and quickening dive. The Prince could arrest the speed by extending the flaps, and he could even attempt a belly landing, but Armstrong knew he would not do this; if his mission had failed he would elect to dive into the ground with a shrug of indifference, and the bombs would detonate and destroy the aircraft.

He got up to extinguish the electric light. At the door he paused, looking out across the grass where the dew had not yet disappeared. Not a soul was in sight, and even the birds had left the grass to fly into the trees; the prospect was as empty as his life had become now that the last friendship had closed. Yes, they were all gone now, and he was alone. The war had one by one taken his companions. And now the Prince had thrown his life away in a senseless gesture when he might have been here on the first morning of peace. He recalled the dead to his memory as he stood looking from the doorway. How brave they had been! What quality they had shown as fighting men! Of course, the Prince must rank as one of the outstanding leaders of the war, even though he had fought a war of his own creation; he had taken a unit into his hand and against the strongest tide he had made it an expression of his will. His was a story that should one day be told, but not now — not until a lifetime had past. The lost airmen filled his mind as the first of the sunlight dispersed the dew, and he saw them strong and upright and in the fullness of their heroism.

The sun was throwing strong shadows when at last he raised his head and expelled his memories. There was nothing to be gained from reflection. He became aware that he was no longer alone, that facing him across the grass at a distance of twenty yards was a young officer who seemed to have halted in the act of approaching him. Armstrong waited, giving him the chance to come forward; as Station Commander he was used to the tentative junior officer. When his eyes cleared, giving the visitor a firmer shape, he saw the officer to have no face, but he suppressed his shock and with an effort kept himself from turning away. Faceless men were not unusual among the aircrew where burning was a common hazard, but Armstrong had never mastered his recoil from them. This man gave the impression of a portrait in paint from which the artist had deleted the features in sudden dissatisfaction. The visitor stayed where he was, moving not at all, watching Armstrong. And then, as if he had decided to say nothing, he walked on across the grass and disappeared.

Poor devil, Armstrong thought, as he returned into the operations room. His mind was still following in the wake of the *Snow Princess* and he could not give his attention to this new casualty. He rang Group operations and reported the aircraft still missing and probably at the end of her endurance.

'If there is no word by midday,' Armstrong said, 'we'll have to assume she went into the sea. Please keep the AOC informed.'

Prince Karol had searched the horizon for so long he could no longer trust his vision. He saw domes and spires, but he knew them to be drawn by his imagination upon a skyline that was void. They had not travelled far enough to be within eyeshot of their destination and now, even if the distance were stained with smoke, they would not have time enough to reach it. They had failed. Like every Polish endeavour this mission had failed not from want of courage but from insufficient strength. They would fall short of the target here in the woodland and no one else would ever raise his hand in memory of Katyn.

The engines cut, resumed, then cut again. Although he had expected it, the sudden fall of the heavy aircraft made his heart jump and locked his limbs in terror. He was aware — as every airman is aware at the moment when the wings no longer support him — of the hard ground beneath; it touched his mind that flight was an impious thing, a wilful intrusion into forbidden places that must lead to expulsion in the end.

He kept the dive straight. Did it matter? Well, he would fall like a meteor and not like a leaf; that choice was left to him.

Zulka — gallant Zulka — did no more than throw down his pencil and brace himself against the aircraft side.

Then — let it fall.

The air sang on the wings as the *Snow Princess* dived towards the forest. His body was weightless, floating within the straps, an insubstantial thing.

Let it fall!

Nothing was left but the screaming of the wind and a long foretaste of eternity.

EIGHTEEN

At nine o'clock the Station Commander took the commemorative parade on the tarmac apron underneath the tower. He stood facing the squadrons while the parade commander ordered a general salute. Next Padre Shenstone read prayers and gave thanks for the victory. When he had finished, the squadrons were placed in open order and Armstrong carried out an inspection of the ranks, the parade commander at his side and the Adjutant and SWO following him. He moved briskly from one rigid figure to the next because he knew that tardy progress led to indiscipline in the rear ranks. He contrived — by the pause, the swift downward movement of his eyes, the murmur of satisfaction or the snort of disapproval — to let each man know that the quality of his turnout and bearing had been noted in the permanent record. To an eye trained in the exacting days of peace, these wartime airmen were a sorry lot who had never learned to stand upright; they lacked the starch of commitment. But none the less they had won a great victory and Armstrong was obliged to be lenient.

He returned to the front of the parade and mounted the dais at the saluting base. The station would march past in column of route. The order was given; the first flight lurched forward at an uncertain pace and he saw the later files searching for the step. He heard the SWO abusing the slovenly and calling the time. Then the station passed in front of him in column, holding the step with difficulty and with unequal distances between the flights. In the years before the war he would have called this a shambles, but for amateur airmen upon their morning of triumph the standard was just sufficient.

When the last file had passed him, he stepped down from the

dais and thanked the parade commander and the other officials who had wheeled from the column and come to a halt behind him. 'Not bad,' he said. 'It will take a little time to correct the laxities of the war. We shall have to start soon ... '

They saluted and went away. Armstrong was about to follow them when he caught sight of an officer under the tower, a spectator who lingered after the parade had passed; an officer who held his attention for the second time that morning; an officer whose face was devoid of feature, displaying nothing but the eyes — young, they seemed, and deeply pained — and below them a formless surface where the fire had passed. Such a face could wear no expression but for a grave watchfulness. Armstrong waited a moment in case the young man wished to speak to him; then, when he made no movement, he walked smartly off the parade ground and went to his office in Station Headquarters, where he had a call to make.

Air Vice-Marshal Teddy French, the Air Officer Commanding, listened with imperfect attention to the quiet voice at the other end of the line while with his free hand he rang impatiently for the Senior Air Staff Officer. The party at Garfield Manor, which had finished only four hours earlier, had left him without resource. French liked the Station Commander at Moreton Valence and knew him to have done a good job in difficult circumstances, but he couldn't share his present concern.

'Listen, old boy,' he said, cutting him short; 'this isn't the only act of high-spirited indiscipline in the Group. Yesterday the officers at Nether Elsham taxied a Halifax into the suburbs of York. Just like that. If your Poles have cut loose, I'm sorry, but I don't know what I can do about it. Where do you think they went?'

'I can't say, sir. It would be improper to speculate. But the deficiency in the explosives inventory is a matter for concern.'

'Great heavens, the volume of explosives passing through the compound would lead to discrepancies of this order. What evidence have you got that the Poles made off with the bombs?'

'None, sir.'

'Well, I can't get excited over a misadventure. I'm sorry to lose two lives, but the aircraft was redundant anyway. We'll have to assemble a court of enquiry, but I don't see how they can do more than declare the aircraft missing.'

The Station Commander did not reply at once.

'Is there something more, David? Something you haven't told me?'

He heard Armstrong clearing his throat at the other end of the line. 'I have told you everything of which I have proof, sir. The rest is guesswork which, if I repeated it, would impugn an officer who is probably dead.'

'I get your point. No sense in looking at every possibility. For myself, I suspect they went into the sea.'

The silence on the line was so prolonged the AOC wondered if the phone was still connected. 'Are you there?' he asked. He had a splitting headache.

'Yes, sir — I am here. As you have said, they almost certainly went into the sea. It is — unlikely we shall find any trace of them.'

'Crazy devils,' French said, and rang off.

When Air Commodore Pratt came into his office a moment later, the AOC told him of the missing aircraft and asked him to convene a court of enquiry. It would be no more than a paper transaction. He stretched his hand from one temple to the other to keep his skull from breaking apart.

'The Poles were always a little mad,' he said, 'but what a way to end the war. The aircraft had only scrap value, of course.'

Air Commodore Pratt, who had drunk not at all, who this morning surveyed the ending of the bomber offensive with marked satisfaction, said concisely, 'It is a pity that such a magnificent campaign should be marred by stupid antics.'

'What did you expect?' the AOC asked, feeling his pain. 'It wasn't a prayer meeting — it was a bloody war.'

'I would have preferred a more sober thankfulness.'

'For what, Stanley? The bombers proved nothing. Christ, I feel rough this morning . . . '

Armstrong sat at his desk, looking at the telephone as if at his own lack of candour. Never in twenty-eight years had he told less than the truth to his superior. He felt shamed and humiliated, as though his achievements in the war had been made void by this act of deception. He could forgive the Prince for his private warfare, and he saw no real objection to suppressing evidence that could only lead to national embarrassment; for plainly the continuing silence from the Soviet Union meant that the Prince had failed and that his aircraft had been blown to pieces. But the murder of an airman and the concealment of his body was another matter which Armstrong had no right to suppress. Had he lived, the Prince should have been brought before a court and obliged to tell his story; but he had given his life in some sort of exchange — the most illustrious of commanders for the most inglorious of airmen — and Armstrong could not destroy his name now that he was gone. Marek knew the story, but Marek would not speak. Nobody had enquired after Aircraftman Haines in the six months that had lapsed since he was deemed to have deserted: no one wanted to know, no one cared . . .

Armstrong turned over in his hand the letter that Nikolski had given him after the parade, and he read again the hasty message:

> *Moreton Valence*
> *7th May 1945*

Friend, I do not tell you where I am going. It is better you do not know. Think only that I am mad and that you bear no responsibility for my madness. I take Zulka with me, but no one else. My officers are ignorant of my purpose and I know very well that you will be fair to them; they are good men who have fought bravely and deserve your magnanimity. The rest was simply the agony of war.

Indeed I feel the greatest sorrow that my strange duty has kept us apart over the months. But I have honoured your name and treasured your friendship, and I do not forget you, dear comrade, even at the end.

> *Karol*
> *Prince of Poland*

Armstrong folded the letter and placed it in his breast pocket. He went out, hoping the fresh air would do something to absolve him from guiltiness, and he walked for a distance across the airfield towards the main runway. Today there was no warning from the tower because Moreton Valence was no longer in use, and at the far end of the field, hidden by the camber, they were cutting hay between the runways. He thought of the man he had known, whose fellowship he most wanted, and whose secret he would now protect. For how long? For his lifetime, at least. Already the lonely and tormented figure of Prince Karol was gathering the substance of myth as the hours following his death mounted one by one. To Armstrong, the withdrawal of that powerful spirit meant a new and more lasting desolation: the events of the night had left him orphaned, friendless ... At the nearer intersection he turned and walked back towards the tower. He was alone except for the insects singing in the grass and for the distant companionship of the haymakers.

No, not alone. His eyes were drawn by another figure. From the shadow of the tower, with a step more purposeful than hitherto, the young officer whose face had been erased by the fire now crossed the apron and waited for him at the edge of the grass.

Armstrong did not let his horror of the injury interrupt his step.

As he drew closer, the outline of the head struck a chord in his memory and he knew he had met this man before; the face contained a mystery that in a minute he would penetrate. Then the jolt of recognition brought him to a halt six paces short of the waiting officer.

His mind lurched into the dimension of wonder. He said, 'I am sorry. I had not known ... '

The officer did not speak but drew himself to attention as if confirming his presence at roll-call.

Armstrong said, 'Simon, I had thought you were dead.'

Speech was difficult for Lampton-Bell, but with painful deliberation he told his commanding officer that he had not died when his aircraft was shot down twelve days earlier. They had fallen, not in the sea but on the Danish island of Falster, and although the aircraft had exploded and burnt killing Chance and the other crew members, he had survived in the rear turret and had struggled out through the flames. 'I was cared for by the Danish resistance until the German capitulation. I came home only yesterday. I tried to speak to you earlier, but you didn't know me.'

'I didn't know you, because I didn't expect to see you,' Armstrong said firmly. 'I gave you up for lost when Chance failed to return. It's wonderful that you have come back!'

He meant it; the quality of consolation was added to the warmth of the sunlight. But Lampton-Bell drew a hand across his lower face where the fire had done terrible work.

'I don't know how you can look at me,' he said.

Armstrong had no difficulty in looking at him now; this officer was no longer a spectre of war but a friend and fellow crew member who had suffered mutilation. He said in his businesslike voice, 'Simon, there is a surgeon at East Grinstead who has restored many faces. A New Zealander, an excellent man. I have seen his work among the aircrews and I have been impressed with his skill. I'll get you down there as soon as the arrangements can be made.'

Lampton-Bell nodded; his face lacked the competence to express either pleasure or pain. His next words showed the answering sympathy of the injured. 'I am sorry to have frightened you, sir.'

'The fright you gave me, Simon, is nothing to my pleasure at finding you alive.'

'I wanted to report to you myself. I have not yet been to sick quarters.'

Armstrong was touched by this consideration and turned away from Lampton-Bell, hiding his own face. 'You should not have waited so long before speaking to me,' he said with something of a station commander's dissatisfaction. 'You should be resting after your journey home. Come now — I will take you to sick quarters in my car.'

He would set aside all other business until Lampton-Bell was cared for. It was the least he could do in recognition of a strange mercy. Together they crossed the tarmac apron under the tower and went towards Station Headquarters, where the car was waiting.

These operations, which took place over thirty years ago, have lain hidden for so long it has been difficult to trace all those who were connected with them. The story may still be modified, but I cannot believe it will be changed in any essential part. At the present time, a proposal to commemorate the life of Prince Karolajczyk with a memorial in a London church is gathering warmth, but plainly the legitimate objections are great. The reader may however wish to know that the group of officers who commissioned this study have been active in other directions.

In the summer of 1977, and with respect for the wishes of the late David Armstrong, a search was made for the body of Aircraftman Haines, with a view to giving it decent burial, but without result: the airfield at Moreton Valence was returned to farmland soon after the war and is now submerged under the loam like so many earlier systems of defence. We found traces of the dispersals, but nothing more. We might as well have turned the soil of Maiden Castle looking for a particular Roman legionary. Haines lies there somewhere; I cannot say where, or at what depth.

But in another field we were more successful. With the generous assistance of the War Graves Commission, seven bodies were recovered from a mountainside in Scotland and reinterred in the little churchyard at Kylorne. Headstones were erected giving their names and their common date of death. More especially, and in fulfilment of Sir Edward French's belief that a brave endeavour can never be suppressed, these stones record the action in which they were engaged and the reason why it was necessary.